The Day of Temptation

The Day of Temptation

William Le Queux

MINT EDITIONS

The Day of Temptation was first published in 1899.

This edition published by Mint Editions 2021.

ISBN 9781513280974 | E-ISBN 9781513285993

Published by Mint Editions®

MINT
EDITIONS

minteditionbooks.com

Publishing Director: Jennifer Newens
Design & Production: Rachel Lopez Metzger
Project Manager: Micaela Clark
Typesetting: Westchester Publishing Services

Contents

I

ALIENS

"O ne fact is plain. Vittorina must not come to England."

"Why? She, a mere inexperienced girl, knows nothing."

"Her presence here will place us in serious jeopardy. If she really intends to visit London, then I shall leave this country at once. I scent danger."

"As far as I can see, we have nothing whatever to fear. She doesn't know half a dozen words of English, and London will be entirely strange to her after Tuscany."

The face of the man who, while speaking, had raised his wine-glass was within the zone of light cast by the pink-shaded lamp. He was about twenty-eight, with dark eyes, complexion a trifle sallow, well-arched brows, and a dark moustache carefully waxed, the points being trained in an upward direction. In his well-cut evening clothes, Arnoldo Romanelli was a handsome man, a trifle foppish perhaps; yet his features, with their high cheek-bones, bore the unmistakable stamp of Southern blood, while in his eyes was that dark brilliance which belongs alone to the sons of Italy.

He selected some grapes from the silver fruit-dish, filled a glass with water and dipped them in—true-bred Tuscan that he was—shook them out upon his plate, and then calmly contemplated the old blue Etruscan scarabaeus on the little finger of his left hand. He was waiting for his companion to continue the argument.

The other, twenty years his senior, was ruddy-faced and clean-shaven, with a pair of eyes that twinkled merrily, square jaws denoting considerable determination, altogether a typical Englishman of the buxom, burly, sport-loving kind. Strangely enough, although no one would have dubbed Doctor Filippo Malvano a foreigner, so thoroughly British was his appearance, yet he was an alien. Apparently he was in no mood for conversation, for the habitual twinkle in his eyes had given place to a calm, serious look, and he slowly selected a cigar, while the silence which had fallen between them still remained unbroken.

The man who had expressed confidence again raised his glass to his lips slowly, regarded his companion curiously across its edge, and smiled grimly.

The pair were dining together in a large, comfortable but secluded house lying back from the road at the further end of the quaint, old-world village of Lyddington, in Rutland. The long windows of the dining-room opened out upon the spacious lawn, the extent of which was just visible in the faint mystic light of the August evening, showing beyond a great belt of elms, the foliage of which rustled softly in the fresh night wind, and still further lay the open, undulating country. Ever and anon the wind, in soft gusts, stirred the long lace curtains within the room, and in the vicinity the sweet mellow note of the nightingale broke the deep stillness of rural peace.

Romanelli ate his grapes deliberately, while the Doctor, lighting his long Italian cigar at the candle the servant handed him, rested both elbows on the table and puffed away slowly, still deep in contemplation.

"Surely this girl can be stopped, if you really think there is danger," the younger man observed at last.

At that instant a second maid entered, and in order that neither domestics should understand the drift of their conversation, the Doctor at once dropped into Italian, answering—

"I don't merely think there's danger; I absolutely know there is."

"What? You've been warned?" inquired Arnoldo quickly.

The elder man raised his brows and slowly inclined his head.

Romanelli sprang to his feet in genuine alarm. His face had grown pale in an instant.

"Good heavens!" he gasped in his own tongue. "Surely the game has not been given away?"

The Doctor extended his palms and raised his shoulders to his ears. When he spoke Italian, he relapsed into all his native gesticulations, but in speaking English he had no accent, and few foreign mannerisms.

The two maid-servants regarded the sudden alarm of their master's guest from London with no little astonishment; but the Doctor, quick-eyed, noticed it, and, turning to them, exclaimed in his perfect English—

"You may both leave. I'll ring, if I require anything more."

As soon as the door had closed, Arnoldo, leaning on the back of his chair, demanded further details from his host. He had only arrived from London an hour before, and, half-famished, had at once sat down to dinner.

"Be patient," his host said in a calm, strained tone quite unusual to him. "Sit down, and I'll tell you." Arnoldo obeyed, sinking again into his chair, his dark brows knit, his arms folded on the table, his eyes fixed upon those of the Doctor.

Outwardly there was nothing very striking about either, beyond the fact that they were foreigners of a well-to-do class. The English of the elder man was perfect, but that of Romanelli was very ungrammatical, and in both faces a keen observer might have noticed expressions of cunning and craftiness. Any Italian would have at once detected, from the manner Romanelli abbreviated his words when speaking Italian, that he came from the Romagna, that wild hot-bed of lawlessness and anarchy lying between Florence and Forli, while his host spoke pure Tuscan, the language of Italy. The words they exchanged were deep and earnest. Sometimes they spoke softly, when the Doctor would smile and stroke his smooth-shaven chin, at others they conversed with a volubility that sounded to English ears as though they were quarrelling.

The matter under discussion was certainly a strangely secret one.

The room was well-furnished in genuine old oak, which bore no trace of the Tottenham Court Road; the table was adorned with exotics, and well laid with cut-glass and silver; while the air which entered by the open windows was refreshing after the heat and burden of the August day.

"The simple fact remains, that on the day Vittorina sets foot in London the whole affair must become public property," said Malvano seriously.

"And then?"

"Well, safety lies in flight," the elder man answered, slowly gazing round the room. "I'm extremely comfortable here, and have no desire to go wandering again; but if this girl really comes, England cannot shelter both of us."

Romanelli looked grave, knit his brows, and slowly twirled the ends of his small waxed moustache.

"But how can we prevent her?"

"I've been endeavouring to solve that problem for a fortnight past," his host answered. "While Vittorina is still in Italy, and has no knowledge of my address, we are safe enough. She's the only person who can expose us. As for myself, leading the life of a country practitioner, I'm respected by the whole neighbourhood, dined by the squire and the parson, and no suspicion of mystery attaches to me. I'm buried here as completely as though I were in my grave."

The trees rustled outside, and the welcome breeze stirred the curtains within, causing the lamp to flicker.

"Yet you fear Vittorina!" observed the younger man, puzzled.

"It seems that you have no memory of the past," the other exclaimed, a trifle impatiently. "Is it imperative to remind you of the events on a certain night in a house overlooking the sea of Livorno; of the mystery—"

"Basta!" cried the younger man, frowning, his eyes shining with unnatural fire. "Can I ever forget them? Enough! All is past. It does neither of us good to rake up that wretched affair. It is over and forgotten."

"No, scarcely forgotten," the Doctor said in a low, impressive tone. "Having regard to what occurred, don't you think that Vittorina has sufficient incentive to expose us?"

"Perhaps," Romanelli answered in a dry, dubious tone. "I, however, confess myself sanguine of our success. Certainly you, as an English country doctor, who is half Italian, and who has practised for years among the English colony in Florence, have but very little to fear. You are eminently respectable."

The men exchanged smiles. Romanelli glanced at his ring, and thought the ancient blue scarabaeus had grown darker—a precursory sign of evil.

"Yes," answered Malvano, with deliberation, "I know I've surrounded myself with an air of the most severe respectability, and I flatter myself that the people here little dream of my true position; but that doesn't effect the serious turn events appear to be taking. We have enemies, my dear fellow—bitter enemies—in Florence, and as far as I can discern, there's absolutely no way of propitiating them. We are, as you know, actually within an ace of success, yet this girl can upset all our plans, and make English soil too sultry for us ever to tread it again." A second time he glanced around his comfortable dining-room, and sighed at the thought of having to fly from that quiet rural spot where he had so ingeniously hidden himself.

"It was to tell me this, I suppose, that you wired this morning?" his guest said.

The other nodded, adding, "I had a letter last night from Paolo. He has seen Vittorina at Livorno. She's there for the sea-bathing."

"What did she say?"

"That she intended to travel straight to London."

"She gave him no reason, I suppose?" Arnoldo asked anxiously.

"Can we not easily guess the reason?" the Doctor replied. "If you reflect upon the events of that memorable night, you will at once recognise that she should be prevented from coming to this country."

"Yes. You are right," Romanelli observed in a tone of conviction. "I see it all. We are in peril. Vittorina must not come."

"Then the next point to consider is how we can prevent her," the Doctor said.

A silence, deep and complete, fell between them. The trees rustled, the clock ticked slowly and solemnly, and the nightingale filled the air with its sweet note.

"The only way out of the difficulty that I can see is for me to hazard everything, return to Livorno, and endeavour by some means to compel her to remain in Italy."

"But can you?"

Romanelli shrugged his shoulders. "There is a risk, of course, but I'll do my best," he answered. "If I fail—well, then the game's up, and you must fly."

"I would accompany you to Italy," exclaimed the other, "but, as you are aware, beyond Modane the ground is too dangerous."

"Do you think they suspect anything at the Embassy?"

"I cannot tell. I called the other day when in London, and found the Ambassador quite as cordial as usual."

"But if he only knew the truth?"

"He can only know through Vittorina," answered the Doctor quickly. "If she remains in Italy, he will still be in ignorance. The Ministry at Rome knows nothing, but her very presence here will arouse suspicion."

"Then I'll risk all, and go to Italy," said the younger man decisively. "I don't relish that long journey from Paris to Pisa this weather. Thirty-five hours is too long to be cramped up in that horribly stuffy sleeping-car."

"If you go, you must start to-morrow, and travel straight through," urged the Doctor earnestly. "Don't break your journey, or she may have started before you reach Livorno."

"Very well," his young companion answered. "I'll go right through, as you think it best. If I start from here at six to-morrow morning, I shall be in Livorno on Monday morning. Shall I wire to Paolo?"

"No. Take him by surprise. You'll have a far better chance of success," urged the other; and, pushing the decanter towards him, added, "Help yourself, and let's drink luck to your expedition."

Romanelli obeyed, and both men, raising their glasses, saluted each other in Italian. The younger man no longer wore the air of gay recklessness habitual to him, but took a gulp of the drink with a forced harsh laugh. In the eyes of the usually merry village doctor there was also an expression of doubt and fear. Romanelli was too absorbed in contemplating the risk of returning to Italy to notice the strange sinister expression which for a single instant settled upon his companion's face, otherwise he might not have been so ready to adopt all his suggestions. Upon the countenance of Doctor Malvano was portrayed at that moment an evil passion, and the strange glint in his eyes would in itself have been sufficient proof to the close observer that he intended playing his companion false.

"Then you'll leave Seaton by the six-thirty, eh?" he inquired at last.

Romanelli nodded.

The Doctor touched the gong, and the maid entered. "Fletcher," he said, "the Signore must be called at half-past five to-morrow. Tell Goodwin to have the trap ready to go to Seaton Station to catch the six-thirty."

The maid withdrew, and when the door had closed, Malvano, his elbows on the table, his cold gaze fixed upon his guest, suddenly asked in a low, intense voice, "Arnoldo, in this affair we must have no secrets from each other. Tell me the truth. Do you love Vittorina?" The foppish young man started slightly, but quickly recovering himself, answered—

"Of course not. What absurd fancy causes you to suggest that?"

"Well—she is very pretty, you know," the Doctor observed ambiguously.

The young man looked sharply at his host. "You mean," he said, "that I might make love to her, and thus prevent her from troubling us, eh?"

The other nodded in the affirmative, adding, "You might even marry her."

At that instant the maid entered, bearing a telegram which a lad on a cycle had brought from Uppingham for the Doctor's guest. The latter opened it, glanced at its few faintly-written words, then frowned and placed it in his pocket without comment.

"Bad news?" inquired Malvano. "You look a bit scared."

"Not at all; not at all," he laughed. "Merely a little affair of the heart, that's all" and he laughed in a happy, self-satisfied way. Arnoldo was fond of the society of the fair sex, therefore the Doctor, shrewd and quick of observation, was fully satisfied that the message was from one or other of his many feminine acquaintances.

"Well, induce Vittorina to believe that you love her, and all will be plain sailing," he said. "You are just the sort of fellow who can fascinate a woman and compel her to act precisely as you wish. Exert on her all the powers you possess."

"I'm afraid it will be useless," his companion answered in a dry, hopeless tone.

"Bah! Your previous love adventures have already shown you to be a past-master in the arts of flattery and flirtation. Make a bold bid for fortune, my dear fellow, and you're bound to succeed. Come, let's take a turn across the lawn; it's too warm indoors to-night." Romanelli uttered no word, but rose at his host's bidding, and followed him out. He felt himself staggering, but, holding his breath, braced himself up, and, struggling, managed to preserve an appearance of outward calm. How, he wondered, would Doctor Malvano act if he knew the amazing information which had just been conveyed to him? He drew a deep breath, set his lips tight, and shuddered.

II

The Silver Greyhound

On the same night as the Doctor and his guest were dining in the remote rural village, the express which had left Paris at midday was long overdue at Charing Cross. Presently a troop of porters assembled and folded their arms to gossip, Customs officers appeared, and at last the glaring headlights of the express were seen slowly crossing the bridge which spans the Thames. Within a couple of minutes all became bustle and confusion. The pale faces and disordered appearance of alighting passengers told plainly how rough had been the passage from Calais. Many were tweed-coated tourists returning from Switzerland or the Rhine, but there were others who, by their calm, unruffled demeanour, were unmistakably experienced travellers.

Among the latter was a smart, military-looking man of not more than thirty-three, tall, dark, and slim, with a merry face a trifle bronzed, and a pair of dark eyes beaming with good humour. As he alighted from a first-class carriage he held up his hand and secured a hansom standing by, then handed out his companion, a well-dressed girl of about twenty-two, whose black eyes and hair, rather aquiline features and sun-browned skin, were sufficient evidence that she was a native of the South. Her dress, of some dark blue material, bore the stamp of the first-class costumier; attached to her belt was the small satchel affected by foreign ladies when travelling; her neat toque became her well; and her black hair, although a trifle awry after the tedious, uncomfortable journey, still presented an appearance far neater than that of other bedraggled women around her.

"Welcome to London!" he exclaimed in good Italian.

For a moment she paused, gazing wonderingly about her at the great vaulted station, dazed by its noise, bustle, and turmoil.

"And this is actually London!" she exclaimed. "Ah! what a journey! How thankful I am that it's all over, and I am here, in England at last!"

"So am I," he said, with a sigh of relief as he removed his grey felt hat to ease his head. They had only hand-baggage, and this having been quickly transferred to the cab, he handed her in. As he placed his foot upon the step to enter the vehicle after her, a voice behind him suddenly exclaimed—

"Hullo, Tristram! Back in London again?"

He turned quickly, and recognised in the elderly, grey-haired, well-groomed man in frock-coat and silk hat his old friend Major Gordon Maitland, and shook him heartily by the hand.

"Yes," he answered. "London once again. But you know how I spend my life—on steamboats or in sleeping-cars. To-morrow I may start again for Constantinople. I'm the modern Wandering Jew."

"Except, that you're not a Jew—eh?" the other laughed. "Well, travelling is your profession; and not a bad one either."

"Try it in winter, my dear fellow, when the thermometer is below zero," answered Captain Frank Tristram, smiling. "You'd prefer the fireside corner at the club."

"Urgent business?" inquired the Major, in a lower tone, and with a meaning look.

The other nodded.

"Who's your pretty companion?" Maitland asked in a low voice, with a quick glance at the girl in the cab.

"She was placed under my care at Leghorn, and we've travelled through together. She's charming. Let me introduce you."

Then, approaching the conveyance, he exclaimed in Italian: "Allow me, signorina, to present my friend Major Gordon Maitland,—the Signorina Vittorina Rinaldo."

"Your first visit to our country, I presume?" exclaimed the Major, in rather shaky Italian, noticing how eminently handsome she was.

"Yes," she answered, smiling. "I have heard so much of your great city, and am all anxiety to see it."

"I hope your sojourn among us will be pleasant. You have lots to see. How long shall you remain?"

"Ah! I do not know," she answered. "A week—a month—a year—if need be."

The two men exchanged glances. The last words she uttered were spoken hoarsely, with strange intonation. They had not failed to notice a curious look in her eyes, a look of fierce determination.

"Terribly hot in Leghorn," observed Tristram, turning the conversation after an awkward pause of a few moments. Vittorina held her breath. She saw how nearly she had betrayed herself.

"It has been infernally hot here in London these past few days. I think I shall go abroad to-morrow. I feel like the last man in town."

"Go to Wiesbaden," Tristram said. "I was at the Rose ten days ago, and the season is in full swing. Not too hot, good casino, excellent cooking, and plenty of amusement. Try it."

"No, I think I'll take a run through the Dolomites," he said. "But why have you been down to Leghorn? Surely it's off your usual track."

"Yes, a little. The Ambassador is staying a few weeks for the sea-bathing at Ardenza, close to Leghorn, and I had important despatches."

"She's exceedingly good-looking," the Major said in English, with a smiling glance at the cab. "I envy you your travelling companion. You must have had quite an enjoyable time."

"Forty hours in a sleeping-car is scarcely to be envied this weather," he answered, as a porter, recognising him in passing, wished him a polite "Good journey, I hope, sir?"

Continuing, Tristram said, "But we must be off. I'm going to see her safe through to her friends before going to the office, and I'm already nearly three hours late in London. So good-bye."

"Good-bye," the other said. "Shall I see you at the club to-night?"

"Perhaps. I'm a bit done up by the heat, but I want my letters, so probably I'll look in."

"Buona sera, signorina," Maitland exclaimed, bending towards the cab, shaking her hand and raising his hat politely.

She smiled, returning his salute in her own sweet, musical Tuscan, and then her companion, shouting an address in Hammersmith, sprang in beside her, and they drove off.

"You must be very tired," he said, turning to her as they emerged from the station-yard into the busy Strand.

"No, not so fatigued as I was when we arrived in Paris this morning," she answered, gazing wonderingly at the long line of omnibuses and cabs slowly filing down the brightly lit thoroughfare. "But what confusion! I thought the Via Calzaiuoli in Florence noisy, but this—!" and she waved her small hand with a gesture far more expressive than any words.

Frank Tristram, remarking that she would find London very different to Florence, raised his hand to his throat to loosen his collar, and in doing so displayed something which had until that moment remained concealed. A narrow ribbon was hidden beneath his large French cravat of black silk tied in a bow. The colour was royal blue,

WILLIAM LE QUEUX

and from it was suspended the British royal arms, surmounted by the crown, with a silver greyhound pendant, the badge known on every railway from Calais to Ekaterinbourg, and from Stockholm to Reggio, as that of a King's Foreign Service Messenger. Captain Frank Tristram was one of the dozen wanderers on the face of the earth whose swift journeys and promptness in delivering despatches have earned for them the title of "The Greyhounds of Europe."

So engrossed was the dark-haired girl in contemplating her strange surroundings that she scarcely uttered a word as the cab sped on swiftly through the deepening twilight across Trafalgar Square, along Pall Mall, and up the Haymarket. Suddenly, however, the blaze of electricity outside the Criterion brought to Frank Tristram's mind cherished recollections of whisky and soda, and, being thirsty after the journey, he shouted to the man to pull up there.

"You, too, must be thirsty," he said, turning to her. "At this café, I think, they keep some of your Italian drinks—vermouth, menthe, or muscato."

"Thank you—no," she replied, smiling sweetly. "The cup of English tea I had at Dover did me good, and I'm really not thirsty. You go and get something. I'll remain here."

"Very well," he said. "I won't be more than a minute" and as the cab drew up close to the door of the bar, he sprang out and entered the long saloon.

His subsequent movements were, however, somewhat curious.

After walking to the further end of the bar, he ordered a drink, idled over it for some minutes, his eyes glancing furtively at the lights of the cab outside. Suddenly, when he had uttered a few words to a passing acquaintance, he saw the vehicle move slowly on, probably under orders from the police; and the instant he had satisfied himself that neither Vittorina nor the cabman could observe him, he drained his glass, threw down a shilling, and without waiting for the change turned and continued through the bar, making a rapid exit by the rear door leading into Jermyn Street.

As he emerged, a hansom was passing, and, hailing it, he sprang in, shouted an address, and drove rapidly away.

Meanwhile the cabman who had driven him from Charing Cross sat upon his box patiently awaiting his return, now and then hailing the plethoric drivers of passing vehicles with sarcasm, as cab and 'bus drivers are wont to do, until fully twenty minutes had elapsed. Then, there being no sign of the reappearance of his fare, he opened the trap-door in the roof, exclaiming—

"Nice evenin' miss."

There was no response. The man peered down eagerly for a moment in surprise then cried aloud—

"By Jove! She's fainted!"

Unloosing the strap which held him to his seat, he sprang down and entered the vehicle.

The young girl was lying back in the corner inert and helpless, her hat awry, her pointed chin upon her chest. He pressed his hand to her breast, but there was no movement of the heart. He touched her ungloved hand. It was chilly, and the fingers were already stiffening. Her large black eyes were still open, glaring wildly into space, but her face was blanched to the lips.

"Good heavens!" the cabman cried, stupefied, as in turning he saw a policeman standing on the kerb. "Quick, constable!" he shouted, beckoning the officer. "Quick! Look here!"

"Well, what's the matter now?" the other inquired, approaching leisurely, his thumbs hitched in his belt.

"The matter!" cried the cabman. "Why, this lady I drove from Charin' Cross is dead?"

III

One of a Crowd

Within half a minute a crowd had gathered around the cab.

The instant the cabman raised the alarm the constable was joined by the burly door-opener of the Criterion in gaoler-like uniform and the round-faced fireman, who, lounging together outside, were ever on the look-out for some diversion. But when the constable agreed with the cab-driver that the lady was dead, their ready chaff died from their lips.

"What do you know of her?" asked the officer of the cab-driver.

"Nothing, beyond the fact that I drove 'er from Charin' Cross with a gentleman. She's a foreigner, but he was English."

"Where is he?" demanded the constable anxiously, at that moment being joined by two colleagues, to whom the fireman in a few breathless words explained the affair.

"He went into the bar there 'arf an hour ago, but he ain't come out."

"Quick. Come with me, and let's find him," the officer said.

Leaving the other policemen in charge of the cab, they entered, and walked down, the long, garish bar, scrutinising each of the hundred or so men lounging there. The cabman, however, saw nothing of his fare.

"He must have escaped by the back way," observed the officer disappointedly. "It's a strange business, this."

"Extremely," said the cab-driver. "The fellow must have murdered her, and then entered the place in order to get away. He's a pretty cute 'un."

"It seems a clear case of murder," exclaimed the other in a sharp, precise, business-like tone. "We'll take her to the hospital first; then you must come with me to Vine Street at once."

When they emerged, they found that the crowd had already assumed enormous proportions. The news that a woman had been murdered spread instantly throughout the whole neighbourhood, and the surging crowd of idlers, all curiosity, pressed around the vehicle to obtain a glimpse of the dead woman's face. Amid the crowd, elbowing his way fiercely and determinedly, was a man whose presence there was a somewhat curious coincidence, having regard to what had previously transpired that evening. He wore a silk hat, his frock-coat was tightly buttoned and he carried in his gloved hand a silver-mounted cane. After considerable difficulty, he obtained a footing in front of the crowd immediately behind the cordon the police had formed around the vehicle, and in a few moments, by craning his neck forward, obtained nil uninterrupted view of the lady's face.

His teeth were firmly set, but his calm countenance betrayed no sign of astonishment. For an instant he regarded the woman with a cold, impassive look, then quickly he turned away, glancing furtively right and left, and an instant later was lost in the surging, struggling multitude which a body of police were striving in vain to "move on."

The man who had thus gazed into the dead woman's face was the man to whom she had been introduced at the station. Major Gordon Maitland.

Almost at the same moment when the Major turned away, the constable sprang into the cab beside the woman, and the driver, at once mounting the box, drove rapidly to Charing Cross Hospital.

To the small, bare, whitewashed room to the left of the entrance hall, where casualties are received, the dark-haired girl was carried, and laid tenderly upon the father-covered divan.

The dresser, who attended to minor accidents, gave a quick glance at the face of the new patient, and at once sent for the house-surgeon. He saw it was a grave case.

Very soon the doctor, a thin, elderly man, entered briskly, asked a couple of questions of the constable outside in the corridor, unloosened her dress, cut the cord of her corsets, laid his hands upon her heart, felt her pulse, slowly moved her eyelids, and then shook his head.

"Dead!" he exclaimed. "She must have died nearly an hour ago."

Then he forced open her mouth, and turning the hissing gas-jet to obtain a full light, gazed into it.

His grey, shaggy eyebrows contracted, and the dresser standing by knew that his chief had detected something which puzzled him. He felt the glands in her neck carefully, and pushing back the hair that had fallen over her brow, reopened her fast-glazing eyes, and peered into them long and earnestly.

He carefully examined the palm of her right hand, which was ungloved, then tried to remove the glove from the left, but in vain. He was obliged to rip it up with a pair of scissors. Afterwards he examined the hand minutely, giving vent to a grunt of dissatisfaction.

"Is it murder, do you think, sir?" the constable inquired as the doctor emerged again.

"There are no outward signs of violence," answered the house-surgeon. "You had better take the body to the mortuary, and tell your inspector that I'll make the post-mortem to-morrow morning."

"Very well, sir."

"But you said that the lady was accompanied from Charing Cross Station by a gentleman, who rode in the cab with her," the doctor continued. "Where is he?"

"He alighted, entered the Criterion, and didn't come back," explained the cabman.

"Suspicious of foul play—very suspicious," the doctor observed. "To-morrow we shall know the truth. She's evidently a lady, and, by her dress, a foreigner."

"She arrived by the Paris mail to-night," the cabman observed.

"Well, it must be left to the police to unravel whatever mystery surrounds her. It is only for us to ascertain the cause of her death—whether natural, or by foul means" and he went back to where the dead woman was lying still and cold, her dress disarranged, her dark hair fallen dishevelled, her sightless eyes closed in the sleep that knows no awakening until the Great Day.

The cabman stood with his hat in his hand; the constable had hung his helmet on his forearm by its strap.

"Then, outwardly, there are no signs of murder?" the latter asked, disappointed perhaps that the case was not likely to prove so sensational as it had at first appeared.

"Tell your inspector that at present I can give no opinion," the surgeon replied. "Certain appearances are mysterious. To-night I can say nothing more. At the inquest I shall be able to speak more confidently."

As he spoke, his cold, grey eyes were still fixed upon the lifeless form, as if held by some strange fascination. Approaching the cupboard, he took from a case a small lancet, and raising the dead woman's arm, made a slight incision in the wrist. For a few moments he watched it intently, bending and holding her wrist full in the glaring gaslight within two inches of his eyes.

Suddenly he let the limp, inert arm drop, and with a sigh turned again to the two men who stood motionless, watching, and said: "Go. Take the body to the mortuary. I'll examine her to-morrow" and he rang for the attendants, who came, lifted the body from the couch, and conveyed it out, to admit a man who lay outside groaning, with his leg crushed.

Half an hour later the cab-driver and the constable stood in the small upper room at Vine Street Police Station, the office of the Inspector of the Criminal Investigation Department attached to that station. Inspector Elmes, a dark-bearded, stalwart man of forty-five, sat at a table, while behind him, arranged over the mantelshelf, were many photographs of criminals, missing persons, and people who had been found dead in various parts of the metropolis, and whose friends had not been traced. Pinned against the grey-painted walls were several printed notices offering rewards, some with portraits of absconding persons, others with crude woodcuts of stolen jewels. It was a bare, carpetless loom, but eminently businesslike.

"Well," the inspector was saying to the constable as he leant back in his chair, "there's some mystery about the affair, you think—eh? Are there any signs of murder?"

"No, sir," the man answered. "At present the doctor has discovered nothing."

"Then, until he has, our Department can't deal with it," replied the detective. "Why has your Inspector sent you up here?"

"Because it's so mysterious, I suppose, sir."

"She may have had a fit—most probable, I should think. Until the doctor has certified, I don't see any necessity to stir. It's more than possible that when the man who left her at the Criterion reads of her death in the papers, he'll come forward, identify her, and clear himself." Then, turning to the cabman, he asked, "What sort of a man was he—an Englishman?"

"Well, I really don't know, sir. He spoke to the dead girl in her own language, yet I thought, when he spoke to his friend at the station, that his English was that of a foreigner. Besides, he looked like a Frenchman, for he wore a large bow for a tie, which no Englishman wears."

"You think him a foreigner because of his tie—eh?" the detective observed, smiling. "Now, if you had noticed his boots with a critical eye, you might perhaps have accurately determined his nationality. Look at a man's boots next time."

Then, taking up his pen, he drew a piece of pale yellow official paper before him, noted the number of the cabman's badge, inquired his name and address, and asked several questions, afterwards dismissing both men with the observation that until a verdict had been given in the Coroner's Court, he saw no reason to institute further inquiries.

Two days later the inquest was held in a small room at St. Martin's Town Hall, the handsome building overlooking Trafalgar Square, and, as may be imagined, was largely attended by representatives of the Press. All the sensationalism of London evening journalism had, during the two days intervening, been let loose upon the mysterious affair, and the remarkable "latest details" had been "worked up" into an amazing, but utterly fictitious story. One paper, in its excess of zeal to outdistance all its rivals in sensationalism, had hinted that the dead woman was actually the daughter of an Imperial House, and this had aroused public curiosity to fever-heat.

When the usual formalities of constituting the Court had been completed, the jury had viewed the body, and the cabman had related his strange story, the Coroner, himself a medical man, dark-bearded and middle-aged, commenced a close cross-examination.

"Was it French or Italian the lady spoke?" he asked.

"I don't know the difference, sir," the cabman admitted. "The man with her spoke just as quickly as she did."

"Was there anything curious in the demeanour of either of them?"

"I noticed nothing strange. The gentleman told me to drive along Pall Mall and the Haymarket, or of course I'd 'ave taken the proper route, up Charin' Cross Road and Leicester Square."

"You would recognise this gentleman again, I suppose?" the Coroner asked.

"I'd know him among a thousand," the man promptly replied.

Inspector Elmes, who was present on behalf of the Criminal Investigation Department, asked several questions through the Coroner, when the latter afterwards resumed his cross-examination.

"You have told us," he said, "that just before entering the cab the gentleman was accosted by a friend. Did you overhear any of their conversation?"

"I heard the missing man address the other as 'Major,'" the cabman replied. "He introduced the Major to the lady, but I was unable to catch either of their names. The two men seemed very glad to meet, but, on the other hand, my gentleman seemed in a great hurry to get away."

"You are certain that this man you know as the Major did not arrive by the same train, eh?" asked the Coroner, glancing sharply up from the paper whereon he was writing the depositions of this important witness.

"I am certain; for I noticed him lounging up and down the platform fully 'arf an hour before the train came in."

"Then you think he must have been awaiting his friend?"

"No doubt he was, sir, for as soon as I drove the lady and gentleman away, he, too, started to walk out of the station."

Then the Coroner, having written a few more words upon the foolscap before him, turned to the jury, exclaiming—"This last statement of the witness, gentlemen, seems, to say the least, curious."

In an instant all present were on tip-toe with excitement, wondering what startling facts were likely to be revealed.

IV

"The Major"

No further questions were put to the cab-driver at this juncture, but medical evidence was at once taken. Breathless stillness pervaded the court, for the statement about to be made would put an end to all rumour, and the truth would be known.

When the dapper elderly man had stepped up to the table and been sworn, the Coroner, in the quick, business-like tone which he always assumed toward his fellow medical men, said—

"You are Doctor Charles Wyllie, house-surgeon, Charing Cross Hospital?"

"I am," the other answered in a correspondingly dry tone.

"The woman was brought to the hospital, I suppose?"

"Yes, the police brought her, but she had already been dead about three-quarters of an hour. There were no external marks of violence, and her appearance was as though she had died suddenly from natural causes. In conjunction with Doctor Henderson, I yesterday made a careful post-mortem. The body is that of a healthy woman of about twenty-three, evidently an Italian. There was no trace whatever of organic disease. From what I noticed when the body was brought to the hospital, however, I asked the police to let it remain untouched until I was ready to make a post-mortem."

"Did you discover anything which might lead to suspicion of foul play?" inquired the Coroner.

"I made several rather curious discoveries," the doctor answered, whereat those in court shifted uneasily, prepared for some thrilling story of how the woman was murdered. "First, she undoubtedly died from paralysis of the heart. Secondly, I found around the left ankle a curious tattoo-mark in the form of a serpent with its tail in its mouth. It is beautifully executed, evidently by an expert tattooist. Thirdly, there was a white mark upon the left breast, no doubt the scar of a knife-wound, which I judged to have been inflicted about two years ago. The knife was probably a long narrow-bladed one, and the bone had prevented the blow proving fatal."

"Then a previous attempt had been made upon her life, you think?" asked the Coroner, astonished.

"There is no doubt about it," the doctor answered. "Such a wound could never have been caused by accident. It had no doubt received careful surgical attention, judging from the cicatrice."

"But this had nothing to do with her death?" the Coroner suggested.

"Nothing whatever," replied the doctor. "The appearance of the body gives no indication of foul play."

"Then you assign death to natural causes—eh?"

"No, I do not," responded Dr. Wyllie deliberately, after a slight pause. "The woman was murdered."

These words produced a great sensation in the breathlessly silent court.

"By what means?"

"That I have utterly failed to discover. All appearances point to the fact that the deceased lost consciousness almost instantly, for she had no time even to take out her handkerchief or smelling-salts, the first thing a woman does when she feels faint. Death came very swiftly, but the ingenious means by which the murder was accomplished are at present entirely a mystery. At first my suspicions were aroused by a curious discoloration of the mouth, which I noticed when I first saw the body; but, strangely enough, this had disappeared yesterday when I made the post-mortem. Again, in the centre of the left palm, extending to the middle finger, was a dark and very extraordinary spot. This I have examined microscopically, and submitted the skin to various tests, but have entirely failed to determine the cause of the mark. It is dark grey in colour, and altogether mysterious."

"There was no puncture in the hand?" inquired the Coroner.

"None whatever. I examined the body thoroughly, and found not a scratch," the doctor answered quickly. "At first I suspected a subcutaneous injection of poison; but this theory is negatived by the absence of any puncture."

"But you adhere to your first statement that she was murdered?"

"Certainly. I am confident that the paralysis is not attributable to natural causes."

"Have you found any trace of poison?"

"The contents of the stomach were handed over by the police to the analyst. I cannot say what he has reported," the doctor answered sharply.

At once the Coroner's officer interposed with the remark that the analyst was present, and would give evidence.

The foreman of the jury then put several questions to the doctor.

WILLIAM LE QUEUX

"Do you think, doctor," he asked, "that it would be possible to murder a woman while she was sitting in a cab in so crowded a place as Piccadilly Circus?"

"The greater the crowd, the less the chance of detection, I believe."

"Have you formed no opinion how this assassination was accomplished? Is there absolutely nothing which can serve as clue to the manner in which this mysterious crime was perpetrated?"

"Absolutely nothing beyond what I have already explained," the witness answered. "The grey mark is on the palm of the left hand, which at the time of the mysterious occurrence was gloved. On the hand which was ungloved there is no mark. I therefore am of opinion that this curious discoloration is evidence in some way or other of murder."

"Was she a lady?"

"She had every evidence of being so. All her clothing was of first-class quality, and the four rings she wore were of considerable value. When I came to make the post-mortem, I found both hands and feet slightly swollen, therefore it was impossible to remove her rings without cutting."

The evidence of Dr. Slade, Analyst to the Home Office, being brief, was quickly disposed of. He stated that he had submitted the contents of the stomach to analysis for poison, but had failed to find trace of anything baneful. It was apparent that the woman had not eaten anything for many hours, but that was, of course, accounted for by the fact that she had been travelling. His evidence entirely dismissed the theory of poison, although Dr. Wyllie had asserted most positively that death had resulted from the administration of some substance which had proved so deadly as to cause her to lose consciousness almost instantly, and produce paralysis of the heart.

Certainly the report of the analyst did not support the doctor's theory. Dr. Wyllie was one of the last persons to indulge unduly in any sensationalism, and the Coroner, knowing him well through many years, was aware that there must be some very strong basis for his theory before he would publicly express his conviction that the woman had actually been murdered. Such a statement, when published in the Press in two or three hours' time, would, he knew, give the doctor wide notoriety as a sensation-monger—the very thing he detested above everything. But the fact remained that on oath Dr. Wyllie had declared that the fair, unknown foreigner had been foully and most ingeniously murdered. If this were really so, then the culprit must be a past master in the art of assassination. Of all the inquiries the Coroner had held during many years of office, this certainly was one of the most sensational and mysterious.

When the analyst had concluded, a smartly-dressed young woman, named Arundale, was called. She stated that she was a barmaid at the Criterion, and related how the unknown man, whose appearance she described, had entered the bar, called for a whisky and soda, chatted with her for a few minutes, and then made his exit by the other door.

"Did he speak to any one else while in the bar?" asked the Coroner.

"Yes, while he was talking to me, an older, well-dressed man entered rather hurriedly. The gentleman speaking to me appeared very surprised—indeed, almost alarmed. Then, drawing aside so that I should not overhear, they exchanged a few hurried words, and the elder left by the back exit, refusing the other's invitation to drink. The younger man glanced at his watch, then turned, finished his whisky leisurely, and chatted to me again. I noticed that he was watching the front door all the time, but believing him to be expecting a friend when, suddenly wishing me a hasty 'Good night,' he threw down a shilling and left."

"What sort of man was it who spoke to him?" inquired the Coroner quickly.

"He was a military man, for I heard him addressed as 'Major.'"

"Curious!" the Coroner observed, turning to the jury. "The cab-driver in his evidence says that a certain Major met the pair at Charing Cross Station. It may have been the same person. This coincidence is certainly striking, and one which must be left to the police to investigate. We have it in evidence that the woman and her companion drove away in the cab, leaving the Major—whoever he may be—standing on the platform. The pair drove straight to the Criterion; yet five minutes later the woman's companion was joined by another Major, who is apparently one and the same."

The constable who took the body to the hospital then related how, while on duty in Piccadilly Circus, he had been called to the cab, and found the woman dead. Afterwards he had searched the pockets of the deceased, and taken possession of the lady's dressing-case and the man's hand-bag—all the luggage they had with them in addition to their wraps. He produced the two bags, with their contents, objects which excited considerable interest throughout the room. In the man's bag was a suit of dress-clothes, a small dressing-case, and one or two miscellaneous articles, but nothing by which the owner could be traced.

"Well, what did you find in the lady's pockets? Anything to lead to her identity?" the Coroner asked at last.

"No, sir. In addition to a purse containing some English money, I found a key, a gentleman's card bearing the name 'Arnoldo Romanelli,' and a small crucifix of ivory and silver. In the dressing-case, which you will see is fitted with silver and ivory fittings," he continued, opening it to the gaze of the jury, "there are a few valuable trinkets, one or two articles of attire, and a letter written in Italian—"

"I have the letter here," interrupted the Coroner, addressing the jury. "Its translation reads as follows:—

Dear Vittorina,

"'Be extremely cautious if you really mean to go to England. It is impossible for me to accompany you, or I would; but you know my presence in Italy is imperative. You will easily find Bonciani's Café, in Regent Street. Remember, at the last table on the left every Monday at five.

"'With every good wish for a pleasant journey,

Egisto

"The letter, which has no envelope," added the Coroner, "is dated from Lucca, a town in Tuscany, a week ago. It may possibly assist the police in tracing friends of the deceased." Then, turning to the constable, he asked, "Well, what else was in the lady's bag?"

"This photograph," answered the officer, holding up a cabinet photograph.

"Why!" cried the cab-driver, who had taken a seat close to where the policeman was standing. "Why, that's a photograph of the Major!"

"Yes," added the barmaid excitedly, "that's the same man who came up to the gentleman while he was speaking to me. Without doubt that's the Major, and an excellent portrait, too."

"Strange that this, of all things, should be in the dead woman's possession, when we have it in evidence that she was introduced to him only half an hour before her death," observed the Coroner. "Very strange indeed. Every moment the mystery surrounding this unknown woman seems to grow more impenetrable."

V

Tristram at Home

The jury, after a long deliberation, returned an open verdict of "Found dead." In the opinion of the twelve Strand tradesmen, there was insufficient evidence to justify a verdict of murder, therefore they had contented themselves in leaving the matter in the hands of the police. They had, in reality, accepted the evidence of the analyst in preference to the theory of the doctor, and had publicly expressed a hope that the authorities at Scotland Yard would spare no pains in their endeavours to discover the deceased's fellow traveller, if he did not come forward voluntarily and establish her identity.

This verdict practically put an end to the mystery created by the sensational section of the evening Press, for although it was not one of natural causes, actual murder was not alleged. Therefore, amid the diversity of the next day's news, the whirling world of London forgot, as it ever forgets, the sensation of the previous day. All interest had been lost in the curious circumstances surrounding the death of the unknown Italian girl in the most crowded of London thoroughfares by reason of this verdict of the jury.

The police had taken up the matter actively, but all that had been discovered regarding the identity of the dead woman was that her name was probably Vittorina—beyond that, absolutely nothing. Among the millions who had followed the mystery with avidity in the papers, one man alone recognised the woman by her description, and with satisfaction learnt how ingeniously her death had been encompassed.

That man was the eminently respectable doctor in the remote rural village of Lyddington. With his breakfast untouched before him, he sat in his cosy room eagerly devouring the account of the inquest; then, when he had finished, he cast the paper aside, exclaiming aloud in Italian—

"Dio! What good fortune! I wonder how it was accomplished? Somebody else, besides ourselves, apparently, feared her presence in England. Arnold is in Livorno by this time, and has had his journey for nothing."

Then, with his head thrown back in his chair, he gazed up at the panelled ceiling deep in thought.

"Who, I wonder, could that confounded Englishman have been who escorted her to London and who left her so suddenly? Some Jackanapes or other, I suppose. And who's the Major? He's evidently English too, whoever he is. Only fancy, on the very night we discussed the desirability of the girl's death, some unknown person obligingly did the work for us!" Then he paused, set his teeth, and, frowning, added, "But that injudicious letter of Egisto's may give us some trouble. What an idiot to write like that! I hope the police won't trace him. If they do, it will be awkward—devilish awkward."

A few minutes later the door opened, and a younger man, slim and pale-faced, entered and wished him "good-morning."

"No breakfast?" the man, his assistant, inquired, glancing at the table. "What's the matter?"

"Liver, my boy, liver," Malvano answered with his usual good-humoured smile. "I shall go to town today. I may be absent the whole week; but there's nothing really urgent. That case of typhoid up at Craig's Lodge is going on well. You've seen it once, haven't you?"

"Yes. You're treating it in the usual way, I suppose?"

"Of course" and the doctor, advancing to the table, poured out a cup of coffee and drank it, at the same time calling to his man Goodwin to pack his bag, and be ready to drive him to the London train at ten-twenty.

His assistant being called to the surgery a few minutes later, Malvano sat down at his writing-table, hastily scribbled a couple of telegrams, which he folded and carefully placed in his pocket-book, and half an hour later drove out of the quiet old-world village, with its ancient church spire and long, straggling street of thatched cottages, on his way to catch the train.

Beside the faithful Goodwin he sat in silence the whole way, for many things he had read that morning sorely puzzled him. It was true that the lips of Vittorina were sealed in death, but the letter signed "Egisto," discovered by the police in her dressing-bag, still caused him the most intense anxiety.

At the same hour that Malvano had been reading the account of the previous day's inquest, Frank Tristram was sitting in his handsome, well-furnished chambers in St. James's Street. He had breakfasted early, as was his wont, and had afterwards started his habitual cigarette. The room in which he sat was a typical bachelor's quarter, filled with all sorts of curios and bric-a-brac which its owner had picked up in the various corners of the earth he had visited bearing despatches from the Foreign Office. Upon the floor lay a couple of fine tiger-skins, presents from an Indian rajah, while around were inlaid coffee-stools and trays of beaten brass from Constantinople, a beautiful screen from Cairo, a rare statuette from Rome, quaint pictures and time-yellowed ivories from the curiosity shops of Florence and Vienna, savage weapons from Africa and South America, and a bright, shining samovar from St. Petersburg. In a corner stood the much-worn travelling-bag which he kept always ready packed, and hanging upon a nail above the mantelshelf was the blue ribbon with its silver greyhound, the badge which carried its owner everywhere with the greatest amount of swiftness, and the least amount of personal discomfort. Over the fireplace, too, were many autographed portraits of British ambassadors and distinguished foreign statesmen, together with those of one or two ladies of this constant traveller's acquaintance.

As he lay back in a wicker deck-chair—the same in which he had taken his after-luncheon nap on board many an ocean steamer—well-shaven, smart, and spruce, his legs stretched out lazily, his hands thrust deep into his pockets, he sighed deeply.

"Italy again!" he grumbled to himself as he took up a scribbled note on official paper. "Just my infernal luck. Italy is the very last place I want to visit just now, yet, by Jove! the Chief sends me a message to start this morning." And rousing himself, he stretched his arms and glanced wearily at the little carriage clock. The discarded newspaper on the floor recalled all that he had read half an hour before.

"I wonder," he went on—"I wonder if any one on Charing Cross platform except the porter spotted the girl?" Then he remained silent for a moment. "No. I oughtn't to go to Italy; it's far too risky. There's plenty of time yet for Marvin to be called. I must feign illness, and await my chance to go on a long trip to Pekin, Teheran, or Washington. Yes, a touch of fever will be a good excuse." But, after a moment's further consideration, he added, "Yet, after all, to be ill will be to arouse suspicion. No, I'll go" and he pressed the electric bell.

In answer to the summons his man-servant, a smart, tall ex-private of Dragoons, entered.

"A foreign telegraph form, Smayle," he said.

The man obeyed with military promptitude, and his master a minute later scribbled a few hasty words on the yellow form, securing a berth in the through sleeping-car leaving Paris that night for Rome.

"Take this to the telegraph office in Regent Street," he said. "I'm leaving this morning, and if anybody calls, tell them I've gone to Washington, to Timbuctoo, or to the devil, if you like—anyhow, I shan't be back for a month. You understand?"

"Yes, sir," answered the man with a smile. "Shall I forward any letters?"

"Yes, Poste Restante, Leghorn."

At that moment the bell of the outer door rang out sharply, and Smayle went in response, returning a moment later, saying—

"Major Maitland, sir."

"Show him in," answered his master in a tone of suppressed excitement.

The man disappeared, and a second later the Major entered jauntily, his silk hat slightly askew, extended his well-gloved hand, greeted his friend profusely with the easy air of a man about town, and sank into one of the comfortable saddle-bag chairs.

"Well, my dear fellow," he exclaimed as soon as they were alone. "Why do you risk London after the events of the other night? I never dreamed that I should find you at home."

"I'm leaving for Italy again by the eleven train," the other answered. "Have you read this morning's paper?"

"Of course I have," answered the Major. "It's an infernally awkward bit of business for both of us, I'm afraid. That introduction at the station was the greatest mistake possible, for the cabman will no doubt identify us. Besides, he overheard you address me by rank."

"But the police have no suspicion," Tristram observed. "At present we are safe enough."

"If I were you I wouldn't arrive or depart from Charing Cross for a few months at least," the Major suggested. "The business is far too ugly for us to run any unnecessary risks, you know."

"No; I shall make a habit of departing from London Bridge and arriving at Cannon Street. I never have more than hand-baggage with me."

"Where are you going to-day?"

"To Leghorn again. Right into the very midst of the enemy's camp," he laughed.

"Suppose any facts regarding the mystery have been published in the local papers, don't you think you'd stand a good chance of being arrested? The police in Italy are very arbitrary."

"They dare not arrest me with despatches in my possession. I have immunity from arrest while on official business." His Majesty's messenger answered.

"That may be so," replied the Major. "But you'd have a considerable difficulty in persuading the police of either London or Leghorn that you were not the amiable young man who arrived at Charing Cross with Vittorina."

"And you would have similar difficulty, my dear old chap, in convincing the detectives that you were not the person who waited for us on the platform," the other replied. "You're so well known about town that, if I were you, I should leave London at once, and not take a return ticket."

"I leave to-night."

"By what route?"

"By a rather round-about one," the Major answered, slowly striking a vesta. "The ordinary Channel passage might disagree with me, you know, so I shall travel this evening to Hull, and sail to-morrow morning for Christiania. Thence I shall get down into Germany via Hamburg."

"A very neat way of evading observation," observed the Captain in a tone of admiration.

"I booked my passage a fortnight ago, in case I might require it," the elder man observed carelessly. "When one desires to cover one's tracks, the ordinary Channel services are worse than useless. I call the Norwegian the circular route. I've used it more than once before. They know me on the Wilson liners."

Tristram glanced at his watch. "I must be off in five minutes. What will be your address?"

"Portland before long, if I'm not wary," the other replied, with a grim smile.

"This is no time for joking, Maitland," Tristram said severely. "Reserve your witticisms for the warders, if you really anticipate chokee. They'll no doubt appreciate them."

"Then address me Poste Restante, Brussels. I'm certain to drift to the Europe there sooner or later within the next three months," the Major said.

"Very well, I must go" and the King's messenger quickly obtained his soft grey felt hat and heavy travelling coat from the hall, filled a silver flask from a decanter, took down the blue ribbon, deftly fastened it around his neck out of sight beneath his cravat, and snatched up his travelling-bag.

"I'm going along to the Foreign Office for despatches. Can I drop you anywhere from my cab?" he asked as they made their way down the stairs together.

"No, my dear fellow," the Major replied. "I'm going up Bond Street."

Then, on gaining St. James's Street, the Captain sprang into a cab, and shouting a cheery adieu to his friend, drove off on the first stage of his tedious thousand-mile journey to the Mediterranean shore.

VI

IN TUSCANY

Leghorn, the gay, sun-blanched Tuscan watering-place known to Italians as Livorno, is at its brightest and best throughout the month of August. To the English, save those who reside permanently in Florence, Pisa, or Rome, its beauties are unknown. But those who know Italy—and to know Italy is to love it—are well aware that at "cara Livorno," as the Tuscans call it, one can obtain perhaps the best sea-bathing in Europe, and enjoy a perfectly delightful summer beside the Mediterranean.

It is never obtrusive by its garishness, never gaudy or inartistic; for it makes no pretension to being a first-class holiday resort like Nice or Cannes. Still, it has its long, beautiful Passeggio extending the whole of the seafront, planted with tamarisks, ilexes, and flowing oleanders; it has its wide, airy piazzas, its cathedral, its Grand Hotel, its pensions, and, lastly, its little open cabs in which one can drive two miles for the not altogether ruinous fare of sixpence halfpenny. Its baths, ingeniously built out upon the bare brown rocks into the clear, bright sea, take the place of piers at English seaside resorts, and here during the afternoon everybody, clad in ducks and muslins, lounge in chairs to gossip beneath the widespread awnings, while the waves beat with musical cadence up to their very feet. At evening there are gay, well-lit open-air cafés and several theatres, while the musical can sit in a stall at the opera and hear the best works performed by the best Italian artists for the sum of one and threepence.

But life at Livorno is purely Tuscan. As yet it is unspoilt by English-speaking tourists; indeed, it is safe to say that not three Cookites set foot within the city in twelve months. In its every aspect the town is beautiful. From the sea it presents a handsome appearance, with its lines of high white houses with their red roofs and closed sun-shutters, backed by the distant blue peaks of the Lucca Mountains, and the serrated spurs of the purple Apennines, while in its sun-whitened streets the dress of the Livornesi, with their well-made skirts of the palest and most delicate tints of blue, grey, and rose, and with their black silk scarves or lace mantillas twisted about their handsome heads, is the most artistic and tasteful in all fair Italy. The men are happy, careless, laughing fellows, muscular, and bronzed by the sun; the women dark-eyed, black-haired, and notable throughout the length and breadth of Europe for their extreme beauty and their grace of carriage.

Little wonder is it that stifled Florentines, from shopkeepers to princes, unable to bear the heat and mosquitoes beside the muddy Arno, betake themselves to this bright little watering-place during August and September, where, even if the heat is blazing at midday, the wind is delightfully cool at evening, and the sea-baths render life really worth living. Unless one has spent a summer in Tuscany, it is impossible to realise its stifling breathlessness and its sickening sun-glare. Unless one has lived among the sly, secretive, proud but carelessly happy Livornesi, has shared their joys, sympathised with their sorrows, fraternised with them and noted their little peculiarities, one can never enjoy Livorno.

At first the newly arrived foreigner is pointed at by all as one apart, and considered an imbecile for preferring Livorno to Florence, or Milano; every shopkeeper endeavours to charge him double prices, and for every trifling service performed he is expected to disburse princely tips. But the Tuscan heart is instantly softened towards him as soon as he seems likely to become a resident; all sorts and conditions of men do him little kindnesses without monetary reward; grave-faced monks will call at his house and leave him presents of luscious fruits and fresh-cut salads; and even his cabman, the last to relent, will one day, with profuse apology for previous extortions, charge only his just fare.

The Italians are indeed an engaging people. It is because they are so ingenuous, so contented, so self-denying, so polite yet so sarcastic, that one learns to love them so well.

Along the Viale Regina Margherita, or esplanade—better known perhaps by its ancient name, the Passeggio—are a number of baths, all frequented by different grades of society, the one most in vogue among the better-class residents and visitors being a handsome establishment with café and skating-rink attached, known as Pancaldi's.

It was here, one evening soon after the mysterious death of Vittorina in London, that two persons, a man and a woman, were sitting, watching the ever-changing hues of one of those glorious blazing sunsets seen nowhere else in the world but in the Mediterranean. The broad, asphalted promenade, covered by its wide canvas awnings, was almost blocked by the hundreds of gaily dressed persons sitting on chairs chattering and laughing, and it seemed as though all the notable people of Florence and

Bologna had assembled there to enjoy the cool breeze after the terrific heat of the August day. Along the Viale the road was sun-bleached, the wind-swept tamarisks were whitened by the dust, and the town that day had throbbed and gasped beneath the terrible, fiery August glare. But here, at Pancaldi's, was light, happy chatter—in Italian of various dialects, of course—a cool, refreshing breeze, and that indefinable air of delicious laziness which Italy alone claims as her birthright.

The pair sitting together at the end of the asphalted walk, at some distance from the crowd, were young and, to a casual observer, well matched. Unlike all others round about her, the woman was of fair complexion, about twenty-five, with that gold-brown hair that Titian loved to paint, eyes of a deep and wondrous blue, a small, adorable mouth, the upper lip of which possessed that rare attribute, the true Cupid's bow, a face sweet, almost childlike in expression, prefect in its purity. Her great beauty was well set off by her black dress and tiny black bonnet, but from the crown of her head to the toe of her pointed patent-leather shoe there was a chic and daintiness about her which, to an English eye, stamped her as foreign, even though her face bore no trace of Italian blood.

Half that gay, gossiping crowd, attracted by her beauty, had already set her down as English, perhaps because her fairness was uncommon in Tuscany, perhaps because they detected by the cut of her companion's clothes that he was English. But Gemma Fanetti was really a native of Florence, a true-bred Tuscan, who knew not half a dozen words of English. She could chatter French a little, and could gabble the nasal Milanese dialect, but it always amused her to be taken for an Englishwoman.

Her dress, although black, and only relieved by a little white lace at the throat and wrists, was made in the latest mode, and fitted her perfectly. On her slim wrist was a single bangle of diamonds, which flashed in the dying sunlight with all the colours of the spectrum as, in chatting idly with her companion, she slowly traced semicircles on the ground with the point of her black sunshade. Undoubtedly she was strikingly beautiful, for men in twos and threes were passing and repassing solely for the purpose of obtaining a glance at her.

Utterly unconscious of their admiration, of the whisperings of those about her, or of the glorious wealth of colour spread before them as the sun sank deep into the grey, glittering sea, they both chatted on, glancing now and then into each other's eyes.

Her companion was about twenty-eight, good-looking, dark-eyed, with a merry face and an air of carelessness as, in a suit of cool, white ducks, and his straw hat tilted slightly over his brow to shade his eyes, he sat back in his chair, joining in her low, well-bred laughter. Truth to tell, Charles Armytage was desperately in love.

For seven years—ever since he came of age and succeeded to his father's property in Wales—he had led a wild, rather dissipated life on the Continent, and had found himself world-weary before his time. His college career had terminated somewhat ignominiously, for he had been "sent down" on account of a rather serious practical joke; he had studied for the Bar, and failed; he had done the whole round of the public gaming establishments, Monte Carlo, Ostend, Spa, Dinant, Namur, and Trouville, losing heavily at each; he had idled on the sands of Scheveningen, flirted on the Promenade des Anglais at Nice, tasted the far-famed oysters at Arcachon, the bouillabaisse at Marseilles, and bathed on San Sebastian's golden sands. Once he had taken a fit into his head to visit all the spas, and, beginning with Royat, he made a tour of all the principal ones as far as Carlsbad. Thus had he developed into a thorough cosmopolitan, travelling hither and thither just as his fancy led him, his only hobby being in occasionally writing a short story or travel article for one or other of the English magazines.

It was in his restless, dejected mood that, six months before, he had arrived in Florence, and by mere chance had first met the woman who was now beside him. He had one morning been walking along the Via Tornabuoni when he first saw her, accompanied by her servant. Suddenly something fell to the pavement, and an urchin instantly snatched it up. Armytage ran after him, recovered the little golden charm, and handed it to its owner, being rewarded by a few words of thanks. Her grace, her beauty, her soft, musical voice rekindled within him a desire for life. Instantly he became fascinated by her wondrous beauty, and she, too, seemed content to chat with him, and to listen to his very faulty Italian, which must have been exceedingly difficult for her to understand.

They did not meet often, but always casually. Once or twice he encountered her cycling in the Cascine, and had joined her in a spin along the shady avenues. They had exchanged cards, but she had never invited him to call, and he, living at a hotel, could scarcely invite her. Italian manners strictly preserve the *convenances*. No unmarried lady in any Tuscan city, not even a woman of the people, ever dreams of going out alone. Even the poorest girl is chaperoned whenever she takes an airing.

Suddenly, just when Armytage found himself hopelessly infatuated, he one morning received an urgent telegram calling him to London, and he had been compelled to leave without a word of farewell, or any knowledge of her address.

As soon as he could, he returned to Florence, but the weather had then grown hot, and all who were able had left the sun-baked city. Then, disappointed at not finding her after an active search, he drifted down to the sea at Livorno, and within three days was delighted to see her strolling in the Passeggio with her ugly, cross-eyed serving woman. The recognition was mutual, and after one or two meetings she explained that she had a flat for the season in one of the great white houses opposite, and expressed a hope that he would call.

He lost no time in renewing the acquaintance, and now they were inseparable. He loved her.

"Do you know, Gemma," he was saying seriously, "when I left Florence in March, I left my heart behind—with you."

She blushed slightly beneath her veil, and raising her clear blue eyes to his, answered with a slight sigh in her soft Italian—

"You say you love me, caro; but can I really believe you?"

"Of course you can, dearest," he answered earnestly, speaking her tongue with difficulty. "I love no other woman in the whole world but you."

"Ah!" she exclaimed sadly, gazing blankly away across the sea, now glittering crimson in the blaze of the dying day. "I sometimes fear to love you, because you may tire of me one day, and go back to some woman of your own people."

"Never," he answered fervently. "As I told you yesterday, Gemma, I love you; and you, in return, have already given me your pledge."

"And you can actually love me like this, blindly, without inquiring too deeply into my past?" she whispered, regarding him gravely with those calm, clear eyes, which seemed to penetrate his very soul.

"Your past matters not to me," he answered in a deep, intense voice under his breath, so that passers-by should not overhear. "I have asked you nothing; you have told me nothing. I love you, Gemma, and trust to your honour to tell me what I ought to know."

"Ah! you are generous!" she exclaimed; and he saw beneath her veil a single tear upon her cheek. "The past life of a man can always be effaced;

that of a woman never. A false step, alas! lives as evidence against her until the grave."

"Why are you so melancholy this evening?" he asked, after a pause.

"I really don't know," she answered. "Perhaps it is because I am so happy and contented. My peace seems too complete to be lasting."

"While you love me, Gemma, I shall love you always," he exclaimed decisively. "You need never have any doubt about my earnestness. I adore you."

Her breast heaved and fell beneath its black lace and jet, and she turned her fine eyes upon him with an expression more eloquent than any words of assurance and affection.

Then, after a brief silence, he glanced around at the crowd about them, saying—

"It is impossible to speak further of our private affairs here. You will dine with me to-night. Where shall it be?"

"Let's dine at the Eden. There's plenty of air there. We can get a table facing the sea, and stay to the performance afterwards. Shall we?" she asked, her face brightening.

"Certainly," he replied. "I'll go across to the hotel and dress, while you go along home and put on another frock. I know you won't go in black to a *café chantant*," he added, laughing.

"You'll call for me?" she asked.

"Yes, at eight."

As these words fell from his lips a man's voice in English exclaimed—

"Hulloa, Charlie! Who'd have thought of finding you here?"

Armytage looked up quickly, and, to his surprise, found standing before him his old college chum and fellow clubman, Frank Tristram.

"Why, Frank, old fellow!" he cried, jumping up and grasping the other's hand warmly. "We haven't met for how long? The last time was one night in the Wintergarden at Berlin, fully two years ago—eh?"

"Yes. Neither of us are much in London nowadays, therefore we seldom meet. But what are you doing here?" asked the King's messenger, looking cool and smart in his suit of grey flannel.

"Killing time, as usual," his friend replied, with a smile.

"Lucky devil!" Tristram exclaimed. "While I'm compelled to race from end to end of Europe for a paltry eight hundred a year, you laze away your days in an out-of-the-world place like this." And he glanced significantly at the sweet, fair-faced woman who, having given him a swift look, was now sitting motionless, her hands idly crossed upon her lap, her eyes fixed blankly upon the sunlit sea.

"Let me introduce you," Armytage exclaimed in Italian, noticing his friend's look of admiration. "The Signorina Gemma Fanetti—my friend, Captain Frank Tristram."

The latter bowed, made a little complimentary speech in excellent Italian, and seated himself with Armytage beside her.

"Well," Tristram said, still speaking in Italian, "this is quite an unexpected pleasure. I thought that in addition to the Ambassador out at Ardenza, and the jovial Jack Hutchinson, the Consul, I was the only Englishman in this purely Tuscan place." Then turning to his friend's companion, he asked, "Are you Livornese?"

"Oh, no," she replied, with a gay, rippling laugh, "I live in Florence; only just now the place is stifling, so I'm down here for fresh air."

"Ah, Florence!" he said. "The old city is justly termed 'La Bella.' I sometimes find myself there in winter, and it is always interesting, always delightful."

At that moment an English lady, the wife of an Italian officer, bowed in passing, and Armytage sprang to his feet and began to chat to her. He had known her well during his stay in Florence earlier in the year.

As soon as Gemma noticed that her lover was no longer listening, her manner at once changed, and bending quickly towards the Captain, she exclaimed in rapid Italian, which she knew Armytage could not understand—

"Well, did you see Vittorina safely to London?"

Tristram started at the unexpected mention of that name.

"Yes," he answered, with slight hesitation. "I saw her safely as far as Charing Cross, but was compelled to leave her there, and put her in a cab for Hammersmith."

"How far is that?"

"About five kilometres," he replied.

"I have had no telegram from her," she observed. "She promised to wire to me as soon as she arrived, and I am beginning to feel anxious about her."

"Worry is useless," he said calmly. "She is no doubt quite safe with her friends. I gave the cabman the right address. My official business was pressing, or I would have gone out to Hammersmith with her."

"You remember what I told you on the night we parted in Florence?" she said mysteriously.

WILLIAM LE QUEUX

He nodded, and his dark face grew a shade paler.

"Well, I have discovered that what I suspected was correct," she said, her eyes flashing for an instant with a strange glint. "Some one has betrayed the secret."

"Betrayed you!" he gasped.

She shrugged her shoulders. Her clear eyes fixed themselves fiercely upon him.

"You alone knew the truth," she said. "And you have broken your promise of silence."

He flinched.

"Well?" he said. "You are, of course, at liberty to make any charge you like against me, but I can only declare that I have not divulged one single word." Then he added quickly, "But what of Armytage? Does he know anything?"

"Absolutely nothing," she answered quickly. "I love him. Remember that you and I have never met before our introduction this afternoon."

"Of course," the Captain answered.

"Curious that Vittorina has disappeared! If I hear nothing of her, I shall go to London and find her," Gemma observed, after a few moments' silence.

"Better not, if you really have been betrayed," he answered quickly.

"I have been betrayed, Captain Tristram," she said rapidly, with withering scorn, her face flushing instantly, her large, luminous eyes flashing. "You are well aware that I have; and, further, you know that you yourself are my bitterest enemy. I spare you now, mean, despicable coward that you are, but utter one word to the man I love, and I will settle accounts with you swiftly and relentlessly."

She held her breath, panting for an instant, then turning from him, greeted her lover with a sweet, winning smile, as at that moment he returned to her side.

VII

Doctor Malvano

Among the thousand notable dining-places in London, Bonciani's Restaurant, in Regent Street, is notable for its *recherche* repasts. It is by no means a pretentious place, for its one window displays a few long-necked, rush-covered flasks of Tuscan wine, together with some rather sickly looking plants, a couple of framed menus, and two or three large baskets of well-selected fruit.

Yet to many, mostly clubmen and idlers about town, the Bonciani is a feature of London life. In the daytime the passer-by sees no sign of activity within, and even at night the place presents an ill-lit, paltry, and uninviting appearance. But among the few in London who know where to dine well, the little unpretentious place halfway up Regent Street, on the left going toward Oxford Street, is well known for its unrivalled cuisine, its general cosiness, and its well-matured wines. The interior is not striking. There are no gilt-edged mirrors, as is usual in Anglo-Italian restaurants, but the walls are frescoed, as in Italy, with lounges upholstered in red velvet, a trifle shabby, extending down the long, rather low room. Upon the dozen little marble-topped tables, with their snow-white cloths, are objects seen nowhere else in London, namely, silver-plated holders for the wine-flasks; for with the dinner here wine is inclusive, genuine Pompino imported direct from old Galuzzo in the Val d'Ema beyond Firenze, a red wine of delicate bouquet which connoisseurs know cannot be equalled anywhere in London.

One evening, about a week after the meeting between Gemma and Tristram at Livorno, nearly all the tables were occupied, as they usually are at the dining hour, but at the extreme end sat two men, eating leisurely, and taking long draughts from the great rush-covered flask before them. They were Tristram and Romanelli.

Four days ago the pair had met late at night at the railway station at Leghorn, and the one hearing the other demand a ticket for London, they got into conversation, and travelled through together, arriving at Victoria on the previous evening. During the three days of travelling they had become very friendly, and now, at the Italian's invitation, Tristram was dining previous to his return on the morrow to Livorno, for at that period Italy was approaching England on the subject of a treaty, and the correspondence between our Ambassador and the Foreign Office was considerable, necessitating despatches being sent to Italy almost daily.

"So you return to-morrow?" Romanelli exclaimed, twirling his tiny black moustache affectedly. To men his foppishness was nauseating; but women liked him because of his amusing gossip.

"Yes," the other answered, sighing. "I expected to get a few days' rest in London, but this afternoon I received orders to leave again to-morrow."

"Your life must be full of change and entertainment," the young Italian said.

"Rather too full," the other laughed. "Already this year I've been to Italy more than twenty times, besides three times to Constantinople, once to Stockholm, twice to Petersburg, and innumerable trips to Brussels and Paris. But, by the way," he added, putting down his glass as if a sudden thought had occurred to him, "you know Leghorn well, I think you said?"

"I'm not Livornese, but I lived there for ten years," the other answered. "I came to London a year ago to learn English, for they said it was impossible to get any sort of good pronunciation in Italy."

"I've passed through Pisa hundreds of times, but have only been in Leghorn once or twice," observed the King's messenger. "Charming place. Full of pretty girls."

"Ah! yes," cried Romanelli. "The English always admire our Livornesi girls."

Tristram paused for a few seconds, then, raising his eyes until they met those of his new acquaintance, asked—

"Do you happen to know a girl there named Fanetti—Gemma Fanetti?"

Romanelli started perceptibly, and for an instant held his breath. He was utterly unprepared for this question, and strove vainly not to betray his surprise.

"Fanetti," he repeated aloud, as if reflecting. "I think not. It is not a Livornese name."

"She lives in Florence, I believe, but always spends the bathing season at Leghorn," Tristram added. His quick eyes had detected the Italian's surprise and anxiety when he had made the unexpected inquiry, and he felt confident that his foppish young friend was concealing the truth.

"I've never, to my recollection, met any one of that name," Romanelli answered with well-feigned carelessness. "Is she a lady or merely a girl of the people?"

"A lady."

"Young?"

"Quite. She's engaged to be married to a friend of mine."

"Engaged to be married?" the young man repeated with a smile. "Is the man an Englishman?"

"Yes, a college chum of mine. He's well off, and they seem a most devoted pair."

There was a brief silence.

"I have no recollection of the name in Florentine society, and I certainly have never met her in Livorno," Romanelli said. "So she's found a husband? Is she pretty?"

"Extremely. The prettiest woman I've ever seen in Italy."

"And there are a good many in my country," the Italian said. "The poor girl who died so mysteriously—or who, some say, was murdered—outside the Criterion was very beautiful. I knew her well—poor girl!"

"You knew her?" gasped the Captain, in turn surprised. "You were acquainted with Vittorina Rinaldo?"

"Yes," replied his companion slowly, glancing at him with some curiosity. "But, tell me," he added after a pause, "how did you know her surname? The London police have failed to discover it?"

Frank Tristram's brow contracted. He knew that he had foolishly betrayed himself. In an instant a ready lie was upon his lips.

"I was told so in Livorno," he said glibly. "She was Livornese."

"Yes," Romanelli observed, only half convinced. "According to the papers, it appears as if she were accompanied by some man from Italy. But her death and her companion's disappearance are alike unfathomable mysteries."

"Extraordinary!" the Captain acquiesced. "I've been away so much that I haven't had a chance to read the whole of the details. But the scraps I have read seem remarkably mysterious."

"There appears to have been absolutely no motive whatever in murdering her," Arnoldo said, glancing sharply across the table at his companion.

"If it were really murder, there must have been some hidden motive," Tristram declared. "Personally, however, in the light of the Coroner's verdict, I'm inclined to the opinion that the girl died suddenly in the cab, and the man sitting beside her, fearing that an accusation of murder might bring about some further revelation, made good his escape."

"He must have known London pretty well," observed Romanelli.

"Of course. The evidence proves that he was an Englishman; and that he knew London was quite evident from the fact that he gave instructions to the cabman to drive up the Haymarket, instead of crossing Leicester Square."

Again a silence fell between them, as a calm-faced elderly waiter, in the most correct garb of the Italian *cameriere*—a short jacket and long white apron reaching almost to his feet—quickly removed their empty plates. He glanced swiftly from one man to the other, polished Tristram's plate with his cloth as he stood behind him, and exchanged a meaning look with Romanelli. Then he turned suddenly, and went off to another table, to which he was summoned by the tapping of a knife upon a plate. The glance he had exchanged with the young Italian was one of recognition and mysterious significance.

This man, the urbane head-waiter, known well to frequenters of the Bonciani as Filippo, was known equally well in the remote Rutlandshire village as Doctor Malvano, the man who had expressed fear at the arrival of Vittorina in England, and who, truth to tell, led the strangest dual existence of doctor and waiter.

None in rural Lyddington suspected that their jovial doctor, with his merry chaff and imperturbable good humour, became grave-faced and suddenly transformed each time he visited London; none dreamed that his many absences from his practice were due to anything beyond his natural liking for theatres and the gaiety of town life; and none would have credited, even had it ever been alleged, that this man who could afford that large, comfortable house, rent shooting, and keep hunters in his stables, on each of his visits to London, assumed a badly starched shirt, black tie, short jacket, and long white apron, in order to collect stray pence from diners in a restaurant. Yet such was the fact. Doctor Malvano, who had been so well known among the English colony in Florence, was none other than Filippo, head-waiter at the obscure little café in Regent Street.

"It is still a mystery who the dead girl was," Tristram observed at last. "The man who told me her name only knew very little about her."

"What did he know?" Romanelli inquired quickly. "I had often met her at various houses in Livorno, but knew nothing of her parentage."

"Nobody seems to know who she really was," Tristram remarked pensively; "and her reason for coming to England seems to have been entirely a secret one."

"A lover, perhaps," Arnoldo said.

"Perhaps," acquiesced his friend.

"But who told you about her?"

"There have been official inquiries through the British Consulate," the other answered mysteriously.

"Inquiries from the London police?"

The King's messenger nodded in the affirmative, adding—

"I believe they have already discovered a good many curious facts."

"Have they?" asked Romanelli quickly, exchanging a hasty glance with Filippo, who at that moment had paused behind his companion's chair.

"What's the nature of their discoveries?"

"Ah!" Tristram answered, with a provoking smile. "I really don't know, except that I believe they have discovered something of her motive for coming to England."

"Her motive!" the other gasped, a trifle pale. "Then there is just a chance that the mystery will be elucidated, after all."

"More than a chance, I think," the Captain replied. "The police, no doubt, hold a clue by that strange letter written from Lucca which was discovered in her dressing-case. And, now that I recollect," he added in surprise, "this very table at which we are sitting is the one expressly mentioned by her mysterious correspondent. I wonder what was meant by it?"

"Ah, I wonder!" the Italian exclaimed mechanically, his brow darkened by deep thought. "It was evident that the mysterious Egisto feared that some catastrophe might occur if she arrived in England, and he therefore warned her in a vague, veiled manner."

Filippo came and went almost noiselessly, his quick ears constantly on the alert to catch their conversation, his clean-shaven face grave, smileless, sphinx-like.

"Well," the Captain observed in a decisive manner, "you may rest assured that Scotland Yard will do its utmost to clear up the mystery surrounding the death of your friend, for I happen to know that the Italian Ambassador in London has made special representation to our Home Office upon the subject, and instructions have gone forth that no effort is to be spared to solve the enigma."

"Then our Government at Rome have actually taken up the matter?" the Italian said in a tone which betrayed alarm.

Tristram smiled, but no word passed his lips. He saw that his new acquaintance had not the slightest suspicion that it was he who had accompanied Vittorina from Italy to London; that it was he who had escaped so ingeniously through the bar of the Criterion; that it was for him the police were everywhere searching.

At last, when they had concluded their meal, Romanelli paid Filippo, giving him a tip, and the pair left the restaurant to pass an hour at the Empire before parting.

Once or twice the young Italian referred to the mystery, but found his companion disinclined to discuss it further.

"In my official capacity, I dare not say what I know," Tristram said at last in an attitude of confidence, as they were sitting together in the crowded lounge of the theatre. "My profession entails absolute secrecy. Often I am entrusted with the exchange of confidences between nations, knowledge of which would cause Europe to be convulsed by war from end to end, but secrets entrusted to me remain locked within my own heart."

"Then you are really aware of true facts?" inquired the other.

"Of some," he replied vaguely, with a mysterious smile.

The hand of his foppish companion trembled as he raised his liqueur-glass to his pale lips. But he laughed a hollow, artificial laugh, and then was silent.

VIII

Her Ladyship's Secret

Filippo, grey-faced, but smart nevertheless, continued to attend to the wants of customers at the Bonciani until nearly ten o'clock. He took their orders in English, transmitted them in Italian through the speaking tube to the kitchen, and deftly handed the piles of plates and dishes with the confident air of the professional waiter.

Evidence was not wanting that to several elderly Italians he was well known, for he greeted them cheerily, advised them as to the best dishes, and treated them with fatherly solicitude from the moment they entered until their departure.

At ten o'clock only two or three stray customers remained, smoking their long rank cigars and sipping their coffee, therefore Filippo handed over his cash, assumed his shabby black overcoat, and wishing "buona notte" to his fellow-waiters, and "good-night" to the English check-taker at the small counter, made his way out and eastward along Regent Street. It was a bright, brilliant night, cool and refreshing after the heat of the day. As he crossed Piccadilly Circus, the glare of the Criterion brought back to him the strange occurrence that had recently taken place before that great open portal, and, with a glance in that direction, he muttered to himself—

"I wonder if the truth will ever be discovered? Strange that Arnoldo's friend knows so much, yet will tell so little! That the girl was killed seems certain. But how, and by whom? Strange," he added, after a pause as he strode on, deep in thought—"very strange."

Engrossed in his own reflections, he passed along Wardour Street into Shaftesbury Avenue, and presently entered the heart of the foreign quarter of London, a narrow, dismal street of high, dingy, uninviting-looking houses known as Church Street, a squalid, sunless thoroughfare behind the glaring Palace of Varieties, inhabited mostly by French and Italians.

He paused before a dark, dirty house, a residence of some importance a century ago, judging from its deep area, its wide portals, and its iron extinguishers, once used by the now-forgotten linkman, and, taking out a latchkey, opened the door, ascending to a small bed-sitting-room on the third floor, not over clean, but nevertheless comfortable. Upon the small side-table, with its cracked and clouded mirror, stood the removable centre of his dressing-bag with its silver fittings, and hanging behind the door were the clothes he wore when living his other life.

He lit the cheap paraffin lamp, pulled down the faded crimson blind, threw his hat and coat carelessly upon the bed, and, after glancing at his watch, sank into the shabby arm-chair.

"Still time," he muttered. "I wonder whether she'll come? If she don't—if she refuses—"

And sighing, he took out a cigarette, lit it, and throwing back his head, meditatively watched the smoke rings as they curled upwards.

"I'd give something to know how much the police have actually discovered," he continued, speaking to himself. "If they've really discovered Vittorina's object in visiting London, then I must be wary not to betray my existence. Already the Ambassador must have had his suspicions aroused, but, fortunately, her mouth is closed for ever. She cannot now betray the secret which she held, nor can she utter any wild denunciations. Our only fear is that the police may possibly discover Egisto in Lucca, make inquiries of him, and thus obtain a key to the whole matter. Our only hope, however, is that Egisto, hearing of the fatal termination of Vittorina's journey, and not desiring to court inquiry, has wisely fled. If he has remained in Lucca after writing that most idiotic letter, he deserves all the punishment he'll get for being such a confounded imbecile."

Then, with an expression of disgust, he smoked on in a lazy, indolent attitude, regardless of the shabbiness and squalor of his surroundings.

"It is fortunate," he continued at last, speaking slowly to himself— "very fortunate, indeed, that Anioldo should have met this cosmopolitan friend of his. He evidently knows something, but does not intend to tell us. One thing is evident—he can't have the slightest suspicion of the real facts as we know them; but, on the other hand, there seems no doubt that the police have ascertained something—how much, it is impossible to tell. That the Italian Ambassador has made representations to the Home Office is quite correct. I knew it days ago. Therefore his other statements are likely to be equally true. By Jove!" he added, starting suddenly to his feet. "By jove! If Egisto should be surprised by the police, the fool is certain to make a clean breast of the whole thing in order to save his own neck. Then will come the inevitable crisis! Dio! Such a catastrophe is too terrible to contemplate."

He drew a deep breath, murmured some inaudible words, and for a long time sat consuming cigarette after cigarette. Then, glancing at his watch again, and finding it past eleven, he rose and stretched himself, saying—

"She's not coming. Well, I suppose I must go to her." Quickly he took from his bag a clean shirt, and assuming a light covert-coat and a crush hat, he was once again transformed into a gentleman. By the aid of a vesta he found his way down the dark carpetless stairs, and, hurrying along, soon gained Shaftesbury Avenue, where he sprang into a hansom and gave the man instructions to drive to Sussex Square, Hyde Park.

In twenty minutes the conveyance pulled up before the wide portico of a handsome but rather gloomy-looking house. His summons was answered by a footman who, recognising him at once, exclaimed, "Her ladyship is at home, sir" and ushered him into a well-furnished morning-room.

A few moments elapsed, when the man returned, and Malvano, with the air of one perfectly acquainted with the arrangements of the house, followed him up the wide, well-lit staircase to the drawing-room, a great apartment on the first floor resplendent with huge mirrors, gilt furniture, and costly bric-a-bric.

Seated in an armchair at the farther end of the room beside a table whereon was a shaded lamp, sat a small, ugly woman, whose aquiline face was wizened by age, whose hair was an unnatural flaxen tint, and whose cheeks were not altogether devoid of artificial colouring.

"So you are determined to see me?" she exclaimed petulantly.

"I am," he answered simply, seating himself without hesitation in a chair near her.

Her greeting was the reverse of cordial. As she spoke her lips parted, displaying her even rows of false teeth; as she moved, her dress of rich black silk rustled loudly; and as she placed her book upon the table with a slight sigh, the fine diamonds in her bony, claw-like hand sparkled with a thousand fires.

"Well, why have you come—at this hour, too?" she inquired with a haughtiness which she always assumed towards her servants and inferiors. She sat rigid, immovable; and Malvano, student of character that he was, saw plainly that she had braced herself for an effort.

"I asked you to come to me, and you have refused," he said, folding his arms calmly and looking straight into her rouged and powdered face; "therefore I have come to you."

"For what purpose? Surely we could have met at the Bonciani?"

"True, but it was imperative that I should see you to-night."

"More complications—eh?"

"Yes," he replied, "more complications—serious ones."

"Serious!" her ladyship gasped, turning instantly pale. "Is the truth known?" she demanded quickly. "Tell me at once; don't keep me in suspense."

"Be patient for a moment, and I'll explain my object in calling," the Doctor said gravely. "Compose yourself, and listen."

The Countess of Marshfield drew her skirts around her and moved uneasily in her chair. She was well known in London society, a woman whose eccentricities had for years afforded plenty of food for the gossips, and whose very name was synonymous with senile coquetry. Her age was fully sixty-five, yet like many other women of position, she delighted in the delusion that she was still young, attractive, and fascinating. Her attitude towards young marriageable men would have been nauseating were it not so absolutely ludicrous; and the way in which she manipulated her fan at night caused her to be ridiculed by all the exclusive set in which she moved.

The dead earl, many years her senior, had achieved brilliant success in the Army, and his name was inscribed upon the roll of England's heroes. Ever since his death, twenty years ago, however, she had been notable on account of her foolish actions, her spasmodic generosity to various worthless institutions, her wild speculations in rotten companies, and her extraordinary eccentricities. As she sat waiting for her visitor to commence, her thin blue lips twitched nervously, and between her eyes was the deep furrow that appeared there whenever she was unduly agitated. But even then she could not resist the opportunity for coquetry, for, taking up her small ivory fan, she opened it, and, slowly waving it to and fro, glanced at him across it, her lips parted in a smile.

But of all men Malvano was one of the least susceptible to feminine blandishments, especially those of such a painfully ugly, artificial person as Lady Marshfield; therefore, heedless of her sudden change of manner towards him, he said bluntly—

"The police have already discovered some facts regarding Vittorina."

"Of her past?" she cried, starting forward.

"No, of her death," he answered.

"Have they discovered whether or not it was murder?" she inquired, her bejewelled hand trembling perceptibly.

"They have no doubt that it was murder," he replied. "They accept the doctor's theory, and, moreover, as you already know, the Italian Embassy in London are pressing the matter."

"They suspect at the Embassy—eh?"

"Without doubt. It can scarcely come as a surprise that they are endeavouring to get at the truth. One thing, however, is in our favour; and that is, she cannot tell what she knew. If she were still alive, I'm confident the whole affair would have been exposed before this."

"And you would have been under arrest."

He raised his shoulders to his ears, exhibited his palms, grinned, but did not reply.

"How have you ascertained this about the police?" her ladyship continued.

"Arnoldo is acquainted with the King's Messenger who carries dispatches between the Foreign Office and the British Ambassador in Italy. The messenger knows everything, but refuses to say much."

"Knows everything!" she cried in alarm. "What do you mean? Has our secret really been divulged?"

"No," answered he. "He is not aware of the true facts, but he knows how far the knowledge of Scotland Yard extends."

"What's his name?"

"Tristram. Captain Tristram."

"Do you know him?"

"No."

"Then don't make his acquaintance," the eccentric woman urged with darkening countenance. "He's no doubt a dangerous friend."

"But we may obtain from him some useful knowledge. You know the old saying about being forewarned."

"Our warnings must come from Livorno," she answered briefly.

"That will be impossible."

"Why?"

"Gemma has unfortunately fallen in love."

"Love! Bah! With whom?"

"With an Englishman," he answered. "Arnoldo saw them together several times when in Livorno last week."

"Who is he?"

"His name is Armytage—Charles Armytage. He—"

"Charles Armytage!" her ladyship echoed, starting from her chair. "And he is in love with Gemma?"

"No doubt he is. He intends to marry her."

"But they must never marry—never!" she cried quickly. "They must be parted immediately, or our secret will at once be out."

"How? I don't understand," he said, with a puzzled expression. "Surely Gemma, of all persons, is still friendly disposed? She owes much to us."

"Certainly," Lady Marshfield answered. "But was she not present with Vittorina on that memorable night in Livorno? Did she not witness with her own eyes that which we witnessed?"

"Well, what of that? We have nothing to fear from her."

"Alas! we have. A word from her would expose the whole affair," the wizen-faced woman declared. "By some means or other we must part her from Armytage."

"And by doing so you will at once make her your enemy."

"No, your own enemy, Doctor Malvano," she exclaimed, correcting him haughtily. "I am blameless in this matter."

He looked straight into her dark, sunken eyes, and smiled grimly.

"It is surely best to preserve her friendship," he urged. "We have enemies enough, in all conscience."

"Reflect," she answered quickly. "Reflect for a moment what exposure means to us. If Gemma marries Armytage, then our secret is no longer safe."

"But surely she has no object to attain in denouncing us, especially as in doing so she must inevitably implicate herself," he observed.

"No," she said gravely, after a brief pause. "In this matter I have my own views. They must be parted, Filippo. Armytage has the strongest motive—the motive of a fierce and terrible vengeance—for revealing everything."

"But why has Armytage any motive in denouncing us? You speak in enigmas."

"The secret of his motive is mine alone," the haggard-eyed woman answered. "Seek no explanation, for you can never gain knowledge of the truth until too late, when the whole affair is exposed. It is sufficient for me to tell you that he must be parted from Gemma."

Her wizened face was bloodless and brown beneath its paint and powder, her blue lips were closed tight, and a hard expression showed itself at the corners of her cruel mouth.

"Then Gemma is actually as dangerous to us as Vittorina was?" Malvano said, deeply reflecting.

"More dangerous," she declared in a low, harsh voice. "She must be parted from Armytage at once. Every moment's delay increases our danger. Exposure and disgrace are imminent. In this matter we must risk everything to prevent betrayal."

IX

Beneath the Red, White, and Blue

August passed slowly but gaily in lazy Leghorn. The town lay white beneath the fiery sun-glare through those blazing, breathless hours; the cloudless sky was of that intense blue which one usually associates with Italy, and by day the deserted Passeggio of tamarisks and ilexes, beside the most waveless sea, was for ever enlivened by the chirp of that unseen harbinger of heat, the cicale. Soon, however, the season waned, the stormy libeccio blew frequently, rendering outdoor exercise impossible; but Charles Armytage still lingered on at Gemma's side, driving with her in the morning along the sea-road to Ardenza and Antignano, or beyond as far as the high-up villa in which lived and died Smollet, the English historian, or ascending to the venerated shrine of the Madonna of Montenero, where the little village peeps forth white and scattered on the green hill-side overlooking the wide expanse of glassy sea. Their afternoons were usually spent amid the crowd of chatterers at Pancaldi's baths, and each evening they dined together at one or other of the restaurants beside the sea.

One morning late in September, when Armytage's coffee was brought to his room at the Grand Hotel, the waiter directed his attention to an official-looking note lying upon the tray. He had just risen, and was standing at the window gazing out upon the distant islands indistinct in the morning haze, and thinking of the words of assurance and affection his well-beloved had uttered before he had parted from her at the door, after the theatre on the previous night. Impatiently he tore open the note, and carelessly glanced at its contents. Then, with an expression of surprise, he carefully re-read the letter, saying aloud—

"Strange! I wonder what he wants?"

The note was a formal one, bearing on a blue cameo official stamp the superscription, "British Consulate, Leghorn," and ran as follows:—

Dear Sir,

"I shall be glad if you can make it convenient to call at the Consulate this morning between eleven and one, as I desire to speak to you upon an important and most pressing matter.

Yours faithfully,
John Hutchinson, His Majesty's Consul

"Hutchinson," he repeated to himself. "Is the Consul here called Hutchinson? It must be the Jack Hutchinson of whom Tristram spoke. He called him 'jovial Jack Hutchinson.' I wonder what's the 'pressing matter'? Some infernal worry, I suppose. Perhaps some dun or other in town has written to him for my address."

He paused, his eyes fixed seriously upon the distant sea.

"No!" he exclaimed aloud at last. "His Majesty's Consul must wait. I've promised to take Gemma driving this morning."

Presently, when he had shaved, and assumed his suit of cool white ducks, the official letter again caught his eye, and he took it up.

"I suppose, after all, it's only decent behaviour to go round and see what's the matter," he muttered aloud. "Yes, I'll go, and drive with Gemma afterwards."

Then he leisurely finished his toilet, strolled out into the Viale, and entering one of the little open cabs, was driven rapidly to the wide, handsome Piazza Vittorio Emanuele, where on the front of a great old galazzo at the further end were displayed a flagstaff surmounted by the English crown and an escutcheon of the British Royal arms. A tall, well-built, fierce moustached Italian *concierge*, who looked as if he might once have been an elegant gendarme of the Prince of Monaco, inquired his business, and took his card into an inner room on the right, the private office of the Consul.

After the lapse of a few minutes the *concierge* returned, and with ceremony ushered him into the presence of the representative of the British Foreign Office.

The room was large, lofty, and airy, with windows overlooking the great Piazza, the centre of Livornese life. The furniture was antique and comfortable, and testified to the taste of its owner; the writing-table littered with documents clearly proved that the office of Consul at Leghorn was no sinecure, and the book-cases were stocked with well-selected and imposing works of reference. Over the fireplace hung a large steel engraving of His Majesty, and on the mantelshelf some signed portraits of celebrities.

"You've enjoyed your stay in Leghorn, I hope," the Consul observed rather stiffly, after inviting his visitor to a seat on the opposite side of the table.

"Very much," Armytage answered, sinking into the chair.

"You'll excuse me for one moment," the Consul said; and scribbling something he touched the bell, and the *concierge* summoned the Vice-Consul, a slim, tall young Englishman, to whom he gave some directions.

Contrary to Charles Armytage's expectations, Mr. Consul Hutchinson had, notwithstanding his professional frigidity and gravity of manner, the easy-going, good-natured bearing of the genial man of the world. He was a fair, somewhat portly man, comfortably built, shaven save for a small, well-trimmed moustache, the very picture of good health, whose face beamed with good humour, and in every line of whose countenance was good-fellowship portrayed.

There were few skippers up or down the Mediterranean—or seamen, for the matter of that—who did not know Consul Hutchinson at Leghorn, and who had not at some time or another received little kindnesses at his hands. From "Gib." to "Constant." Jack Hutchinson had the reputation of being the best, most good-natured, and happiest of all His Majesty's Consuls, devoted to duty, not to be trifled with certainly, but ever ready to render immediate assistance to the Englishman in difficulties.

"Well," he exclaimed, looking across at Armytage at last, when they were alone again, "I am glad you have called, because I have something to communicate in confidence to you."

"In confidence?" Armytage repeated, puzzled.

Mr. Consul Hutchinson, still preserving his professional air of dignity as befitted his office, leaned one elbow upon the table, and looking straight into his visitor's face, said—

"The matter is a purely private, and somewhat painful one. You will, I hope, excuse what I am about to say, for I assure you it is in no spirit of presumption that I venture to speak to you. Remember, you are a British subject, and I am here in order to assist, sometimes even to advise, any subject of His Majesty."

"I quite understand," Armytage said, mystified at the Consul's rather strange manner.

"Well," Hutchinson went on slowly and deliberately, "I am informed that you are acquainted with a lady here in Leghorn named Fanetti—Gemma Fanetti. Is that so?"

"Certainly. Why?"

"How long have you known her? It is not out of idle curiosity that I ask."

"Nearly seven months."

"She is Florentine. I presume you met her in Florence?"

"Yes."

"Were you formally introduced by any friend who knew her?"

"No," he answered, after slight hesitation. "We met quite casually."

"And you followed her here?"

"No. We met here again accidentally. I had no idea she was in Leghorn. Since our first meeting I have been in London several months, and had no knowledge of her address," he replied.

"And you are, I take it, in ignorance of her past?" Hutchinson said.

Armytage sat silent for a few moments, then quickly recovering himself said a trifle haughtily—

"I really don't think I'm called upon to answer such a question. I cannot see any reason whatever for this cross-examination regarding my private affairs."

"Well," the Consul exclaimed seriously, "the reason is briefly this. It is an extremely painful matter, but I may as well explain at once. You are known by the authorities here to be an associate with this lady— Gemma Fanetti."

"What of that?" he cried in surprise.

"From what I can understand, this lady has a past—a past which the police have investigated."

"The police? What do you mean?" he cried, starting up.

"Simply this," answered the Consul gravely. "Yesterday I received a call from the Questore, and he told me in confidence that you, a British subject, were the close associate of a lady whose past, if revealed, would be a startling and unpleasant revelation to you, her friend. The authorities had, he further said, resolved to order her to leave Leghorn, or remain on penalty of arrest; and in order that you, an English gentleman, might have time to end your acquaintance, he suggested that it might be as well for me to warn you of what the police intended doing. It is to do this that I have asked you here to-day."

Armytage sat pale, silent, open-mouthed.

"Then the police intend to hound the Signorina Fanetti from Leghorn?" he observed blankly.

"The Italian police possess power to expel summarily from a town any person of whom they have suspicion," the Consul replied calmly.

"But what do they suspect?" he cried, bewildered. "You speak as if she were some common criminal or adventuress."

"I have, unfortunately, no further knowledge of the discovery they have made regarding her. It must, however, be some serious allegation, or they would not go the length of expelling her from the city."

"But why should she be expelled?" he protested angrily. "She has committed no offence. Surely there is some protection for a defenceless woman!"

Hutchinson raised his eyebrows and shrugged his shoulders, an expressive gesture one soon acquires after residence in Italy.

"The Questore has supreme power in such a matter," he said. "He is a very just and honourable official, and I'm sure he would never have taken these steps to avoid you disgrace if there were not some very strong reasons." Charles Armytage, leaning upon the edge of the Consul's table, held down his head in deep contemplation.

"Then to-morrow they will order her to quit this place?" he observed thoughtfully. "It's unjust and brutal! Such treatment of a peaceful woman is scandalous!"

"But remember you've admitted that you have no knowledge of her past," Hutchinson said. "Is it not possible that the police have discovered some fact she has concealed from you?"

"It's an infernal piece of tyranny!" Armytage cried fiercely. "I suppose the police have fabricated some extraordinary allegations against her, and want money to hush it up. They want to levy blackmail."

"No, no," Jack Hutchinson said, his manner at once relaxing as he rose and crossed to the window, his hands behind his back. "The position is a simple one," he continued, looking him straight in the face. "The police have evidently discovered that this lady is either not what she represents herself to be, or that some extraordinary mystery is attached to her; therefore cut her acquaintance, my dear sir. Take my advice. It will save you heaps of bother."

"I can't," the other answered hoarsely. "I'll never forsake her!"

"Not if she's hounded from town to town by the police, like this?"

"No. I love her," he replied brokenly.

Hutchinson sighed. A silence fell between them deep and complete.

At last the Consul spoke in a grave tone. His professional air had relaxed, as it always did when he desired to assist an Englishman in distress.

"Before you love her," he suggested, "would it not be as well to ask her what chapter of her life she has concealed? If she really loves you, she will no doubt tell you everything. Is it not an excellent test?"

"But that will not alter the decision of the Questore." Armytage observed woefully.

"No, that's true. The lady must leave Leghorn this evening. Take my advice and part from her," he added sympathetically. "In a few weeks you will forget. And if you would spare her the disgrace of being sent out of Leghorn, urge her to leave of her own accord. If you will pledge your word that she shall leave to-day, I will at once see the Questore, and beg him to suspend the orders he is about to give."

"I love Gemma, and intend to marry her."

"Surely not without a very clear knowledge of her past?"

"Already I have decided to make her my wife," Armytage said, his face set and pale. "What the police may allege will not influence me in any way."

"Ah! I fear you are hopelessly infatuated," Hutchinson observed.

"Yes, hopelessly."

"Then I suppose you will leave Leghorn with her? That she must go is absolutely imperative. In that case if I may advise you, I should certainly not only leave Leghorn, but leave Italy altogether."

"What!" he cried indignantly. "Will the police of Milan or Venice act in the same cowardly way that they have done here?"

"Most probably. When she leaves, the police will without doubt take good care to know her destination, and inform the authorities of the next town she enters. Your only plan is to leave Italy."

"Thanks for your advice," the other replied in a despondent tone. "Loving her as I do, what you have just told me, and what you have hinted, have upset me and destroyed my peace of mind. I fear I'm not quite myself, and must apologise for any impatient words I have used. I shall act upon your suggestion, and leave Italy." Then he paused, but after a few moments raised his head, saying—

"You have been good enough to give me friendly advice upon many points; may I encroach upon your good nature still further? Tell me, do you think it wise to acquaint her with the facts you have told me?" Hutchinson looked at the man before him, and saw how hopelessly he was in love. He had seen them driving together, and had long ago noticed how beautiful his companion was.

"No," he answered at last. "If you intend to marry her, there is really no necessity for demanding an immediate explanation. But as soon as you are out of Italy, and you have an opportunity, I should certainly invite her to tell you the whole truth."

Then, after some further conversation, the two men shook hands, and Charles Armytage slowly made his way downstairs and out across the wide, sunlit Piazza.

From the window Consul Hutchinson watched his retreating figure, and noticed how self-absorbed he was as he strode along. His heart had gone out to sympathise in this brief interview, and a strong desire came upon him to help and protect the lonely Englishman. "Poor devil!" he muttered, "he's badly hit, and I fear he has a troublous time before him. I wish to God I could help him."

X

The Mystery of Gemma

When Armytage entered Gemma's pretty salon, the window of which commanded a wide view of the blue Mediterranean, she rose quickly from the silken divan with a glad cry of welcome. She was veiled and gloved ready to go out, wearing a smart costume of pearl grey, with a large black hat which suited her fair face admirably.

"How late you are!" she exclaimed a trifle impetuously, pouting prettily as their lips met. "You said eleven o'clock, and it's now nearly one."

"I've had a good deal to see after," he stammered. "Business worries from London."

"Poor Nino!" she exclaimed sympathetically in her soft Italian, putting up her tiny hand and stroking his hair tenderly. Nino was the pet name she had long ago bestowed upon him. "Poor Nino! I didn't know you were worried, or I would not have complained. Excuse, won't you?"

"Of course, dearest," he answered, sinking a trifle wearily into a chair; whilst she, regarding him with some surprise, reseated herself upon the divan, her little russet-brown shoe stretched forth coquettishly from beneath the hem of her well-made skirt.

The room was small, but artistic. Its cosiness and general arrangement everywhere betrayed the daily presence of an artistic woman; and as he sat there with his eyes fixed upon her, he became intoxicated by her marvellous beauty. There was a softness about her face, an ingenuous sweetness which always entranced him, holding him spell-bound when in her presence.

"You are tired," she said in a low, caressing tone. "Will you have some vermouth or marsala? Let me tell Margherita to bring you some."

"No," he answered quickly; "I had a vermouth at Campari's as I passed. I'm a trifle upset to-day."

"Why?" she inquired quickly, regarding him with some astonishment.

He hesitated. His eyes were riveted upon her. The sun-shutters were closed, the glare of day subdued, and he was debating whether or not he should relate to her in that dim half-light all that had been told him an hour ago. In those brief moments of silence he remembered how, on the afternoon he had encountered Tristram at Pancaldi's, she had expressed surprise that he should love her so blindly, without seeking to inquire into her past. He remembered his foolish reply. He had told her he wished to know nothing. If he demanded any explanation now, it would convince her that he doubted. Yes, Hutchinson's advice was best. At present he must act diplomatically, and remain silent.

"The reason why I am not myself to-day is because I must leave you, Gemma," he said slowly at last, in a low, earnest voice.

"Leave me!" she gasped, starting and turning pale beneath her veil.

"Yes," he replied quickly. "It is imperative that I should start for Paris to-night."

"Has my Nino had bad news this morning?" she asked in a sympathetic tone, bending and extending her hand until it touched his.

Its contact thrilled him. In her clear blue eyes he could distinguish the light of unshed tears.

"Yes," he answered—"news which makes it necessary that I should be in Paris at the earliest possible moment."

"And how long shall you remain?" she inquired. "I shall not return to Italy," he replied decisively, his eyes still upon hers.

"You will not come back to me?" she cried blankly. "What have I done, Nino? Tell me, what have I done that you should thus forsake me?"

"I do not intend to forsake you," he answered, grasping her hand. "I will never forsake you; I love you far too well."

"You love me!" she echoed, tears coursing down her cheeks. "Then why go away and leave me alone? You must have seen how fondly I love you in return."

"I shall not go alone," he answered her, rising and placing his arms tenderly about her neck. "That is, if you will go with me."

"With you?" she exclaimed, her face suddenly brightening. "With you, Nino?"

There was a deep silence. She gazed into his dark, serious eyes with an expression of love and devotion more eloquent than words; and he, still holding her hand, bent until their lips met in a fierce, passionate caress.

"Surely you do not fear to travel with me without regard for the *convenances*?" he said.

"Have we not already set them at naught?" she answered, looking earnestly into his face. "Unfortunately, I have no *chaperone*, no friends; therefore, according to Italian manners, your presence here in my house is against all the laws of etiquette" and she laughed a strange, hollow laugh through her tears.

"We can, I think, Gemma, set aside etiquette, loving each other as we do!" he exclaimed, pressing her hand. "Let us go together to London, and there marry."

"Why not marry in Italy?" she suggested, after a pause. "Marriage at your British Consulate is binding."

The mention of the Consulate brought back to his memory all that Hutchinson had said. Her words seemed to imply that she did not wish to leave Tuscany.

"Why in Italy?" he inquired. "You have no tie here!"

She hesitated for a moment.

"No, none whatever," she assured him in a voice which sounded strangely harsh and unconvincing. He attributed her agitation to the excitement of the moment and the fervency of her love.

"Then why do you wish to remain?" he inquired bluntly.

"I have reasons," she replied mechanically, her eyes slowly wandering around the room. Suddenly she rose, and hastily snatching up an open letter that was lying upon the mantelshelf, crushed it within the palm of her gloved hand. He was sitting with his back to the mantel, therefore he saw nothing of this strange action, and believed, when she went out of the room a moment later, that she went to speak with her servant.

True, she spoke some words with Margherita in the kitchen, but placing the letter upon the burning charcoal, she watched the flame slowly consume it. Then, with a parting order to Margherita uttered in a tone distinctly audible to her lover, she returned smilingly to his side.

"For what reason do you want to remain here?" he inquired when she had reseated herself with a word of apology for her absence.

"It is only natural that I should be loth to leave my own country," she answered evasively, laughing.

"No further motive?" he asked, a trifle incredulously. "Well, I have many acquaintances in Florence, in Milan, and Rome."

"And you desire to remain in Italy on their account?" he exclaimed. "Only the other day you expressed satisfaction at the suggestion of leaving Italy."

"I have since changed my mind."

"And you intend to remain?"

"Not if you are compelled to leave Livorno, Nino," she answered with that sweet smile which always entranced him.

In her attitude he detected mystery. She appeared striving to hide from him some important fact, and he suddenly determined to discover what was its nature. Why, he wondered, should she desire to remain in Tuscany after the satisfaction she had already expressed at the prospect of life in England?

"I am compelled to go to-night," he said. "The train leaves at half-past nine, and we shall take the through wagon-lit from Pisa to Paris at midnight. If you'll be ready, I'll wire to Rome to secure our berths in the car."

"Then you really mean to leave?" she asked in a tone of despair.

"Certainly," he replied, puzzled at her strange manner.

"It will perhaps be better for me to remain," she observed with a deep sigh.

"Why?"

"If we marry, you would tire of me very, very soon. Besides, you really know so little of me" and she regarded him gravely with her great, clear, wide-open eyes.

"Ah, that's just it!" he cried. "You have told me nothing."

She shrugged her shoulders with a careless air, and smiled.

"You have never inquired," she answered.

"Then I ask you now," he said.

"And I am unable to answer you—unable to tell the truth, Nino," she replied brokenly, her trembling hand seeking his.

"Why unable?" he demanded, sitting erect and staring at her in blank surprise.

"Because—because I love you too well to deceive you," she sobbed. Then she added, "No, after all, it will be best for us to part—best for you. If you knew all, as you must some day—if we married, you would only hate me" and she burst into a torrent of blinding tears.

"Hate you—why?" he asked, slipping his arm around her slim waist.

With a sudden movement she raised her veil and wiped away the tears with her little lace handkerchief.

"Ah! forgive me," she exclaimed apologetically. "I did not believe I was so weak. But I love you, Nino. I cannot bear the thought of being parted from you."

"There is surely no necessity to part," he said, purposely disregarding the strange self-accusation she had just uttered.

"You must go to Paris. Therefore we must part," she said, sighing deeply.

"Then you will not accompany me?"

Her blue eyes, child-like in their innocence, were fixed upon his. They were again filled with tears.

"For your sake it is best we should part," she answered hoarsely.

"Why? I cannot understand your meaning," he cried. "We love one another. What do you fear?"

"I fear myself."

"Yourself?" he echoed. Then, drawing her closer to him, he exclaimed in a low intense voice, "Come, Gemma, confide in me. Tell we why you desire to remain here; why you are acting so strangely to-day."

She rose slowly from the divan, a slim, woeful figure, and swayed unevenly as she answered—

"No, Nino. Do not ask me."

"But you still love me?" he demanded earnestly. "Have you not just expressed readiness to marry me?"

"True," she replied, pale and trembling. "I will marry you if you remain here in Livorno. But if you leave—if you leave, then we must part."

"My journey is absolutely necessary," he declared. "If it were not, I should certainly remain with you."

"In a week, or a fortnight at most, you can return, I suppose? Till then, I shall remain awaiting you."

"No," he replied firmly. "When I leave Italy, I shall not return." Then, after a slight pause, he added in a low, sympathetic tone, "Some secret oppresses you. Gemma. Why not take me into your confidence?"

"Because—well, because it is utterly impossible."

"Impossible! Yet, we love one another. Is your past such a profound secret, then?"

"All of us, I suppose, have our secrets, Nino," she replied earnestly. "I, like others, have mine."

"Is it of such a character that I, your affianced husband, must not know?" he asked in a voice of bitter reproach.

"Yes," she answered nervously. "Even to you, the man I love, I am unable to divulge the strange story which must remain locked for ever within my heart."

"Then you have no further confidence in me?"

"Ah! Yes, I have, Nino. It is my inability to tell everything, to explain myself, and to present my actions to you in a true light, that worries me so."

"But why can't you tell me everything?" he demanded.

"Because I fear to."

"I love you, Gemma," he assured her tenderly. "Surely you do not doubt the strength of my affection?"

"No," she whispered, agitated, her trembling fingers closing upon his. "I know you love me. What I fear is the dire consequences of the exposure of my secret."

"Then, to speak plainly, you are in dread of the actions of some person who holds power over you?" he hazarded.

She was silent. Her heart beat wildly, her breast heaved and fell quickly; her chin sank upon her chest in an attitude of utter dejection.

"Have I guessed the truth?" he asked in a calm, serious voice.

She nodded in the affirmative with a deep-drawn sigh. "Who is this person whom you fear?"

"Ah! no, Nino," she burst forth, trembling with agitation she had vainly striven to suppress. "Do not ask me that. I can never tell you—never!"

"But you must—you shall!" he cried fiercely. "I love you, and will protect you from all your enemies, whoever they may be."

"Impossible," she answered despairingly. "No, let us part. You can have no faith in me after my wretched admissions of to-day."

"I still have every faith in you, darling," he hastened to reassure her. "Only tell me everything, and set my mind at rest."

"No," she protested. "I can tell you nothing—absolutely nothing."

"You prefer, then, that we should be put asunder rather than answer my questions?"

"I cannot leave Italy with you," she answered simply but harshly.

"Not if we were to marry in England as soon as the legal formalities can be accomplished?"

"I am ready to marry you here—to-day if you desire," she said. "But I shall not go to London."

"Why?"

"I have reasons—strong ones," she answered vehemently.

"Then your enemies are in London?" he said quickly. "Are they English?"

At that instant the door-bell rang loudly, and both listened intently as Margherita answered the somewhat impetuous summons. There were sounds of low talking, and a few moments later the servant, pale-faced and scared, entered the room, saying—

"Signorina! There are two officers of police in the house, and they wish to speak with you immediately."

"The police!" Gemma gasped, trembling. "Then they've discovered me!"

There was a look of unutterable terror in her great blue eyes; the light died instantly out of her sweet face; she reeled, and would have fallen had not her lover started up and clasped her tenderly. Her beautiful head, with its mass of fair hair, fell inert upon his shoulder. This blow, added to the mental strain she had already undergone, had proved too much.

"Nino," she whispered hoarsely, "you still love me—you love me, don't you? And you will not believe what they allege against me—not one single word?"

XI

SILENCE IS BEST

L et the police enter," Armytage said, still pressing her slim figure in his arms. "You know, Gemma, that I love you."

"No, no," she cried trembling; "I will see them alone. I must see them alone."

"Why?"

"I cannot bear that you should stand by and hear the terrible charge against me," she answered hoarsely. "No, let me go alone to them" and she struggled to free herself.

But he grasped her slim wrist firmly, saying, "I love you, and will be your protector. If they make allegations against you, they must prove them. I, the man who is to be your husband, may surely know the truth?"

"But promise me that you will not heed what they say—you will not believe their foul, unfounded charges," she implored, lifting her pale face to his.

"I believe implicitly in you, Gemma," he answered calmly. "Let them come in."

Gemma, her hand in that of her lover, stood blanched and trembling in the centre of the room as the two police officers in plain clothes entered.

One was a tall, broad-shouldered, middle-aged man with a pleasant face, a pair of dark, piercing eyes, and tiny coal-black moustache; while the other was younger, and, from the bronze of his countenance, evidently a Silician.

"We are police officers," the elder man exclaimed. "We would prefer to speak to the signorina alone."

"I am the closest friend of the signorina," Armytage said calmly. "I am about to make her my wife."

The officer shrugged his shoulders, exhibited his palms, and a sarcastic smile played about his lips.

"If I may presume to advise the Signor Conte," he said, "I certainly think that it would be best if I spoke to her alone."

And Gemma, clinging to her lover, gazed imploringly into his face, adding—"Yes, caro. Let them speak to me alone."

"No," the young Englishman answered firmly.

"But the matter is a delicate one—extremely delicate," urged the delegato. "I certainly think that the signorina should be allowed to decide whether or not you should be present."

"In a week or so we shall marry," declared Armytage. "What concerns signorina also concerns myself."

"To please me, caro, will you not go out of the room for a moment?" Gemma cried in a low voice of earnest supplication.

Her attitude was that of one who feared the revelation of some terrible secret, and in those moments her lover had become filled with a keen desire to penetrate the cloak of mystery which enveloped her.

"No," he answered her, after a brief silence; "I have decided to remain and hear what the signor delegato has to say."

The police official and the trembling woman exchanged quick glances. In the officer's gaze was a look of sympathy, for perhaps her beauty had softened his impressionable Italian nature; in her blue eyes was an expression of humiliation and abject fear.

"My mission is very quickly accomplished," the delegato exclaimed slowly.

"You intend to arrest!" Gemma cried hoarsely. "I—I have dreaded this for a long time past. I knew that, one day or other, you would come for me, and my reputation would be ruined for ever."

"Listen, signorina," the official said gravely. "Certain information has been obtained by the Questore, and upon that information I have been sent here to you. Much as I regret to disturb you, signorina, the Questore, after carefully considering certain statements before him, has decided that your presence is undesirable in Livorno, and, further, he wishes me to inform you that to-day you must leave this city."

Gemma, her face white and drawn, humiliated and abased, sighed deeply, then breathed again more freely. She had expected arrest, but instead was ordered out of Livorno. To say the least, the police had been merciful towards her.

"Then I must leave to-day?" she repeated mechanically.

"Yes, signorina. The penalty for remaining here after this order of the Questore is immediate arrest," he said.

"But why is this course pursued?" Armytage asked. "For what reason is the presence of the signorina deleterious in the city? It all seems very remarkable to me."

"The information before the Questore is of a very confidential character, signore."

"Are you not aware of the allegations against her?"

"No," he replied; "I have only been deputed to warn her to leave Livorno."

"Is such a measure frequently resorted to?"

"Usually we arrest the suspected individual, question him, and afterwards deport him to the railway station, if there is not sufficient ground to justify a prosecution. In this case there is just a simple warning. Only in very exceptional cases is the course followed which the Questore is now pursuing."

"Then you have no knowledge of the actual charge in this case?"

"No, signore, I have not. But," he added, "the signorina must herself know the reason."

Armytage turned quickly to her. Their eyes met for a single instant. Then she slowly nodded, saying in an indistinct voice: "Yes, yes, I know only too well the reason of this. I must leave Livorno—leave Italy, my own country that I love, never to return."

"That would be the very best course to pursue," the delegato urged. "If you leave Italy, signorina, you will, I think, hear no more of the unfortunate affair. Indeed, I have strong reasons for believing that the Questore has acted in the manner he has done purposely, in order that you should be afforded an opportunity to leave Italy."

"He thinks that exile is preferable to imprisonment," she said aloud, as if reflecting. "Well, perhaps he is right" and she laughed a short, hollow laugh.

"Yes," urged Armytage, "you must leave to-night." She was silent. The police official exchanged glances with the tall, good-looking young Englishman, then said, bowing politely—

"I will wish you adieu, signore. A thousand pardons for disturbing you; but it was my duty, therefore pray forgive me."

"Certainly, certainly," he replied; and both men went out bowing, leaving Armytage alone with the woman he loved.

"All this is strange—very strange," he observed when they had gone. He was puzzled; for, after all, he now knew no more than what Consul Hutchinson had already told him.

"Yes," she said slowly, "to you it must appear extraordinary, but to me, who expected it and who dreaded it, it was only what might be anticipated. They have warned me out of Italy, it's true; but if they knew everything," she added—"if they knew everything, I should to-night be placed in a criminal's cell."

"Why?"

"Already I have told you it is impossible for me to explain," she answered vehemently, in her voluble Italian. "If you really love me, it is surely sufficient to know that the police are in ignorance of facts which I feared were revealed; and that they have not obtained the one item of information necessary to effect my ruin and disgrace."

"Why do you speak like this?" he demanded quickly. "Has your past life in Florence been so full of mystery that you fear its exposure?"

"There are certain matters which I desire to keep secret—which I will keep secret, even if it costs me the loss of you, the man I adore," she answered fiercely.

"Then they are matters which surely concern me—if I am to be your husband," he said gravely.

"No," she answered calmly, still pale to the lips; "they only concern myself. I admit freely that there is a secret connected with my past—a secret which I shall strive to preserve, because its revelation would, I know, cause you, my beloved, much worry and unnecessary pain. I therefore prefer to hide this truth and fight my enemies alone."

"Is not this secret one that, before marrying you, I ought to know?" he demanded earnestly.

"It cannot concern you in any way," she declared. "True, it has reference to my past life, but surely you don't believe me to be an adventuress—do you?"

"Of course not, piccina," he answered, laughing, as he again placed his arm tenderly around her waist. "You an adventuress! What made you suggest such a thing?"

"I must be an enigma to you," she said. "But believe me, I would tell you everything if I could see that you could be benefited in the least. The story is a long and wretched one; and when I reflect upon the closed chapter of my life's history, I am always dolorous and unhappy. The more so because I'm unable to confide in you, the man I love."

"Will you explain all to me some day?"

"Yes, everything. At present, if I were to tell you, the result would only be disastrous to myself, and in all probability wreck your happiness. Silence is best now—far the best."

His face wore a heavy expression of disappointment and dissatisfaction. Truth to tell, the whole matter was so utterly inexplicable

WILLIAM LE QUEUX

that he entertained serious misgivings. She noticed this, and raising her sweet face, now no longer haggard, but pale and sweet-looking, she added—

"Cannot you trust me further, Nino?"

"Trust you, darling!" he cried. "Why, of course I can. Only all this secrecy worries me."

"Ah no! Don't think of it any more," she urged. "To-night I will leave with you for Paris. I have a friend there to whom I can go. Afterwards, in London, we will marry—if you still desire that we should."

The last words were uttered in a low, tremulous, hesitating tone.

"Still desire!" he echoed. "I still love you as fondly—ah! even more fervently than before. If you would only confide in me, I should be entirely happy."

"At present that is impossible," she declared. "Some day, before long, I hope to be in a position to tell you everything."

"And you are ready to go to London?" he observed. "Half an hour ago you said you did not wish to go to England!"

"True, because I feared to go. Now I no longer fear. I am ready, even eager to accompany you if you still wish."

"Then we will go straight to Paris; and when I have concluded my business, which will occupy perhaps a couple of days, we'll go on to London."

"Benissimo!" she answered, raising her full, red lips to his. "I so want to see your great and wonderful London, caro. I've read so much about it. It must be gigantic. I shall be so happy and content with you as my guide. To see London has ever been the dream of my life."

"Ah! I'm afraid you'll be sadly disappointed, piccina," he said, again smiling. "After your bright, beautiful Italy, our busy, bustling, smoke-blackened city will seem terribly dull, monotonous, and dreary. The sky is seldom blue, and the atmosphere never clear and bright like this. In your Tuscany everything is artistic—the country, the towns, the people; but in England—well, you will see for yourself."

"But there are lots of amusements in London," she said, "and life there is always gay."

"For the rich, London offers the greatest and most diverse attractions of any place in the world; but for the poor, herded together in millions as they are, it is absolutely the worst. In Italy you have much poverty and distress, but the lot of the poor man is far easier here than in toiling, turbulent, over-crowded London."

"One never appreciates the town in which one lives, be it ever so beautiful," she laughed.

"Well, be patient, and you shall see what London is like," he said. "But it is already two o'clock. You must lunch, and afterwards pack your trunks. Our train leaves at half-past nine to-night, and at Pisa we shall join the night-mail to the frontier. I'll wire to the sleeping-car office in Rome, and secure our berths in the through car for Paris."

"Ah! Nino," she exclaimed happily, "I am content, very content to leave Italy with you. An hour ago I had reasons for remaining; but now it is, of course, impossible; and, strangely enough, I have no further object in staying here."

"And you will not regret leaving?"

"Of course not," she said, flinging herself into his ready arms and shedding tears of joy. "I fear nothing now, because I know that you love me, Nino," she sobbed. "I know you will not believe anything that is alleged against me. You have asked me to marry you, and I am content—ah! absolutely content to do so. But even now I do not hold you to your promise, because of my inability to divulge to you my secret. If you think me untrue or scheming, then let us part. If you believe I love you, then let us marry in England and be happy."

"I love you, Gemma," he answered low and earnestly. "Let us go together to London, and let this be the last hour of our doubt and unhappiness."

XII

A Word with His Excellency

One morning, about ten days after Armytage had left Leghorn with Gemma, a rather curious consultation took place at the Italian Embassy in Grosvenor Square between Count Castellani, the Ambassador to the Court of St. James', and Inspector Elmes, of the Criminal Investigation Department.

The Ambassador, a handsome, grey-haired man of sixty with courtly manner as became the envoy of the most polite nation in the world, stroked his beard thoughtfully while he listened to the detective. He was sitting at his big writing-table in the small, well-furnished room where he was in the habit of holding private conference with those with whom the Chief Secretary of Embassy had no power to deal. Elmes, smart, well-shaven, and ruddy, sat in a large easy chair close by, and slowly explained the reason of his visit.

"I remember the case quite well," His Excellency exclaimed when the detective paused. "Some papers regarding it were placed before me, but I left my Secretary to deal with them. The girl, if I remember aright, arrived in London from Livorno accompanied by an unknown Englishman, and was found dead in a cab at Piccadilly Circus—mysteriously murdered, according to the medical evidence."

"The jury returned an open verdict, but without doubt she was the victim of foul play," Elmes said decisively.

"One moment," the Ambassador interrupted, placing his hand upon an electric button upon the table.

In answer to his summons the thin, dark-faced Neapolitan man-servant appeared, and by him the Ambassador sent a message to the Secretary, who in a few moments entered.

He was younger by ten years than the Ambassador, foppishly dressed, but nevertheless pleasant-faced, with manners which were the essence of good breeding.

"You remember the case of the girl—Vittorina, I think her name was—who was found dead in a cab outside the Criterion?"

"Yes."

"Did we make any inquiries of the police in Livorno regarding her identity?"

"Yes. Do you wish to see the reply?"

"You might send it in to me at once," the Ambassador said; and the Secretary withdrew.

"What you have told me is certainly extraordinary—most extraordinary," exclaimed His Excellency, addressing Elmes.

"All the inquiries I have made point to the one fact I have already suggested," the detective said. "At Scotland Yard we received a request from your Excellency that we should carefully investigate the matter, and we are doing so to the very best of our ability."

"I'm sure you are. I well recollect now signing a formal request to your Department to make searching investigation."

At that moment a clerk entered, bearing a file of papers, which he placed before His Excellency.

"Now," exclaimed the latter, "let us see what reply we received from the police of Livorno" and he slowly turned over letter after letter. The correspondence had evidently been considerable. Its magnitude surprised the detective.

Suddenly the Count paused, and his brows contracted as he read one of the official letters. He glanced at the signature, and saw it was that of the Marquis Montelupo, Minister of Foreign Affairs at Rome. Twice he read it through. It was a long despatch, closely written, and as the Ambassador re-read it his brow darkened.

Again he touched the electric bell, and a second time summoned the Secretary of Embassy.

When the latter appeared His Excellency beckoned him into an inner room, and, taking the file of papers with him, left the Inspector alone with *The Times*.

After the lapse of some ten minutes both men returned.

"But what I desire to know, and that clearly, is, why this despatch was never handed to me," His Excellency was saying angrily as they emerged.

"You were away at Scarborough, therefore I attended to it myself," the Secretary answered.

"Did you not appreciate its extreme importance?" His Excellency cried impetuously. "Surely, in the interests of our diplomacy, this matter should have been placed immediately before me! This despatch, a private one from the Minister, has apparently been lying about the Embassy for the servants or any chance caller to read. The thing's disgraceful! Suppose for one moment the contents of this despatch have leaked out! What would be the result?"

The Secretary made no reply, but shrugged his shoulders.

"Such gross carelessness on the part of any one connected with this Embassy amounts almost to treason," the Ambassador continued, livid with rage and indignation. "We are here to do our utmost to preserve the honour and prestige of our nation. Is not our national motto, 'For the country and the king'? Yet, because I was absent a week, a matter of the most vital importance is calmly shelved in this manner! Moreover, it was sent by special messenger from Rome; yet it has been allowed to lie about for anybody to copy!"

"Pardon me, your Excellency," exclaimed the Secretary. "The file has been kept in the private safe until this moment, and the key has never left my pocket."

"Then why did you send it in here by a clerk, and not bring it yourself?" was His Excellency's withering retort.

"It was impossible for me to return at that moment," the Secretary explained. "I was dictating an important letter to catch the post."

"I see from these papers that we wrote direct to the Questore at Livorno, and his reply came by special messenger, under cover from the Foreign Minister. Surely that in itself was sufficient to convince you of its extreme importance! Your previous experiences in Vienna and Berlin ought to have shown you that the Minister does not send despatches by special messenger unless he fears the *cabinet noir*."

"I wrote formally to the Questore at Livorno, according to your instructions, and certainly received from the Ministry at Rome the reply attached. I must confess, however, that it did not strike me as extraordinary until this moment. Now that I read it in the light of recent occurrences, I see how secret is its nature. It is impossible, however, that any one besides myself has read it."

"Let us hope not," His Excellency snapped as he reseated himself. "It was most injudicious, to say the least" and then with politeness he bowed to the Secretary as a sign that he had concluded his expressions of displeasure.

"It is most fortunate that you called," the Ambassador observed, turning to Elmes when the Secretary had left. "If you had not, a most important matter would have escaped my attention. As it is, I fear I shall be too late in intervening, owing to the gross negligence which has been displayed. After the inquest had been held upon the body of the unfortunate girl, we wrote, it appears, to the police at Livorno to endeavour to discover who she was" and he slowly turned over the papers one by one until he came to a formidable document headed, "Questura di Livorno," which he glanced through.

"The police, it seems, have no knowledge of any person missing," he continued slowly and deliberately, when he had read through the report. "The name Vittorina is, of course, as common in Tuscany as Mary is in England. The photograph taken by your Department after death had been seen by the whole of the detectives in Livorno, but no one has identified it. If we had had the surname, we might possibly have traced her by means of the register, which is carefully kept in every Italian town; but as it is, the Questore expresses regret that he is unable to furnish us with more than one item of information."

"What is that?" asked Elmes eagerly.

"It is stated that by the last train from Livorno, one night in August, two persons, a man and a woman, inquired for tickets for London. They were informed that tickets could only be issued as far as Milan or Modane. The man was English, and the woman Italian. The detective on duty at the station took careful observation of them, as persons who ask for through tickets for London are rare. The description of the woman tallies exactly with that of the unknown Vittorina, and that of the man with the fellow who so cleverly escaped through the Criterion bar."

"We already knew that they came from Leghorn," the Inspector observed disappointedly; but the Ambassador took no notice of his words. He was rereading for the third time the secret instructions contained in the despatch from the Minister at Rome, and stroking his pointed greybeard, a habit when unusually puzzled.

"You, of course, still have the original of that curiously worded letter found in the dead girl's dressing-bag, and signed 'Egisto'?" Count Castellani exclaimed presently, without taking his keen eyes off the despatch before him.

"Yes, your Excellency," Elmes answered. "I have it in my pocket."

"I should like to see it, if you'll allow me," he said in a cold, dignified voice.

The detective took out a well-worn leather wallet containing many notes of cases on which he was or had been engaged, and handed to the Ambassador the strange note which had so puzzled the police and the readers of newspapers.

His Excellency carefully scrutinised the note.

"It is strangely worded—very strangely," he said. "Have you formed any opinion regarding the mention of Bonciani's Restaurant in Regent Street? What kind of place is it? I've never heard of it."

"The Bonciani is a small restaurant half-way up Regent Street, frequented by better-class Italians; but what the veiled references to appointments on Mondays can mean, I've at present utterly failed to discover."

"This Egisto, whoever he is, writes from Lucca, I see," His Excellency remarked. "Now, Lucca is only half an hour from Pisa, and if the man wished to say adieu to her, he might have taken half an hour's journey and seen her off in the train for the frontier. Have you made any inquiries regarding this strange communication?"

"A letter has been written to the British Consul at Leghorn, in whose district Lucca is, sending him a copy of the letter, together with the evidence, and asking him to communicate with the authorities."

"Has that letter been sent?" the Ambassador inquired quickly.

"No. I only made application for it to be sent when I was round at the Chief Office this morning."

"Then stop it," His Excellency said. "In this matter Consular inquiries are not required, and may have the effect of thwarting the success of the police. If you will leave this letter in my hands I shall be pleased to make inquiries through the Ministry, and at once acquaint you with the result."

"That will be extremely kind of you, your Excellency," the Inspector said; for he at once saw that the Ambassador had far greater chance of discovering some clue than he had. A request from the Italian representative in London would, he knew, set the police office in a flutter, and all their wits would be directed towards discovering the identity of the writer of the extraordinary missive.

"This piece of evidence will be quite safe in my hands, of course," added the Count. "If I am compelled to send it to Italy, in order that the handwriting should be identified, I shall make it a condition that it shall be returned immediately. Do you speak Italian?"

"A little, your Excellency," he answered. "I've been in Italy once or twice on extradition cases."

"Then you can read this letter, I suppose?" the courtly diplomat asked, eyeing him keenly.

"Yes. I made the translation for the Coroner," answered Elmes, with a smile.

"Well, it does you credit. Very few of our police, unfortunately, know English. In your inquiries in this case, what have you discovered?" the Ambassador asked. "You may be perfectly frank with me, because the woman was an Italian subject, and I am prepared to assist you in every way possible."

"Thanks," the detective said. "Already I've made—and am still making—very careful investigations. The one fact, however, which I have really established is the identity of the mysterious Major—who was waiting on the platform of Charing Cross Station, who was introduced to the girl, who afterwards spoke to her English companion in the Criterion, and whose photograph, fortunately enough, was found in the dead girl's dressing-bag."

"The Major?" repeated His Excellency, as if reflecting. "Ah! yes, of course; I recollect. Well, who is that interesting person?" he asked.

"The photograph has been identified by at least a dozen persons as that of a Major Gordon Maitland, who lives in the Albany, and who is a member of the Junior United Service Club."

"Maitland!" echoed the Ambassador, starting at the mention of the name. "He's rather well known, isn't he? I fancy I've met him somewhere or other."

"He's very well known," answered Elmes. "It is strange, however, that he left London a few days after the occurrence, and has not left his address either at his chambers or his club."

"That is certainly curious," the Ambassador agreed. "It may, however, be only accidental that he left after the tragic affair."

"I have made judicious inquiries in quarters where he is best known, but absolutely nothing is discoverable regarding his whereabouts, although I have three officers engaged on the case."

"You have found out nothing regarding his friend, the mysterious Englishman, I suppose?"

"Absolutely nothing. All trace of him has vanished as completely as if the earth had swallowed him up."

"He may have been an American, and by this time is in New York, or even San Francisco," the Count hazarded.

"True, he might have been. Only Major Maitland can tell us that. We are certain to find him sooner or later."

"I sincerely hope you will," the Ambassador said. "I am here to guard the interests of all Italian subjects, and if the life of one is taken, it is my duty to press upon your Department the urgent necessity of discovering and punishing the assassin. If, however, I can be of any service to you in this matter, or can advise you, do not hesitate to call on me. You can always see me privately if you send in your card" and rising, as a sign the interview was at an end, His Excellency bowed, and wished the detective "good-morning."

The instant Inspector Elmes had closed the door the Ambassador took up the letter found in the dead girl's bag, together with the file of papers lying before him. Carrying them swiftly to the window, he readjusted his gold-rimmed pince-nez, and hurriedly turned over folio after folio, until he came to the secret despatch with the sprawly signature of the Italian Minister of Foreign Affairs. Then, placing the letter beside the despatch, he closely compared the signature with the handwriting of the letter.

His face grew pale, his grey brows contracted, and he bit his lip.

The "l's," "p's" and "t's" in the strange missive were exactly identical with those in the signature to the closely written despatch which had been penned by the private secretary.

With trembling hand he held the soiled scrap of paper to the light.

"The watermark shows this to be official paper," he muttered aloud. "There is certainly some deep, extraordinary mystery here—a mystery which must be fathomed."

Again he glanced at the long formal despatch. Then the Ambassador added, in a low, subdued, almost frightened tone: "What if it proved that the Marquis Montelupo and 'Egisto' are one and the same?"

XIII

A Discovery in Ebury Street

The soft, musical Tuscan tongue, the language which Gemma spoke always with her lover, is full of quaint sayings and wise proverbs. The assertion that "L'amore della donna é come il vino di Champagni; se non si beve subito, ricade in fondo al calice" is a daily maxim of those light-hearted, happy, indolent dwellers north and south of Arno's Valley, from grey old Lucca, with her crumbling city gates and ponderous walls, across the mountains, and plains to where the high towers of Siena stand out clear-cut like porcelain against the fiery blaze of sunset. Nearly every language has an almost similar proverb—a proverb which is true indeed, but, like many another equally wise, is little heeded.

When Armytage and Gemma had arrived in London, he had not been a little surprised at the address where she stated some friends of hers resided. While still in the train, before she reached London, she took from her purse a soiled and carefully treasured piece of paper, whereon was written, "76, Bridge Avenue, Hammersmith"; and to this house they drove, after depositing their heavy baggage in the cloak-room. They found it a poor, wretched thoroughfare off King Street, and in the wet evening it looked grey, depressing, and unutterably miserable after the brightness of Italy. Suddenly the cab pulled up before the house indicated—a small two-storied one—but it was evident that the person they sought no longer lived there, for a board was up announcing that the house was to let. Armytage, after knocking at the door and obtaining no response, rapped at the neighbouring house, and inquired whether they were aware of the address of Mr. Nenci, who had left. From the good woman who answered his inquiries he obtained the interesting fact that, owing to non-payment of the weekly rent, the landlord had a month ago seized the goods, and the foreigner, who had resided there some six months, had disappeared, and, being deeply in debt among the neighbouring small shops, had conveniently forgotten to leave his address.

"Was Mr. Nenci married?" asked Charlie Armytage, determined to obtain all the information he could.

"Yes, sir," the woman answered. "His wife was a black-faced, scowling Italian, who each time she passed me looked as though she'd like to stick a knife into me. And all because I one day complained of 'em throwing a lot of rubbish over into my garden. My husban', 'e says 'e'd go in and talk to 'em, but I persuaded him not to. Them foreigners don't have any manners. And you should just have seen the state they left the 'ouse in! Somethin' awful, the lan'lord says."

"Then you haven't the slightest idea where they've gone?"

"No, sir. Back to their own country, I hope, for London's better off without such rubbish."

Returning to the cab, he told Gemma of the departure of her friends, and suggested that for the present she should stay at the Hotel Victoria, in Northumberland Avenue, while he took up his bachelor quarters in Ebury Street. Therefore they drove back again to Charing Cross; and having seen her comfortably installed in the hotel, he drove to his own rooms.

He had written to his housekeeper from Paris, and on entering his cosy little flat, with its curiously decorated rooms with their Moorish lounges and hangings, found a bright fire, a comfortable chair ready placed for him, his spirit-stand and a syphon of soda ready to hand, and Mrs. Wright, his housekeeper, welcoming him back cordially, and expressing the hope that his journey had been a pleasant one.

Having deposited his bag, he washed, dressed, swallowed a whisky-and-soda, and drove back to the Victoria, where he dined with his well-beloved.

At eleven o'clock next morning, according to his promise, he came to the hotel, and they drove out in a taxi to see some of the principal streets of London. She had chosen a dress of dark grey, which fitted her perfectly, and beneath her large black hat her fair face and blue eyes looked the perfect incarnation of innocence and ingenuousness. As he had anticipated, all was strange to her, and in everything she became deeply interested. To her, London was a revelation after the quiet idleness of Tuscany. They drove along the busy Strand, past the Law Courts, down Fleet Street with its crowd of lounging printers, and up Ludgate Hill. At St. Paul's they alighted and entered the Cathedral. Its exterior was admired, but at its bare interior she was disappointed. She had expected the Duomo of London to be resplendent in gilt and silver altars, with holy pictures, but instead found a great, gaunt building, grey, silent, and depressing.

Armytage noticed the blank look upon her beautiful countenance, and asked her her opinion.

"It is fine, very fine," she answered in her pure Tuscan. "But how bare it is!"

"This is not a Catholic country, like yours," he explained. "Here we don't believe in gaudy altars, or pictures of the Vergine Annunziata."

"Are all your churches the same, Nino?" she inquired. "Are there no altars?"

"Only the central one, and that is never golden, as in Italy."

He pointed out to her tombs of great men about whom she had read long ago in her school days at the Convent of San Paolo della Croce, in Florence, and in them she was much interested. But afterwards, when they drove round St. Paul's churchyard, into Cheapside, where the traffic was congested and progress was slow, she looked upon the mighty, crowded city with eyes wide open in wonder as a child's. At every point she indicated something which she had never before seen, and Bennett's clock striking midday caused her as much delight as if she had been a girl of twelve. Hers was an extraordinary temperament. As he sat beside her, listening to her original remarks anent things which to his world-weary eyes were so familiar as to be unnoticeable, he saw how genuinely ingenuous she was, how utterly unlike the callous adventuress which once, in Livorno, he feared her to be.

To show and explain to her all the objects of interest they passed was to him an intense pleasure.

They returned by way of Cannon Street, where he pointed out the great warehouses whence emanated those objects so dear to the feminine heart—hats and dresses; past the Post Office, with its lines of red mail-carts ready to start for the various termini; along Newgate Street with its grim prison, across the Holborn Viaduct, and thence along Oxford and Regent Street to the hotel.

"How busy and self-absorbed every one seems!" she again remarked. "How gigantic this city seems! Its streets bewilder me."

"Ah, piccina mia," he answered, "you've only seen a very tiny portion of London. There are more people in a single parish here than in the whole of Florence."

"And they all talk English, while I don't understand a word!" she said, pouting prettily. "I do so wish I could speak English."

"You will learn very soon," he answered her. "In a couple of months or so you'll be able to go out alone and make yourself understood."

"Ah no!" she declared with a slight sigh. "Your English is so difficult— oh, so very difficult!—that I shall never, never be able to speak it."

"Wait and see," he urged. "When we are married, I shall speak English to you always, and then you'll be compelled to learn," he laughed.

"But, Nino," she said, her eyes still fixed upon the crowd of persons passing and repassing, "why are all these people in such a dreadful hurry? Surely there's no reason for it?"

"It is business, dearest," he answered. "Here, in London, men are bent on money-making. Nine-tenths of these men you see are struggling fiercely to live, notwithstanding the creases in their trousers, and the glossiness of their silk hats; the other tenth are still discontented, although good fortune has placed them beyond the necessity of earning their living. In London, no man is contented with his lot, even if he's a millionaire; whereas in your country, if a man has a paltry ten thousand lire a year, he considers himself very lucky, takes life easily, and enjoys himself."

"Ah," she said, just as the cab pulled up before the hotel entrance, where half a dozen Americans, men and women, lounging in wicker chairs, began to comment upon her extreme beauty, "in London every one is so rich."

"No, not every one," he answered, laughing. "Very soon your views of London will become modified" and he sprang out, while the grey-haired porter, resplendent in gilt livery, assisted her to alight.

An incident had, however, occurred during the drive which had passed unnoticed by both Gemma and her companion. While they were crossing Trafalgar Square, a man standing upon the kerb glanced up at her in quick surprise, and, by the expression on his face, it was evident that he recognised her.

For a few moments his eyes followed the vehicle, and seeing it enter Northumberland Avenue, he hurried swiftly across the Square, and halted at a respectable distance, watching her ascend the hotel steps with Armytage.

Then, with a muttered imprecation, the man turned on his heel and strode quickly away towards St. Martin's Lane.

When, a quarter of an hour later, Armytage was seated with her at luncheon in the great table d'hote room, with its heavy gilding, its flowers and orchestral music, she, unconscious of the sensation her beauty was causing among those in her vicinity expressed fear of London. It was too enormous, too feverish, too excited for her ever to venture out alone, she declared. But he laughed merrily at her misgivings, and assured her that very soon she would be quite at home among her new surroundings.

"Would you think very ill of me, piccina, if I left you alone all day to-morrow?" he asked presently, not without considerable hesitation.

"Why?" she inquired, with a quick look of suspicion.

"No, no," he smiled, not failing to notice the expression on her face. "I'm not going to call on any ladies, piccina. The fact is, I've had a pressing invitation for a day's shooting from an uncle in the country, and it is rather necessary, from a financial point of view, that I should keep in with the old boy. You understand?"

"I'll go down by the early train," he said, "and I'll be back again here by nine to dine with you." Then, turning to the waiter standing behind his chair, he inquired whether he spoke Italian.

"I am Italian, signore," the man answered.

"Then, if the signorina is in any difficulty to-morrow, you will assist her?"

"Certainly, signore; my number is 42," the man said, whisking off the empty plates and rearranging the knives.

"I wouldn't go, only it is imperative for one or two reasons," he explained to her. "In the morning you can take a cab, and the waiter will tell the driver that you want to go for an hour or so in the West—remember, the West End—not the East End. Then you will return to lunch, and have a rest in the afternoon. You know well that I'll hasten back to you, dearest, at the earliest possible moment."

"Yes," she said, "go, by all means. You've often told me you like a day's shooting, and I certainly do not begrudge my poor Nino any little pleasure."

"Then you are sure you don't object to being left alone?"

"Not in the least," she laughed, as with that chic which was so charming she raised her wine-glass to her pretty lips.

When they had finished luncheon she went to her room, while he smoked a cigarette; then, when she re-appeared, he drove her to his own chambers in Ebury Street.

"My place is a bit gloomy, I'm afraid," he explained on the way. "But we can chat there without interruption. In the hotel it is impossible."

"No place is gloomy with my Nino," she answered.

His arm stole around her slim waist, and he pressed her to him more closely.

"And you must not mind my servant," he exclaimed. "She's been in our family for twenty years, and will naturally regard you with considerable suspicion, especially as you are a foreigner, and she can't speak to you."

"Very well," she laughed. "I quite understand. Woman-servants never like the advent of a wife."

Presently they alighted, and he opened the door of the flat with his latchkey.

"Welcome to my quarters, piccina," he exclaimed as she entered the tiny, dimly lit hall, and glanced round admiringly.

"How pretty!" she exclaimed. "Why, it is all Moorish!" looking up at the silk-embroidered texts from the Koran with which the walls were draped.

"I'm glad you like it," he said happily; and together they passed on into his sitting-room, a spacious apartment, the windows of which were filled with wooden lattices, the walls draped with embroidered fabrics, the carpet the thickest and richest from an Eastern loom, the stools, lounges, and cosy-corners low and comfortable, and the ceiling hidden by a kind of dome-shaped canopy of yellow silk.

Slowly she gazed around in rapt admiration.

"I delight in a Moorish room, and this is the prettiest and most complete I have ever seen," she declared. "My Nino has excellent taste in everything."

"Even in the choice of a wife—eh?" he exclaimed, laughing, as he bent swiftly and kissed her ere she could draw away.

She raised her laughing eyes to his, and shrugged her shoulders.

"Don't you find the place gloomy?" he asked.

"My friends generally go in for old oak furniture, or imitation Chippendale. I hate both."

"So do I," she assured him. "When we are married, Nino, I should like to have a room just like this for myself—only I'd want a piano," she added, with a smile.

"A piano in a Moorish room!" he exclaimed. "Wouldn't that be somewhat out of place? Long pipes and a darbouka or two, like these, would be more in keeping with Moorish ideas" and he indicated a couple of drums of earthenware covered with skin, to the monotonous music of which the Arab and Moorish women are in the habit of dancing.

"But you have an English table here," she exclaimed, crossing to it, "and there are photographs on it. Arab never tolerate portraits. It's entirely against their creed."

"Yes," he admitted; "that's true. I've never thought of it before."

At that instant she bent quickly over one of the half-dozen photographs in fancy frames.

Then, taking it in her hand, she advanced swiftly to the window, and examined it more closely in the light. "Who is this?" she demanded in a fierce, harsh voice. "A friend of mine," he replied, stepping up to her and glancing over her shoulder at the portrait. "He's an army officer—Major Gordon Maitland."

"Maitland!" she cried, her face in an instant pale to the lips. "And he is a friend of yours, Nino—you know him?"

"Yes, he is a friend of mine," Armytage replied, sorely puzzled at her sudden change of manner. "But why? Do you also know him?"

She held her breath; her face had in that instant become drawn and haggard, her pointed chin sank upon her breast in an attitude of hopeless despair, her clear blue eyes were downcast; but no answer passed her trembling lips.

This sudden, unexpected discovery that the Major was acquainted with the man she loved held her dumb in shame, terror, and dismay. It had crushed from her heart all hope of love, of life, of happiness.

XIV

The Doctor's Story

Doctor Malvano, in a stout shooting-suit of dark tweed, his gun over his shoulder, his golf-cap pulled over his eyes to shade them, was tramping jauntily along, across the rich meadow-land, cigar in mouth, chatting merrily with his host, a company promoter of the most pronounced Broad Street type named Mabie, who had taken Aldworth Court, in Berkshire, on a long lease, and who, like many of his class, considered it the best of form to shoot. The ideal of most men who make money and spend it in London city is to have "a place in the country" and in this case the "place" was a great, old, time-mellowed, red-brick mansion, inartistic as was architecture in the early Georgian days, but nevertheless roomy, comfortable, and picturesque in its ivy mantle, and surrounded by its spacious park.

The party with whom he was shooting was a decidedly mixed one. At a country house, Malvano was always a welcome guest on account of his good humour, his easy temperament, and his happy knack of being able to entertain all and sundry. Ladies liked him because of his exquisite Italian courtesy, and perhaps also because he was a merry, careless bachelor; while among the men of a house-party, he was voted good company, and the excellence of his billiard-playing and shooting always excited envy and admiration. In the hours between breakfast and luncheon, few birds had that day escaped his gun. To his credit he had placed a good many brace of partridges and pheasants, half a dozen snipe, a hare or two, and held the honours of the morning by bringing down the single woodcock which the beaters had sent up.

They had lunched well at an old farmhouse on his host's estate, a table being well spread in the great oak-beamed living-room, with its tiny windows and a fire on the wide hearth, and, in the enjoyment of an unusually good cigar, the Doctor felt disinclined to continue his feats of marksmanship. Indeed, he would have much preferred the single hour's rest in an easy chair, to which he had always been accustomed in Italy, than to be compelled to tramp along those high hedgerows. Yet he was a guest, and could make no complaint.

Malvano possessed a very curious personality. Keen-eyed and far-sighted, nothing escaped him. He had a deep, profound knowledge of human nature, and could gauge a man accurately at a glance. His merry, careless manner, thoughtless, humorous, and given to laughing immoderately, caused those about him to consider him rather too frivolous for one of his profession, and too much given to pleasure and enjoyment. The popular mind demands the doctor to be a person who, grave-faced and care-lined, should study the *Lancet* weekly, and carefully note every new-fangled idea therein propounded; should be able to diagnose any disease by looking into a patient's mouth; and who should take no pleasure outside that morbid one derived from watching the growth or decline of the maladies in persons he attended. Malvano, however, was not of that type. Without doubt he was an exceedingly clever doctor, well acquainted with all the most recent Continental treatments, and whose experience had been a long and varied one. He could chatter upon abstruse pathological subjects as easily as he could relate a story in the smoking-room, and could dance attendance upon the ladies, and amuse them by his light brilliant chatter with that graceful manner which is born in every Italian, be he peasant or prince. Within twenty miles or so of Lyddington, no house-party was complete without the jovial doctor, who delighted the younger men with his marvellous collection of humorous tales, and whom even the elder and grumpy admired on account of his perfect play at Bridge.

But Filippo Malvano was not in the best spirits this autumn afternoon, tramping across the meadows from Manstone Farm, at the Pangbourne and Hampstead Norris cross-roads, towards Clack's Copse, where good sport had been promised by the keeper. He was careful enough not to betray to his host the fact that he was bored, but as he strode along, his heavy boots clogged with mud, he was thinking deeply of a curious incident that had occurred half an hour before, while they had been lunching up at the farm.

The remainder of the party, half a dozen guns, were on ahead, piloted by the keeper, the beaters were before them on either side of the tall hazel hedge, but beyond one or two rabbits, the spot seemed utterly destitute of game.

"What kind of sport have you this season up in Rutland?" the City merchant was asking with the air of wide experience which the Cockney sportsman is so fond of assuming.

"Fair—very fair," Malvano replied mechanically. "Just now I'm shooting somewhere or other two or three days each week, and everywhere pheasants seem plentiful."

His dark eyes were fixed upon the moving figures before him, and especially upon one—that of a lithe athletic man in a suit of grey homespun, who walked upright notwithstanding the uneven nature of the ground, and who carried his gun with that apparent carelessness which showed him to be a practised sportsman.

It was this man who was occupying all the Doctor's attention. To his host he chatted on merrily, joking and laughing from time to time, but, truth to tell, he was sorely puzzled. While sitting around the farmer's table, Mabie, turning to him, had made some observation regarding the autumn climate in Tuscany, whereupon, the young man now striding on before him, had looked up quickly, asking—

"Do you know Tuscany?"

"Quite well," the Doctor had answered, explaining how for some years he had practised in Florence.

"I know Florence well," his fellow-guest had said. "While there I made many friends." Then, after a second's hesitation, he gazed full into the Doctor's face, and asked, "Do you happen to know any people named Fanetti there?"

This unexpected inquiry had caused the Doctor to start; but he had been sufficiently self-possessed to repeat the name and calmly reply that he had never heard of it. He made some blind inquiry as to who and what the family were, and in which quarter they resided; and then, with that tactful ingenuity which was one of his most remarkable characteristics, he turned the conversation into an entirely different channel.

This incident, however, caused the jovial, careless Malvano considerable anxiety; for here, in the heart of rural England, across the homely board of the simple, broad-faced farmer, a direct question of the most extraordinary kind had been put to him. He did not fail to recollect the keen, earnest look upon the man's face as he uttered the name of Fanetti—a name he had cause to well remember—and when he recalled it, he became seized with fear that this man, his fellow-guest, knew the truth. Having for the past half-hour debated within himself what course was the best to pursue, he had at last decided upon acting with discretion, and endeavouring to ascertain how far this stranger's knowledge extended.

Turning to his host as they walked on side by side, he removed his cigar, and said, in his habitual tone of carelessness—

"I, unfortunately, didn't catch the name of the young man to whom you introduced me this morning—the one in the light suit yonder."

"Oh, my nephew, you mean," Mabie answered. "A good fellow—very good fellow. His name's Armytage—Charles Armytage."

"Armytage!" gasped the Doctor. In an instant he remembered his conversation with Lady Marshfield. She had said that she knew a certain Charles Armytage. But Malvano betrayed no sign, and remained quite calm. "Yes," he continued; "he seems a very decent fellow. He's a good shot, too. Several times this morning I've—"

At that instant a partridge rose before them, and Malvano raised his gun swift as lightning, and brought it down almost before the others had noticed it.

"Several times to-day I've admired his shooting," continued the Doctor, at the same time reloading.

"He's only just back from the Continent," his host explained, "and I asked him to run down from town to-day, thinking a little English sport would be pleasant after the idleness of a summer in Italy."

"A summer in Italy!" Malvano exclaimed in surprise. "He was rather ill-advised to go there during the hot weather. Every one strives to get away during summer. Where has he been?"

"In Florence, and afterwards at Leghorn, I believe. He's been away all this year."

"He has no profession?"

"None," Mabie answered. "His father died and left him comfortably off. For a couple of years he led a rather wild life in Brussels and Paris, sowed the usual wild oats, and afterwards took to travelling. On the average, he's in England about a couple of months in the year. He says he only comes home to buy his clothes, as he can't find a decent tailor on the Continent."

"I well understand that," Malvano laughed. "Is he making a long stay at home this time?"

"I believe so. He told me this morning that he was tired of travelling, and had come back to remain."

Malvano smiled a trifle sarcastically. It was evident that his host did not know the true story of his nephew's fascination, or he would have mentioned it, and perhaps sought the Doctor's opinion. Therefore, after tome further ingenious questions regarding his nephew's past and his present address dropped the subject.

WILLIAM LE QUEUX

An hour later he found himself alone with Armytage. They had passed through Clack's Copse, and, after some splendid sport, had gained the road which cuts through the wood from Stanford Dingley to Ashampstead, where they were waiting for the remainder of the party, who, from the repeated shots, were in the vicinity finding plenty of birds.

"Your uncle tells me you know Italy well," Malvano observed.

"I don't know it well," Armytage replied, looking the picture of good health and good humour as he stood astride in his well-worn breeches and gaiters, and his gun across his arm. "I've been in Tuscany once or twice at Florence, Pisa, Viareggio, Lucca, Leghorn, and Monte Catini. I'm very fond of it. The country is lovely, the garden of Italy, and the people are extremely interesting, and of such diverse types. Nowhere in the world, perhaps, is there such pride among the lower classes as in Tuscany."

"And nowhere in the world are the people more ready to charge the travelling Englishman excessively—if they can," added Malvano, laughing. "I'm Italian born, you know, but I never hesitate to condemn the shortcomings of my fellow-countrymen. The honest Italian is the most devoted friend in the world; the dishonest one is the brother of the very devil himself. You asked me at lunch whether I knew any one named Fanetti—was Fanetti the name?—in Florence," said the Doctor, after a pause, watching the younger man's face narrowly. "At the time I didn't recollect. Since lunch, I have remembered being called professionally to a family of that name on one occasion."

"You were?" cried Armytage, immediately interested. He felt that, perhaps, from this careless, easy going doctor, he might obtain some clue which would lead him to the truth regarding Gemma's past.

Malvano recalled Lady Marshfield's words, and with his keen dark eyes looked gravely into the face of the tall, broad-shouldered young Englishman.

"Yes," he said. "There was a mother and two daughters, if I remember aright, and they lived in a small flat in the Via Ricasoli, a few doors from the Gerini Palace. I was summoned there in the night under somewhat mysterious circumstances, for I found, on arrival, that one of the daughters had a deep-incised wound in the neck, evidently inflicted with a knife. I made inquiry how it occurred, but received no satisfactory reply. One thing was evident, namely that the wound could not have been self-inflicted. There had been an attempt to murder the girl."

"To murder her!" Armytage cried.

"No doubt," the Doctor answered. "The wound had narrowly proved fatal, therefore the girl was in too collapsed a condition to speak herself. I dressed the wound, and advising them to call their own doctor, went away."

"Didn't you see the girl again?" asked Armytage. "No. There was something exceedingly suspicious about the whole affair, and I had no desire to imperil my professional reputation by being party at hushing up an attempted murder. Besides, from what I heard later, I believe they were decidedly a family to avoid."

"To avoid! What do you mean?" the young man cried, dismayed.

Malvano saw that the words were producing the effect he desired, namely, to increase suspicion and mistrust in his companion's heart, and therefore resolved to go even further.

"The family of whom I speak held a very unenviable reputation in Florence. Some mystery was connected with the father, who was said to be undergoing a long term of imprisonment. They were altogether beyond the pale of society. But, of course," he added carelessly, "they cannot be the same family as those of whom you speak. Where did you say your friends live?"

"They no longer live in Florence," he answered hoarsely, his brow darkened, and his eyes downcast in deep thought. All that he learnt regarding Gemma seemed to be to her detriment. None had ever spoken generously of her. It was, alas! true, as she had told him, she had many enemies who sought her disgrace and ruin. Then, after a pause, he asked, "Do you know the names of the girls?"

"Only that of the one I attended," Malvano answered, his searching eyes on the face of young Armytage. "Her name was Gemma."

"Gemma!" he gasped. His trembling lips moved, but the words he uttered were lost in the two rapid barrels which the Doctor discharged at a couple of pheasants at that instant passing over their heads.

XV

The Shadow

In an old and easy dressing-gown, Gemma was idling over her tea and toast in her room on the morning after her lover had been shooting down in Berkshire, when one of the precocious messenger-lads delivered a note to her.

At first she believed it to be from Armytage, but, on opening it, found scribbled in pencil on a piece of paper, the address, "73, St. James's Street, second floor" while enclosed were a few words in Italian inviting her to call at that address on the first opportunity she could do so secretly, without the knowledge of her lover. The note was from Tristram.

With a cry of anger that he should have already discovered her presence in London, she cast the letter from her and stamped her tiny foot, crying, in her own tongue—

"Diavolo! Then ill luck has followed me—even here!" For a long time she sat, stirring her tea thoughtfully, and gazing blankly at her rings.

"No," she murmured aloud in a harsh, broken voice; "I won't see this man. Let him act as he thinks fit. He cannot wreck my happiness more completely than it is already. Major Maitland is a friend of the man I love. Is not that fact in itself sufficient to show me that happiness can never be mine; that it is sheer madness to anticipate a calm, peaceful life with Charles Armytage, as my husband? But Dio! Was it not always so?" she sighed, as hot tears rose in her clear blue eyes, and slowly coursed down her cheeks. "I have sinned; and this, alas! is my punishment." Again she was silent. Her breast heaved and fell convulsively, and with hair disordered and unbound she presented an utterly forlorn appearance. Her small white hands were clenched, her lips tightly compressed and in her eyes was an intense expression as if before her had arisen some scene so terrible that it froze her senses.

At last the striking of the clock aroused her, and she slowly commenced to dress. She looked at herself long and earnestly in the mirror, and saw how deathly pale she had become, and how red were her eyes.

Presently, as she crossed the room, she noticed the letter, and, snatching it up, slipped the paper with the address into her purse, tearing up the note into tiny fragments.

It was past eleven when she descended to the great hall, and there found her lover seated on one of the lounges, smoking and patiently awaiting her.

They sat together in the hall for a few minutes, then took a taxi and drove about the West End. Armytage did not fail to observe how Gemma's beauty and foreign chic were everywhere remarked. In the streets men stared at her admiringly, and women scanned her handsome dresses with envious eyes; while in the hotel there were many low whisperings of admiration. Yet he could not conceal from himself the fact that she was as mysterious as she was beautiful.

While passing across Grosvenor Square, she had been suddenly seized with excitement, for her quick eyes caught sight of a red, white, and green flag, hanging limp and motionless from a flagstaff upon one of the largest houses.

"Look! There's our Italian flag! Why is it there?" she cried, thrilled at sight of her own national colours.

"That's the Embassy," he replied. "I suppose today is some anniversary or other in Italy."

"The Embassy!" she repeated, turning again to look at it. "Is that where Count Castellani lives?"

"Yes. He's your Ambassador. Do you know him?"

"I met him once in Florence. He was at a ball at the Strossi Palace."

"Then you know Prince Strossi?" he exclaimed. "Quite well," she answered. "The Strossis and my family have long been acquainted."

Her prompt reply made it apparent to him that she had moved in the most exclusive set in Florence. She had never before mentioned that she was acquainted with people of note. But next instant he recollected the strange story which the Florentine Doctor had told him on the previous afternoon. Had not Malvano declared that her family was an undesirable one to know? What, he wondered, was the reason of this curious denunciation?

Again she fixed her eyes upon the Embassy, and seemed as though she were taking careful observation of its appearance and position.

"Did you go much into society in Florence?" he inquired presently.

"Only when I was forced to," she answered ambiguously. "I do not care for it."

"Then you will not fret even if, after our marriage, you know only a few people?"

The word "marriage" caused her to start. It brought back to her the hideous truth that even now, after he had brought her to England, their union was impossible.

"No," she answered, glancing at him with eyes full of love and tenderness. "I should always be happy with you alone, Nino. I should want no other companion."

"You would soon grow dull, I fear," he said, taking her hand in his.

"No, never—never," she declared. "You know well how I love you, Nino."

"And I adore you, darling," he answered. Then, after looking at her in hesitation for a moment, he added. "But you speak as though you still fear that we shall not marry. Why is that?" He had not failed to notice her sudden change of manner when he had spoken of marriage.

"I really don't know," she answered, with a forced laugh. "I suppose it is but a foolish fancy, yet sometimes I think that this happiness is too complete to be lasting."

"What causes you to fear this?" he asked earnestly. "When I reflect upon the unhappiness of the past," she said with a sigh—"when I remember how bitter was my life, how utterly blank and hopeless was the world prior to our meeting, I cannot rid myself of the apprehension that my plans, like all my others, will be thwarted by the one great secret of my past; that all my castles are merely air-built; that your love for me, Nino, will soon wane, and we shall part."

"No, no, piccina," he cried, placing his arm tenderly around her waist, beneath the warm cape she wore. "It is foolish—very foolish to speak like that. You surely have no reason to doubt me?"

"I do not doubt your love, Nino. I doubt, however, whether you have sufficient confidence in me to await the elucidation of the strange mystery which envelops me—a mystery which even I myself cannot penetrate."

"Have I not already shown myself patient?" he asked with a reproachful look.

"Yes, yes, mio adorato," she hastened to reassure him. "You are good and kind and generous, and I love you. Only—only I fear the future. I fear you—I fear myself."

"Why do you fear me, little one?" he asked. "Surely I'm not so monstrous—eh?"

The hand he held trembled.

"I distrust the future—because I know the fate cruel and terrible—which, sooner or later, must befall me," she exclaimed, with heart-sinking.

"You steadily decline to tell me anything," he said. "If you would only confide in me, we might together find some means to combat this mysterious catastrophe."

"I cannot! I dare not!"

"But you must!" he cried. "You shall!"

"I refuse?" she answered fiercely.

"You shall not suffer this constant terror merely because of a foolish determination to preserve your secret. After all, I suppose it is only some curious and unfounded dread which holds you awe-stricken, when you could afford to laugh it all to scorn."

"You will never wring confession from me, Nino—never!"

Her eyes met his fixedly, determinedly. On her countenance was an expression as if she were haunted by a shadow of evil, as if even then she saw before her the dire disaster which she had declared must ere long wreck her life, and extinguish all hope of happiness. No further word passed her lips, and a silence fell between them until the cab drew up at the hotel.

The afternoon being bright and sunny, they went down to the Crystal Palace.

To Gemma, all was fresh and full of interest; she even found in the plaster imitations of well-known statues something to criticise and admire, although she admitted that, living within a stone's throw of the world-famed Uffizi Gallery, she had never entered the Tribuna there, nor seen the Satyr, the Wrestlers, or the Medici Venus.

After spending an hour in the Palace, they emerged into the grounds, and, descending the many flights of steps, passed the great fountains, and strolled down the long, broad walk towards Penge, it being their intention to return to town from that station. The sun was going down, a grey mist was rising, and the chill wind of evening whisked the dead leaves in their path. The spacious grounds were silent, deserted, cheerless.

She had taken his arm, and they were walking in silence beneath the fast-baring branches through the half-light of the fading day, when suddenly he turned to her, saying—"I've been thinking, Gemma—thinking very deeply upon all you told me this morning. I must tell you the truth—the truth that it is impossible for me to have complete confidence in you if you have none in me. The more I reflect upon this strange secret, the more am I filled with suspicion. I cannot help it. I have struggled against all my doubts and fears—but—"

"You do not trust me?" she cried hoarsely. "Did I not express fear only this morning that you would be impatient, and grow tired of the steady refusals I am compelled to give you when you demand the truth?"

"Having carefully considered all the facts, I can see no reason—absolutely none—why you should not explain the whole truth," he said rather brusquely.

"The facts you have considered are those only within your own knowledge," she observed. "There are others which you can never know. If you could only understand the situation aright, you would at once see plainly the reason that I am prepared for any sacrifice—even to lose your love, the most precious gift that Heaven has accorded me—in order to preserve my secret."

"Then you are ready to wish me farewell if I still press for the truth?" he cried, dismayed; for the earnestness of her words impressed him forcibly.

"I am," she answered in a low, intense voice.

They had halted in the broad, gravelled walk, and were alone.

"Listen!" he cried fiercely, as a sudden resolve seized him. "This cannot go on longer, Gemma. I have brought you here to London because I love you, because I hoped to make you my you wife. But you seem determined to keep all the story of your past from me." Then, recollecting Malvano's words when they had been shooting together, he added, "If you still refuse to tell me anything, then, much as it grieves me, we must part."

"Part!" she echoed wildly. "Ah yes, Nino! I knew you would say that. Did I not tell you long, long ago, that it would be impossible for us to marry in the present circumstances? You doubt me? Well, I am scarcely surprised!" and she shuddered pale as death.

"I doubt you because you are never frank with me."

"I love you, Nino," she protested with all the ardour of her hot Italian blood as she caught his hand suddenly and raised it to her fevered lips. "You are my very life, for I have no other friend in the world. Surely you have been convinced that my affection is genuine, but I have not deceived you in this!"

"I believe you love me," he answered coldly, in a half-dubious tone nevertheless.

"Ah no, caro!" she lisped softly, reproachfully, in her soft Tuscan. "Do not speak like that. I cannot bear it. If you can trust me no longer, then let us part. I—I will go back to Italy again." And she burst into a torrent of hot tears.

"You'll go back and face the mysterious charge against you?" he asked, with a twinge of sarcasm in his voice, as he drew his hand firmly from hers.

His words caused her to start. She looked him fiercely in the face for an instant, a strange light in her beautiful, tearful eyes, then cried huskily—

"Yes, if you cast me from you, Nino, I care no longer to live. I cannot live without your love."

XVI

"Traitors Die Slowly"

They had returned to the hotel, and Armytage had dined with her, but the meal had been a very dismal one. Gemma, with woman's instinct, knew that she looked horribly untidy, and that her eyes betrayed unmistakable signs of recent tears, therefore she was glad when the meal concluded, and she could escape from the staring crowd of diners.

From her lover's manner, it was also plain that, notwithstanding his protestations of blind affection in Leghorn, he had suddenly awakened to the fact that some deep mystery lay behind her, and that he was disinclined to carry their acquaintance much further without some explanation. Time after time, as she sat opposite him at the table, she had watched him narrowly, looking into his dark, serious eyes in silence, and trying to divine his thoughts. She wondered whether, if he left her, his love for her would be sufficient to cause him to return to her side. Or had he met, as she once feared he would, some other woman—a woman of his own people; a woman, perhaps, that he had loved long ago? This thought sank deeply into her mind. As she watched him and listened to his low, jerky speech, it seemed plain to her that she had guessed the truth. He had grown tired of her, and was making her enforced silence an excuse for parting. When this thought crossed her mind, her bright, clear eyes grew luminous with unshed tears.

He told her that to meet next morning was impossible, as he had business to transact. This she knew to be a shallow excuse, as only that morning he had told her that his time was completely at her disposal. Yes, there was no disguising the truth that he had grown weary of her, and now meant to discard her. Yet she loved him.

When an Italian woman loves, it is with a fierce, uncontrollable passion, not with that too often sickly admiration for a man's good looks which is so characteristic of love among the more northern nations. In no country is love so ardent, so passionate, so enduring, as in the sunny garden of Europe. The Italian woman is slow to develop affection, or even to flirt with the sterner sex; but when she loves, it is with all the strength of her being; she is the devoted slave of her lover, and is his for life, for death. Neither the strength of Italian affection nor the bitterness of Italian jealousy can be understood in England, unless by those who have lived among the hot-blooded Tuscans in that country where the sparkle of dark eyes electrify, and where the knives are cheap, and do their work swiftly and well.

They passed out of the table d'hote room into the hall. Then he stretched forth his hand.

"You are not coming to see me to-morrow, Nino?" she asked in a low, despondent voice.

"No," he replied. "I have an appointment."

"But you can surely dine here?"

"I am not quite certain," he answered. "If I can, I will send you a telegram."

"You are impatient—you who promised me to wait until I could give you some satisfactory explanation. It is cruel of you—very cruel, Nino," she said in a voice scarcely above a whisper.

"You are never straightforward," he replied quickly. "If you confessed to me, all this anxiety would at once cease."

"I cannot."

"No," he said meaningly; "you will not. You dare not, because your past has not been what it should have been! Buona sera!" and with this parting allegation he lifted his hat and bowed stiffly.

"Felicissima notte, Nino," she answered so low as to be almost inaudible.

Then he turned and passed out of the great glass doors which the porters held open for him.

Gemma went to her room, and, bursting into tears, sat for a long time alone, despairing, plunged in grief. She knew by her lover's manner that he had forsaken her, and she felt herself alone in gigantic London, where the language, the people, the streets, all were strange to her. As she sat in her low easy chair, a slim, graceful figure in her pale-blue dinner-dress, she clenched her tiny hands till the nails embedded themselves in the palms, as she uttered with wild abandon the name of the man she so fondly loved.

"Ah!" she cried aloud. "You, Nino, who have treated me with this suspicion and contempt—you who have brought me here among your people and deserted me—can never know how much I have sacrificed for your sake. Nor can you ever know how fondly I love you. Why have I acted with all this secrecy must for ever remain a mystery. You have left me," she added in a hoarse, strained voice, half inaudible on account of her sobs—"you have left me now; but some day when I am free—when I can show you things in their true light—you will regret that to-night you have broken a woman's heart." And she bent forward and gave way to a flood of hot, passionate tears.

Fully half an hour she sat plunged in a deep melancholy, but at last she rose and crossed the room unsteadily. Her fair brow bore a look of determination, her face was hard set, and in her tear-stained eyes was an expression of strength of will.

"Yes," she murmured, "I'll risk all. My life cannot be rendered more hopeless, more wretched, than it now is in this atmosphere of doubt and suspicion." Then she bathed her face in eau-de-Cologne, sniffed her smelling-salts, rubbed her cheeks with a towel to take away their ghastly pallor, and assuming her travelling coat, with its wide fur collar and cuffs, which, being long, hid her dress, she put on her hat and went out.

She went up to one of the porters in the hall hastily, and said—

"Prendetimi una vettura."

The man looked at her in surprise, unable to understand her. She pointed outside to where several hansoms were passing.

"Oh! a cab you want, miss!" he cried, the fact suddenly dawning upon him; and as he touched the electric bell which calls cabs from the rank, she handed him the slip of paper she had that morning received.

The porter read it, descended the steps with her, handed her into the cab, and, having shouted the address to the man, she was driven rapidly away to St. James's Street, where she ascended to the second floor, and found upon a door a brass plate bearing Captain Tristram's name.

She rang the bell, and in response the smart, soldier-servant Smayle appeared, and looked at her in surprise.

"The Signor Capitano Tristram?" she inquired.

"Yes, miss," the man answered; and she entered the hall, and glanced around her while he closed the door.

At that moment Tristram's voice, from one of the rooms beyond, cried—

"Show the lady in, Smayle."

She followed the servant into the cosy sitting-room redolent of cigars. She was gazing round the apartment, noting how comfortable it was, when suddenly the door reopened and Tristram entered. He had evidently been dining out, or to a theatre, and had now discarded his dress-coat for an easy velvet lounge-jacket. When he had closed the door, he stood for a moment regarding her in silence.

"Well," he said at length in Italian. "So you have come, eh?" His welcome was certainly the reverse of cordial.

"Yes," she faltered; "I have come. How did you know I was in London?"

Certain furrows on Tristram's brow revealed profound thought.

"A woman who is wanted by the police always has some difficulty in concealing her whereabouts," he answered meaningly. His countenance was hard and vengeful; his features expressed so much disdain and cruelty at that moment that one would scarcely believe they could ever be susceptible of any gentle emotion.

"Why do you throw that in my face?" she asked angrily.

"My dear signorina," he answered, crossing the room, "come here to this chair and sit down. I want to talk to you very seriously, if you'll allow me."

She moved slowly across, and, sinking into the armchair near the fire, unbuttoned her long coat.

"No," he said; "it's hot in this room: take it off, or you won't find the benefit of it when you leave. See how solicitous I am after your health" and he laughed.

In silence she rose and allowed him to help her divest herself of the heavy garment.

"How charming you look!" he said. "I really don't wonder that you captivate the hearts of men—those who don't know you."

"It seems that you've invited me here for the purpose of raking up all my past," she cried, darting at him a fierce look. "I have accepted your invitation because you and I are old friends, because our interests are identical."

"How?" he asked, puzzled.

"There is a certain episode in my career that must for ever remain a profound secret," she said in a low but distinct tone. "And there is one in yours which, if revealed, would bring you to disgrace, to ruin—nay, to death."

He started, and his dark face paled beneath its bronze of travel.

"What do you mean?" he cried, standing astride before her, his back to the fire, his arms folded resolutely.

"What I have said!"

"And you are foolish enough to think that I fear you?" he cried with biting sarcasm.

"I think nothing, caro," she answered in a voice of the same intense disdain. "The truth is quite obvious. We fear each other."

"I fear you?" And he laughed, as if the absurdity of the idea were humorous.

"Yes," she said fiercely. "I am no longer powerless in your hands. You know well my character, signore—you know what kind of woman I am."

"Yes, I do, unfortunately," he answered. "And what, pray, does all this extraordinary exhibition of bitterness imply?" he asked.

"You force me to speak plainly," she said, her eyes flashing angrily. "Well, then, reflect upon the strange death of Vittorina, and bear in mind by whom was her death so ingeniously compassed."

He sprang towards her suddenly in a fierce ebullition of indignation, his hand uplifted as if he intended to strike her.

"Enough! Curse you!" he muttered.

"Take care," she said calmly, without stirring from her seat. "If you touch me, it is at your own peril."

"Threats?"

"Threats! And to prove to you that they are not in vain," she said, "learn in the first place, that the police have discovered the identity of the Major, and that a warrant is already issued for his arrest."

"I don't believe it," he cried. "You have no proof."

"Inquire of your friends at the Embassy," she replied ambiguously. "You will there learn the truth."

"Listen!" he cried wildly, grasping her roughly by the wrist. "What allegation do you make against me? Come, speak!"

"You have shown yourself at enmity with me, therefore it will remain for you to discover that afterwards," she answered, shaking him off. "One does not show one's hand to one's adversaries."

"You mentioned the death of your friend Vittorina—well?"

"Well?" she repeated, still coldly and calmly. "It is of no use to further refer to that tragic circumstance, except to say that I am aware of the truth."

"The truth!" he cried blankly. "Then who killed her?"

"You know well enough with what devilish ingenuity her young life was taken; how at the moment when she least expected danger she was cut off by a means so curious and with such swiftness as to baffle even the cleverest doctors in London. You know the truth, Signor Capitano—so do I."

"You would explain how her life was taken; you would tell the world the strange secret by which she was held in bondage. But you shan't," he cried, standing before her with clenched fists. "By Heaven, you shan't!"

"Traitors die slowly in London, but they do die," she said slowly, with deep meaning.

"Curse you!" he cried. "What do you intend to do?"

"Listen!" she answered, rising slowly from her chair and standing before him resolute, desperate, and defiant. "I came here to-night for one purpose—to make a proposal to you."

"A proposal! To marry me, eh?" he laughed.

"This is no time for weak jokes, signore," she answered angrily. "Silence is best in the interests of us both, is it not?"

He paused, his eyes fixed on the hearthrug.

"I suppose it is," he admitted at last.

"Think," she urged, "what would be the result were the whole of those strange facts exposed. Who would suffer?"

He nodded, but no word passed his hard lips. She noticed that what she uttered now impressed him.

"Our acquaintance," she went on in a more sympathetic tone, "was formed in curious circumstances, and it has only been fraught with unhappiness, sorrow, and despair. I come to you to-night, Frank," she added in a low despondent voice, "to ask you to help me to regain my freedom."

He laughed aloud a harsh, cruel laugh, saying—"You have already your freedom. I hope you are enjoying it. No doubt Armytage loves you, and London is a change after Tuscany."

His laugh aroused within her a veritable tumult of hatred.

"You speak as if I were not an honest woman," she cried, her eyes glistening. "Even you shall not brand me as an adventuress."

"Well, I think your adventures in Florence and in Milan were curious enough," he said, "even if we do not mention that night in Livorno when Vittorina—"

"Ah no!" she exclaimed, interrupting him. "Why should you cast that into my face? Now that we are friends no longer, you seek to heap disgrace upon me by recalling all that has gone by. In this conversation I have not sought to bring back to your memory any of the many recollections which must be painful. My object in coming to you is plain enough. I am perfectly straightforward—"

"For the first time in your life."

She took no heed of his interruption, but went on saying—

"Charles Armytage has promised me marriage."

"He's a fool!" was the abrupt rejoinder. "When he knows the truth, he'll hate you just as much as I do."

"You certainly pay me delicate compliments," she said, drawing herself up haughtily. "Your hatred is reciprocated, I assure you. But surely this is not a matter of either love or hatred between us. It is a mere arrangement for our mutual protection and benefit."

"What do you want me to do?" he asked, leaning back upon the mantelshelf in affected laziness—"you want my silence?"

"Yes," she answered eagerly, looking straight into his dark countenance.

"You're afraid that if you marry Charlie Armytage I may expose you—eh?"

She nodded, with downcast eyes.

He was silent for a few moments.

"Then," he answered at last in a deep, determined voice, "understand once and for all that Armytage is a friend of mine. He shall never marry you."

She knit her brows, and her pale lips twitched nervously. "Then you are still bent upon wrecking my life?" she said slowly and distinctly as she faced him. "I offer you silence in exchange for my freedom, for it is you alone who can give me that. Yet you refuse."

"Yes," he said. "I refuse absolutely."

"Then you would debar me from happiness with the man I love?" she said in a low, deep whisper. "You, the man to whose machinations I owe my present wretchedness, refuse to free me from the trammels you yourself have cast about me—you refuse to tell the truth in exchange for my silence."

He looked at her calmly with withering contempt.

"I have no desire for the silence of such as you," he answered quickly. "I fear nothing that you may say. Threats from you are mere empty words, cara."

"Then listen!" she cried, her brilliant eyes again flashing in desperation. "To-morrow I shall call upon Castellani at the Embassy, and tell him the truth."

"You dare not!" he gasped fiercely. His face had blanched instantly as, advancing a couple of steps towards her with clenched hands, he gazed threateningly into her eyes.

"I have given you an alternative which you have rejected, Signor Capitano," she said, taking up her fur-trimmed coat. "You defy me; and I wish you good-night."

"You intend to expose the whole of the facts?" he cried in dismay. "You will incriminate yourself!"

"I care nothing for that. My happiness is now at an end. For the future I have no thought, no care, now that you and I are enemies. As I have already said, traitors die slowly in London, but they do die."

"You shall not go to Castellani," the Captain muttered between his set teeth; and with a cry of uncurbed, uncontrollable rage he sprang upon her before she could defend herself or raise an alarm, and seizing her, he compressed his strong, sinewy fingers upon her slim white throat. "You shan't go!" he cried. "No further word shall pass your pretty lips—curse you! I'll—I'll kill you!"

XVII

SMAYLE'S DILEMMA

Tristram's sinewy fingers tightened upon the slender white throat of the helpless woman until her breath was crushed from her, her face became crimson, and in her wild, starting eyes was a ghastly expression of suffering and despair.

"Mercy!" she managed to gasp with difficulty. "Ah, no! Let me go! let me go!"

"Your evil tongue can ruin me. But you shall not!" he cried in a frenzy of anger, his face suffused by a fierce, murderous passion. "By Heaven, you shall die!"

"If—if you kill me," she shrieked, "you will suffer; for even though I'm outcast, there is a law here, in your England, to deal with murderers."

"Outcast!" he echoed wildly, with an imprecation. "Yes; curse you! Is there any wonder that you are hounded out of Italy, after all that has occurred? Is there any wonder, after what took place in Tuscany, that I now hold you within my hands, eager to extinguish the last remaining spark of your life?"

"You're a brute!" she cried in a hoarse, gurgling voice. "Release me! I—I can't breathe!"

"No, by Heaven, you shall die!" he declared, his strong, muscular hands trembling with uncurbed passion. "Your infernal tongue shall utter no more foul slanders, for to-night, now—this moment—I'll silence you!" She uttered a low, agonised cry, then, fainting, panting, breathless, sank upon her knees, unable any longer to resist the frightful pressure upon her throat. At that instant, however, Smayle, hearing an unusual noise, dashed in, and, taking in the situation at a glance, seized his master firmly.

"Good heavens, sir! what's the matter?" he cried. "Why, you're killing the lady!"

"Get out?" cried the Captain with an oath, shaking himself free, and still holding the fainting woman at his feet. "Get out quickly! Leave the house, and—and don't come back!"

"But you're killing her!" he cried. "See, there's blood in her mouth!"

"Obey me this instant!" he roared. "Leave me!"

"No," Smayle answered, "I won't!" And, springing upon his master, he managed, after a desperate struggle, to drag his hands free of the kneeling woman's throat and fling him back with a smothered oath. "I won't see a woman murdered in that cowardly way," he declared vehemently, "even if you are my master?"

"What the devil do my affairs concern you, Smayle?" Tristram demanded fiercely, glaring at his servant, and glancing at Gemma, now fallen back prostrate on the floor, her hat crushed beneath her, her fair hair escaping from its pins.

"They concern me as far as this, sir—that you shall leave this room at once. If the lady is dead, then you've committed murder, and I am witness of it!"

"You'd denounce me, would you?" the Captain shrieked with rage, his hands still clenched in a fierce paroxysm of anger. Then, next instant he sprang at him.

But Smayle was a slim, athletic fellow, and, like most of the genus Tommy Atkins, knew how to use his fists when occasion required. He jumped aside, nimbly evaded the blow his master aimed at him, and cleverly tripped up his adversary, so that he fell headlong to the ground, bringing down from its pedestal a pretty Neapolitan statuette, which was smashed to atoms.

Tristram quickly rose with an imprecation, but Smayle, again grappling with him, succeeded at length, after an encounter long and fierce, in flinging him out of the room, and locking the door.

Then instantly he turned towards the white-faced woman, and, kneeling beside her, endeavoured to restore her to consciousness. With his handkerchief he staunched the blood slowly trickling from the corners of her pale lips, placed a cushion beneath her head, and snatching some flowers from a bowl, sprinkled her face with the water. Her white, delicate throat was dark and discoloured where his master's rough hands had pressed it in his violent attempt to strangle her, her dress was torn open at the neck, and her gold necklet she had worn, with its tiny enamelled medallion, lay upon the ground, broken by the sudden, frantic attack. Tenderly the soldier-servant stroked her hair, chafed her hands, and endeavoured to restore her to consciousness, but all in vain. Inert and helpless she remained while he held her head, gazing upon her admiringly, but unable to determine the best course to pursue.

The outer door banged suddenly, and he knew his master had fled.

With every appearance of one dead, Gemma lay upon the carpet where she had sunk from the cruel, murderous hands of the man who had attempted to kill her, while Smayle again rose, and obtaining some brandy from the liquor-stand, succeeded in forcing a small quantity of it down her throat.

This revived her slightly, for she opened her great clear eyes, gazing into Smayle's with an expression of fear and wonder.

"Drink a little more of this, miss," the man said eagerly, holding the glass to her lips, delighted to find that she was not, after all, dead as he had at first feared.

Unable to understand what he said, she nevertheless allowed him to pour a few more drops of the spirit down her dry, parched throat, but it caused her to cough violently, and she made a gesture that to take more was impossible.

For fully ten minutes she remained silent, motionless, her head lying heavily upon Smayle's arm, breathing slowly, but each moment more regularly. The deathly pallor gradually disappeared as the blood came back to her cheeks, but the dark rings about her eyes, and the marks upon her throat, still remained as evidence how near she had been to an agonising and most terrible death.

At last Gemma again opened her eyes and uttered some words faintly, making a frantic gesture with her hands. The man who had rescued her understood that she wished to rise, and, grasping her beneath the arms, gradually lifted her into the Captain's great leather-covered armchair, in which she reclined, a frail, beautiful figure, with eyes half closed and breast panting violently after the exertion.

Then again she closed her eyes, her tiny hands, cold and feeble, trembled, and in a few minutes her regular breathing made it apparent to the Captain's man that, exhausted, she had sunk into a deep and peaceful sleep.

He left her side, and creeping from the room noiselessly, searched all the other apartments. His master had gone. He had taken with him his two travelling-bags—a sign that he had set out upon a long journey. As far as Constantinople, one bag always sufficed; to Teheran he always took both. The fact that the two bags were taken made it plain that his absence would be a long one—probably some weeks, if not more.

Smayle stole back to the sitting-room, and saw that the blue official ribbon with its silver greyhound hung no longer upon its nail, and that his revolver was gone. He returned to the Captain's bedroom, and upon the dressing-table found a ten-pound note lying open. Across its face had been scribbled hastily, in pencil, the words, "For Smayle." Upon the floor were some scraps of paper, letters that had been hurriedly destroyed, while in the empty grate lay a piece of tinder and a half-consumed wax vesta, showing that some letters of more importance than the others had been burnt.

The man, mystified, gathered the scraps together, examined them closely and placed them in a small drawer in the dressing-table. Then putting the banknote in his pocket, exclaimed to himself—

"This is curious, and no kid. The Captain ain't often so generous as to give me a tenner, especially when he only paid me yesterday. I wonder who the lady is? I wish I could speak to her. She's somebody he's met, I suppose, when abroad."

He went to the hall, and noted what coats his master had taken, when suddenly it occurred to him that without assistance it was impossible that he could have carried them all downstairs; somebody must have helped him.

Into the small bachelor's kitchen he passed, pondering deeply over the strange occurrence. Only an hour before, his master had arrived home from dining at the club, and putting on his well-worn velvet lounge-coat, had announced his intention of remaining at home and smoking. Smayle had asked him whether he was under orders to leave with despatches, when he had answered that it was not yet his turn, and that he expected to have a fortnight in London. Three days ago he had returned from St. Petersburg, tired, hungry, irritable, as he always was after that tedious journey. A run home from Brussels, Paris, or even Berlin, never made him short-tempered, but always when he arrived from Petersburg, Madrid, or "Constant," he grumbled at everything; always declared that Smayle had been drinking his whisky; that the place was dirty; that the weather in London was brutal; and ten thousand a year wouldn't repay him for the loss of nerve-power on "those infernal gridirons they call railways."

Yet he had made a serious attempt upon the life of a strange lady who had called, and had left hurriedly with sufficient kit to last him six months.

He was reflecting deeply, wondering what he should do with the lady, when suddenly he was startled by the door-bell ringing. With military promptness he answered it, and found his master's new acquaintance, Arnoldo Romanelli. The latter had spent several evenings at Tristram's

WILLIAM LE QUEUX

chambers since the night they had dined together at Bonciani's, therefore Smayle knew him well.

"The Captain's not at home, sir," he answered, in reply to the visitor's inquiry.

"Is he away?"

"He left this evening suddenly."

"On important business, I suppose?"

"Yes, sir," Smayle answered. Then he added, "Excuse me, sir, but you are Italian, aren't you?"

"Yes; why?" Arnoldo asked in surprise.

Smayle hesitated, fidgeted a moment, and then answered—

"Well, sir, there's a lady there, in the Captain's sitting-room, and she's not well, and she can't speak English."

"A lady?" cried Romanelli, suddenly interested. "Young or old?"

"Young, sir. She's Italian, I believe. And I thought, sir, that perhaps you wouldn't mind assisting a friend of my master's."

"Of course not. Take me to her at once," he said. "Is she very ill?"

"She had a bad fainting fit," answered the servant as he led the way to the sitting-room. She was still lying back in the chair, now quite conscious, but still pale, dishevelled, and so exhausted as to be scarcely able to move her limbs. They seemed paralysed by the excruciating torture she had undergone.

The opening of the door aroused her, and looking up, her eyes met those of the young Italian.

"You—Gemma!" he cried in profound surprise, rushing forward. "Why are you here—in London? And in Tristram's rooms?"

She held her breath in amazement at this unexpected meeting.

"I—I called here," she explained in a low, weak voice, "and became seized with a sudden faintness. I—I think I fell."

"I trust you're not hurt," he said quickly. "You are pale and trembling. Shall I call a doctor?"

"No, no," she answered. "In a few minutes I shall be quite right again."

Romanelli noticed her necklet at his feet, and picked it up. Then he glanced across the room and saw the broken statuette, and his quick, dark eyes detected signs of a struggle in the disarranged hearth-rug and the chairs pushed out of place.

"Merely fainting did not break this," he said gravely, holding up the chain and picking up the tiny medallion enamelled with the picture of a dog's head with the words beneath, "Toujours Fidèle." The chain and its pendant were simple and old-fashioned, the one remaining link of her girlhood days at the Convent of San Paolo della Croce.

She held out her hand in silence, and the young man placed both chain and medallion in her palm. Then, with her great, pain-darkened eyes fixed upon him, she kissed the chain reverently, afterwards slipping both into her glove, and sighing.

"Gemma," continued Romanelli, bending beside her chair, "what does this mean? Tell me. Why have you come to London?"

She shook her head.

"This man can't speak Italian," he explained, glancing at Smayle, who stood beside wondering. "We can talk quite freely. Come, tell me what has happened."

"Nothing," she assured him.

"But why are you in London? Were you not afraid?"

"Afraid?" she echoed. "Why should I be? I am just as safe here in England, as I was in Florence or Livorno."

"Vittorina died within the first hour she set foot in London," he observed with a grave, meaning look.

"You loved her," she said. "You have all my sympathy, Arnoldo. Some day we shall know the truth; then those responsible for her death shall receive no mercy at our hands."

"That chapter of my life has closed," the young Italian said, with a touch of sorrow in his voice. "She has been murdered, but by whom we cannot yet tell." He paused, then added, "What object had you, Gemma, in leaving Italy? And why have you come here? Surely you know that you have enemies in London—enemies as cruel, as unrelenting, as cunning as those who killed poor Vittorina."

"I am well aware of that," she answered, stirring uneasily in her chair, and putting up her hand to her bruised throat. "I know I have enemies. To one person, at least, my death would be welcome," she added, remembering the fierce struggle in that room an hour before.

"Then why have you risked everything and come here? You were safer in Italy," he said.

"I was not safer there. I am safe nowhere," she replied. "The police have discovered some of the facts, and—"

"The police!" he gasped in alarm. "Our secret is out, then?"

"Not entirely. I was warned to leave Livorno within twenty-four hours, and advised to leave Italy altogether. Then—well, I came here."

"With your lover, eh?"

She nodded.

"And you will marry him?" the young Italian observed slowly. "You do not fear the exposure which afterwards must come? These English are fond of looking closely into the woman's past, you know."

She shrugged her shoulders, answering: "My past is secret. Fortunately the one person who knows the truth dares not speak."

"Then what I know is of no account?" he said, somewhat surprised.

She laughed.

"If you and I have ever flirted, or even exchanged foolish letters, it was long ago, when we had not the experience of the world we now have. I do not dread exposure of your knowledge of my past."

"But this lover of yours, this Englishman—why does he believe in you so blindly?" Romanelli inquired. "Is he so utterly infatuated that he thinks you absolutely innocent of the world and its ways?"

"My affairs of the heart are of no concern to you now, Arnoldo," she answered a trifle coquettishly.

"But if I come here to a man's rooms, and find you in his sitting-room in a half-conscious state, trembling and afraid, with every sign of a desperate struggle in your dress and in the room, and therefore I, once your boy-lover, seek an explanation," he said. "True, the affection between us is dead long, long ago, but remember that you and I both have interests in common, and that by uniting we may effect the overthrow of our enemies. If we do not—well, you know the fate that awaits us."

"Yes," she answered in a voice that sounded low and distant. "I know, alas! too well—too well!"

XVIII

What Lady Marshfield Knew

Some days passed. Charles Armytage had not called again at the hotel, having resolved to end the acquaintance. He regretted deeply that he had brought Gemma to London; yet when he pondered over it in the silence of his own rooms in Ebury Street, he told himself that he still loved her, that she was chic, beautiful, and even this mystery surrounding her might one day be elucidated.

The action of the authorities in Leghorn puzzled him. Gemma's secret was, without doubt, of a character which would not bear the light of day. Still, as days went on and he heard nothing of her, he began to wonder whether she was at the hotel, or whether she had carried out her intention of returning to Italy.

He loved her. This brief parting had increased his affection to such an extent that he thought of her hourly, remembering her sweet, musical voice, her pretty broken English, her happy smiles whenever he was at her side. Her face, as it rose before him in his day-dreams, was not that of an adventuress, but of a sweet, loving woman who existed in mortal terror of some terrible catastrophe; its childlike innocence was not assumed; her blue eyes had the genuine clearness of those of an honest woman.

Thoughts such as these filled his mind daily. He passed the hours at the rooms of friends, at the club, at the theatres, anywhere where he could obtain distraction, but in all he saw the same face, with the same calm look of reproach, those same eyes glistening with tears as had been before him in the hall of the Victoria on that well-remembered evening when they parted.

At last, one morning, he could bear the suspense no longer. Bitterly reproaching himself for having acted so harshly as to leave her alone in a country where she was strange and did not know the language, he took a cab and drove down to Northumberland Avenue.

He inquired at the bureau of the hotel, and was informed that the Signorina Fanetti had left three days ago, and that she had given no address to which letters might be forwarded. He thanked the clerk, turned, and went blindly down the steps into the street, crushed, grief-stricken, the sun of his existence blotted out.

He remembered his protestations in Livorno; he remembered all that had passed between them, and saw that he had acted as a coward and a cad. That she loved him he had no doubt, and it was also plain to him that she had left London heart-broken.

Armytage was very well known in London, and as soon as his friends knew he was back again, the usual flow of invitations poured in upon him. In his endeavour to divert his thoughts, he accepted all and sundry, and one evening went to Lady Marshfield's, whose receptions were always a feature of London life.

The eccentric old lady had long been his friend. Like so many other young and good-looking men, he had been "taken up" by her ladyship, flattered, petted, and feted, utterly unconscious that by allowing this to be done he was making himself the laughingstock of the whole set in which he moved. But the ugly old woman's attentions had at last nauseated him, as they had done every other young man, and his absence abroad had for a time prevented him calling at Sussex Square.

But to the card for this particular evening was added, in her ladyship's own antiquated handwriting, a few words expressing pleasure at his return to London, and a hope that he would call and see her.

Lady Marshfield's junketings were distinctly brilliant on account of the large number of the diplomatic corps which she always gathered about her and this evening there was a particularly noteworthy crowd. There were many young attaches, many pretty girls, a few elderly diplomats, a fair sprinkling of members of Parliament, and a large gathering of the exclusive set in which her ladyship moved. The rooms were well-lit, the electricity bringing joy to every feminine heart, as it always does, because it shows their jewels to perfection; the flowers were choice and abundant, and the music was by one of the most popular orchestras in London. But it was always so.

When Charles Armytage shook the old lady's hand at the head of the stairs, her thin blue lips parted in what she considered her sweetest smile, and she said: "You have quite deserted me, Charles. I hear you've been in London a whole fortnight, and yet this is your first visit!"

"I've been busy," he answered. "I was away so long that I found such lots of things wanting my attention when I came back."

"Ah! no excuses, no excuses," the old lady croaked. "You young men are always full of excellent reasons for not calling. Well, go in; you're sure to find some people you know. When I can, I want to have a serious chat with you, so don't leave before I've seen you again. Promise me?"

"Certainly," he said, as he passed on into the apartment filled to overflowing with its distinguished crowd.

Careless of all about him, he wandered on through the great salons until he met several people he knew, and then the evening passed quite gaily.

At last, an hour past midnight, he found himself again at Lady Marshfield's side.

"Well," she said as they passed into one of the small rooms then unoccupied, for the guests were already departing—"well, why have you been so long away?"

"I had no incentive to stay in England," he said. "I find life much more amusing on the Continent, and I'm a bit of a Bohemian, you know."

"When you are in love—eh?" she laughed.

Her words stabbed him, and he frowned.

"If I want a wife, I suppose I can find one in London," he snapped, rather annoyed.

"But it was love which kept you in Tuscany so long," she observed with sarcasm. "Because you love Gemma Fanetti."

He started in surprise.

"How did you know?" he inquired.

"News of that sort travels quickly," the old lady answered, glancing at him craftily. "It is to be regretted."

"Why?"

"Because a woman of her character could never become your wife, Charles," she replied after a moment's hesitation. "Take my advice; think no more of her." Strange, he pondered, how every one agreed that her past would not bear investigation, yet all seemed to conspire against him to preserve the secret.

"We have already parted," he said in a low voice. On many previous occasions they had spoken together confidentially.

At that moment a man-servant entered, glanced quickly across the room, and noticing with whom his mistress was conversing, turned and rapidly made his exit. Armytage was seated with his back to the door, therefore did not notice that the eminently respectable servant was none other than the man in whose company he had shot down in Berkshire— the jovial Malvano. That evening the movements of the village doctor of Lyddington had been somewhat mysterious. He had arrived about dinner-time as an extra hand, and had served refreshments in the shape of champagne-cup, coffee, sandwiches and biscuits to the hungry ones—and it is astonishing how hungry and thirsty people always are at other people's houses, even if they have only finished dinner half an hour before. His face was imperturbable, his manner stiff, and the style in which he handled plates and glasses perfect.

One incident, at least, would have struck the onlooker as curious. While standing behind the improvised buffet serving champagne, Count Castellani, the Italian Ambassador, a tall, striking figure with his dozen or so orders strung upon a tiny golden chain in his lapel, approached and demanded some wine. Malvano opened a fresh bottle, and while pouring it out His Excellency exclaimed in a low half-whisper in Italian—

"To-morrow at twelve, at the Embassy."

"Si, signore," the other answered without raising his head, apparently still engrossed in pouring out the wine.

"You're still on the alert?" asked the Ambassador in an undertone.

"Si, signore."

"Good! To-morrow I must have a consultation with you," answered His Excellency, tossing off the wine.

By the secret confidences thus exchanged, it was evident that Count Castellani and Doctor Malvano thoroughly understood each other; and, further, it was plain that upon some person in that assembly Filippo, head-waiter at the Bonciani, was keeping careful observation. Yet he apparently attended to his work as a well-trained servant should; and even when he discovered Armytage with her ladyship, he was in no way confused, but retreated quietly without attracting the young man's attention.

"Why have you parted from Gemma?" her ladyship asked.

"Well," answered Armytage, hesitating, "have you not said that she's an impossible person?"

"Of course. But when a man's in love—"

"He alters his mind sometimes," he interrupted, determined not to tell this woman the truth.

"So you've altered your mind?" she said. "You ought really to congratulate yourself that you've been able to do so."

"Why?"

Lady Marshfield regarded her visitor gravely, fanned herself slowly in silence for some moments, then answered—

"Because it is not wise for a man to take as wife a woman of such an evil reputation."

"Evil reputation?" he echoed. "What do you mean by evil?"

"Her reputation is wide enough in Italy. I wonder you did not hear of her long ago," her ladyship answered. "You speak as if she were notorious."

"Ask any one in Turin, in Milan, or Florence. They will tell you the truth," she replied. "Your idol is, without doubt, the most notorious person in the whole of Italy."

"The most notorious?" he cried. "You speak in enigmas. I won't have Gemma maligned in this way," he added fiercely.

She smiled. It was a smile of triumph. She was happy that they were already parted, and she sought now to embitter him against her, in order that he should not return to her.

"Have you never heard of the Countess Funaro?" she asked in a calm voice.

"The Countess Funaro!" he cried. "Of course I have. Her escapades have lately been the talk of society in Rome and Florence. Only a couple of months ago a duel took place at Empoli, the outcome of a quarrel which she is said to have instigated, and the young advocate Cassuto was shot dead."

"He was her friend," her ladyship observed.

"Well?"

"Well," said Lady Marshfield, "don't you think you were rather foolish to fall in love with a woman of her reputation?"

"Good Heavens!" he cried, starting up. "No, that can't be the truth! Gemma cannot be the notorious Contessa Funaro!"

"If you doubt me, go out to Italy again and make inquiries," the eccentric old lady answered calmly.

"But the Countess Funaro has the most unenviable reputation of any person in Italy. I've heard hundreds of extraordinary stories regarding her."

"And the latest is your own interesting experience—eh!"

"I—I really can't believe it," Armytage said, dumbfounded.

"No; I don't expect you do. She's so amazingly clever that she can cause her dupes to believe in her absolutely. Her face is so innocent that one would never believe her capable of such heartless actions as are attributed to her."

"But what experience have you personally had of her?" he inquired, still dubious. He knew that this elderly woman of the world was utterly unscrupulous.

"I met her in Venice last year," her ladyship said. "All Venice was acquainted with her deliciously original countenance. Her notoriety was due to her pretty air of astonishment, the purity of her blue eyes, and the expression of chaste innocence which she can assume when it so pleases her—an expression which contrasts powerfully with her true nature, shameless creature that she is."

"And are you absolutely positive that the woman I love as Gemma Fanetti is none other than the Contessa Funaro, the owner of the great historic Funaro palace in Florence, and the Villa Funaro at Ardenza?"

"I have already told you all I know."

"But you have given me no proof."

"I merely express satisfaction that you have been wise enough to relinquish all thought of marrying her."

"I really can't believe that this is the truth. How did you know she was in London?"

"I was told so by one who knows her. She has been staying at the Victoria," her ladyship answered.

"I don't believe what you say," he cried wildly. "No, I won't believe it. There is some mistake."

"She has left the hotel," Lady Marshfield said, fixing her cold eyes on him. "Follow her, and charge her with the deception."

"It is useless. I am confident that Gemma is not this notorious Contessa."

Her ladyship made a gesture of impatience, saying—"I have no object in deceiving you, Charles. I merely think it right that you should be made aware of the truth, hideous as it is."

"But is it the truth?" he demanded fiercely. "There is absolutely no proof. I certainly never knew her address in Florence, but at Livorno she lived in a little flat on the Passeggio. If she were the Contessa, she would certainly have lived in her own beautiful villa at Ardenza, only a mile away."

"She may have let it for the season," his hostess quickly observed.

"The Countess Funaro is certainly wealthy enough, if reports be true, without seeking to obtain a paltry two or three thousand lire for her villa," he said.

"She no doubt had some object in living quietly as she did, especially as she was hiding her identity from you."

"I don't believe it. I can't believe it," he declared, as the remembrance of her passionate declarations of love flooded his mind. If what her ladyship alleged were actually the truth, then all her ingenuousness had been artificial; all her words of devotion feigned and meaningless; all her kisses false; all mere hollow shams for the purpose of deceiving and ensnaring him for some ulterior object. "Until I have proof of Gemma's perfidy and deceit, I will believe no word against her," he declared decisively.

"You desire proof?" the old woman said, her wizened face growing more cruel as her eyes again met his. "Well, you shall have it at once" and, rising, she crossed a small escritoire, and took from it a large panel portrait, which she placed before him. "Read the words upon this," she said, with an evil gleam in her vengeful gaze.

He took the picture with trembling hands, and read the following, written boldly across the base:—

"T'invio la mia fotografia, cosi ti sara sempre presente la mia efige, che ti obblighera a ricordarmi. Tua aff.—Gemma Luisa Funaro."

The photograph was by Alvino, of Florence, from the same negative as the one at that moment upon the table in his chambers. The handwriting was undoubtedly that of a woman he loved dearer than life.

Charles Armytage stood pale and speechless. Indeed, it was a hideous truth.

XIX

A Secret Despatch

At noon next day Count Castellani, the Italian Ambassador to the Court of St. James, stood at the window of his private room gazing out upon cabs and carriages passing and repassing around Grosvenor Square.

In his hand was a secret and highly important despatch which had only ten minutes before arrived from Rome by special messenger. His brows were knit, and he was pondering deeply over it. He stroked his grey beard and sighed, murmuring to himself—

"Extraordinary! Most extraordinary! If I had suspected such a complication as this, I should have never accepted this Embassy. True, this is the highest office in our diplomatic service—an office which I have coveted ever since I was a young attache at Brussels. And now that I have fame in my own country, and honour among these English, I am unable to enjoy it. Ah! the fruits of life are always bitter—always!"

Then he drew another heavy sigh, and remained silent, gazing moodily out, his dark eyes fixed blankly upon the handsome square. No sound reached that well-furnished room with its double windows and hangings of dark-red velvet, the chamber in which the greatest of English statesmen had often sat discussing the future of the European situation and the probabilities of war; the room in which on one memorable day a defensive alliance had been arranged between Italy and England, the culminating master-stroke of diplomacy which had obviated a great and disastrous European war. And it was the tall, handsome, grey-bearded man, at that moment standing at his window plunged in melancholy, who had thus successfully saved his own country, Italy, by concluding the treaty whereby the fine Italian Navy would, in the event of war, unite with the British fleet against all enemies—the alliance whereby England would be strengthened against all the machinations of the Powers, and bankrupt Italy would still preserve her dignity among nations. It had been a truly clever piece of diplomacy. By careful observation and cunning ingenuity, Count Castellani had obtained knowledge of the projected action of France, of Germany, and of Russia, while the British Foreign Office had remained in utter ignorance. Then one day he had invited Lord Felixtowe, His Majesty's principal Secretary of State for Foreign Affairs, and in that room he had plainly told the story of the conspiracy in progress against England. The Foreign Minister was so surprised that at first he could not credit that the Powers implicated could have the audacity to contemplate the invasion of our island; but when His Excellency brought forward certain undeniable proofs, he was compelled to admit the truth of his assertion.

Then, without a moment's hesitation, the subject of a defensive alliance was mooted. United with the magnificent vessels of the Italian Navy, the battleships of Britain could hold the seas against all comers. There was no time to be lost, for Russian diplomacy was shrewdly at work in Rome with the object of contracting an alliance between the Government of the Czar and that of King Humbert. Therefore, without consulting the Cabinet, Lord Felixtowe had accepted the Ambassador's proposals, and within twenty-four hours a treaty was signed, which has ever since been Europe's safeguard against war. It was a short document, its draft only covering half a sheet of foolscap; but it was a bond between two friendly nations, which, it is to be hoped, will never be severed.

Yet the life of an Ambassador is by no means enviable. Even when promoted to the first rank, he obtains but little thanks from his chief, and less from his own compatriots at home. In this instance, Count Castellani, through whose ingenuity and far-sightedness England, and perhaps the whole of Europe, had been saved from an encounter of so fierce, sanguinary, and frightful a nature as the world has never yet witnessed, obtained not a word of thanks from the Italian people. Indeed, beyond a private autograph note from his sovereign and a long and formal despatch from the Marquis Montelupo, his master-stroke had passed by unnoticed and unknown save to those who had for years been plotting the down fall of the British Empire. The result was that in this, as in nearly every case where clever diplomacy is needed, the result of the negotiations remained hidden from the public. In this case, as in so many others, the alliance was entirely secret, and only after some months was its existence allowed to leak out, and only then in order that the enemies of England should hesitate before embarking upon any desperate step.

Sometimes, in his fits of melancholy, Count Castellani, like all other men, could not help feeling discontented. He was but human. When he reflected upon the glory which the German and French Ambassadors were accorded in their own countries each time they carried through some paltry, unimportant little piece of diplomacy, his heart grew weary

WILLIAM LE QUEUX

within him. It was in this mood, unhappy and discontented, that he stood at the window with the secret despatch in his white, nervous hand. What he had read there brought back to him a recollection of days bygone—a recollection that was painful and bitter now that he had risen to be chief of the service in which he had spent the greater part of his life.

Yet it held him stupefied.

Again he sighed. His daughter Carmenilla, a slim, dark-haired girl of twenty, entered softly and, seeing her father silent and pensive, moved noiselessly across the room. He was wifeless, and all his love was bestowed upon his daughter, who held her father in absolute reverence. Carmenilla was not beautiful, but she was her father's companion, helpmate, and friend. She stood behind him, and heard him exclaim, in a low voice only just audible—

"If what I suspect is true, then the secret is out. I must obtain leave of absence and go to Rome. Perhaps even now my letters of recall are on their way! Nevertheless, it is too strange to believe. No; at present I must wait. I can't—I won't believe it!"

At that moment there was a tap at the door, and as Carmenilla slipped out noiselessly, the liveried Italian servant announced that Dr. Malvano had called.

"Show him in here," His Excellency answered, crossing instantly to his writing-table, unlocking one of the drawers, and placing the secret despatch therein.

When Malvano entered, rosy, buxom, and smiling, well dressed in frock-coat, and carrying his silk hat and stick with that air adopted by members of the medical profession, the Count shook him by the hand and greeted him cordially. Without invitation, His Excellency's visitor tossed his hat and stick upon the sofa, sank into the nearest chair, and stretched out his legs, apparently quite at home.

The Ambassador, first raising the heavy velvet *portiere*, and slipping the small brass bolt of the door into its socket, took a seat at his table, and fixing his eyes upon the man who had served him with wine the night before, said, with a sigh—

"Well, Filippo. A crisis appears imminent."

"You have heard from Rome?" Malvano exclaimed quickly. "I met Varesi, the messenger, in the hall."

"Yes," His Excellency said. "I've received certain instructions from the Minister, but it is impossible to act upon them."

"Why?"

"For the prestige of Italy, for our own reputations, for the personal safety of the one to whom we owe our knowledge, it is impossible to act," the Count answered gravely. "My hands are tied absolutely."

"And you will stand by and see murder committed without seeking to bring pressure to bear against those who seek our ruin? This is not like you, Castellani."

"No, Filippo," the other said, in a tone of confidence quite unusual to him, for he was a stern, rather harsh, diplomat, who never allowed any personal interest to interfere with his duties as Ambassador. "Not a word of reproach from you, of all men. You alone know that I have secretly done my best in this affair; that I have more than once risked my appointment in order to successfully accomplish the work which you and I have in hand."

"And I, too, have done my utmost," Malvano observed. "Up to the present, however, our enemies have been far too wary to be caught napping."

"Yes," the Ambassador said. "In this matter I have relied absolutely upon your patriotism. Like myself, you have run great risks; but I fear that all is to no purpose."

"Why?"

"Because we have not yet fathomed the mystery of the death of the girl Vittorina Rinaldo. If we could do that it would give us a clue to the whole affair."

"Exactly," Malvano answered. "In that matter we are no nearer the truth than we were on the first day we commenced our investigation. And why? Because of one thing—we fear 'La Gemma.'"

"Where is she now?"

"Ah! Unfortunately she quarrelled with young Armytage, left the Hotel Victoria suddenly, and—"

"And her whereabouts are unknown," His Excellency gasped. "Dio mio!" he cried. "Then she may actually have gone back to Italy and betrayed everything!"

"I think that very probable," Malvano said gravely. "For the past fortnight I've been daily at the Bonciani, and have kept my ears open. There is something secret in progress."

"What's its nature?"

"I don't know."

"Then you ought to know," His Excellency cried petulantly. "You must find out. Remember, you are the secret agent of this Embassy, and it is your duty to keep me well informed."

Malvano smiled. The expression upon his round ruddy face at that moment was the same as when, on the night Romanelli dined with him at Lyddington, he had urged his young friend to travel to Livorno, and make a declaration of love to the unfortunate Vittorina. It was a covert glance of cunning and double dealing. "I always report to you all I know," he answered. "Yes, yes," His Excellency said hastily, in a more conciliatory tone. "I withdraw those words, Filippo. Forgive me, because to-day I'm much worried over a matter of delicate diplomacy. In this affair our interests are entirely mutual. You and I love our country, our beloved Italia, and have taken an oath to our Sovereign to act always in his interests. It therefore now becomes our duty to elucidate this mystery. In you Italy has a fearless man of marvellous resource and activity—a man who has, in the past, obtained knowledge of secrets in a manner which has almost passed credence. Surely you will not desert us now and relinquish all hope of obtaining the key to this extraordinary enigma. What have you heard at Lady Marshfield's?"

"I sent in my daily report this morning," the Doctor answered rather coldly. "You have, I suppose, read it?"

"I have," His Excellency said, leaning both his arms upon the table. "I cannot, however, believe that your surmise has any foundation. It's really too extraordinary."

"Why?"

"Such a thing seems not only improbable, but absolutely impossible," the Count replied.

There was a pause, brief and painful. The men looked at one another deeply in earnest. At last Malvano spoke.

"I know well the conflicting interests in this matter. If we do our best for Italy, we do the worst for ourselves—eh?"

The Ambassador nodded. "My political enemies in Rome have, I fear, ingeniously plotted my downfall," the Count replied in a low tone, as he pressed the other's hand. "A single spark is only required to fire the mine. Then the Ministry will be overthrown, and the country must inevitably fall into the hand of the Socialists. Look what they have already done in Venice and in Milan. At the latter city they've closed La Scala, one of the finest theatres in the world; they've dissolved the dancing-school, and have done their worst in every direction. Venice has been revolutionised and now at every local election one reads, written with black paint upon the walls, 'Down with the King and the robbers! Long live the Revolution!' I'm a staunch supporter of law and order, a firm upholder of country and of King, therefore my days of office are numbered."

"Not if we successfully solve this enigma."

"Why? By doing so I shall defeat the plots of my enemies, and thus embitter them against me far more than before."

"You fear La Gemma?"

His Excellency nodded.

"Why?"

"She knows too much."

"So did Vittorina. She was silenced."

"What do you mean, Malvano?" the Ambassador cried, pale and agitated. "That she should share the same fate?"

"No," the other answered gravely. "As far as I can see no life need be taken if we act with cunning and discretion. Can you trust me?"

"I do so implicitly," His Excellency answered, seeing that the secret agent was now entirely in earnest. "More than once you have obtained knowledge by means little short of miraculous."

"Briefly, I'm an excellent spy—eh?" the Doctor laughed. "Well, I didn't spend ten years at the Questura in Firenze, and practise as a doctor at the same time, without obtaining a little wholesome experience. If you'll give this affair entirely into my hands, I'll promise to do my level best, and to assist you out of your dilemma. Your position at this moment is, I know, one of the most extreme peril; but by playing a desperate game we may succeed in discovering what is necessary, thereby placing ourselves and our country in a position of absolute security."

"You are an extremely good friend, Filippo," the Count answered quickly. "In this country, surrounded as I am by traitors and spies, you are the only one in whom I can absolutely trust—except Carmenilla."

"Your daughter must know nothing," the Doctor exclaimed quickly. "This is no woman's affair. If life must be sacrificed, then she might inadvertently expose us—women are such strange creatures, you know."

"Whose life, then, do you fear may be taken?" His Excellency eagerly asked.

The Doctor raised his shoulders with a gesture expressive of profound ignorance.

"Not Gemma's?"

"Why not Gemma's?" Malvano inquired, in an intense voice. "In this affair we must speak plainly. Is she not your enemy?"

"Certainly."

"Then, if a life must be taken, why not hers?"

There was a silence, broken only by the low rumble of carriages and cabs outside.

"No," His Excellency answered. "Before I give you perfect freedom in this matter you shall promise me that she shall be spared. I have reasons—strong ones."

"Certainly, if you desire it," the secret agent replied. The thought at that moment flashed across his mind that, if for the preservation of their secret her lips must necessarily be closed, there were others beside himself who would compass her death. The life of a man or woman can always be taken for a sovereign in London, if one knows where to look for men ready to accomplish such work.

"Then you give me your promise?" the Count asked eagerly.

"On one condition only," Malvano replied in a firm voice, while his eyes fixed themselves upon those of the Ambassador.

"What is your condition?" His Excellency inquired.

"There must be no secret between you and me, for in order to successfully accomplish this stroke of diplomacy we must act deliberately, with forethought, and yet boldly face the facts, risking everything—even our lives," he answered. Then, gazing straight into the other's face, he added, "I shall not act unless you allow me to read the despatch you received to-day from Rome." The Ambassador's brows instantly contracted, and he held his breath. For the first time, he became seized with a suspicion that this man, whose deep cunning as a secret agent was almost miraculous, was now playing him false.

"No," he answered, "that is impossible. My oath to the King prevents me showing any one a despatch marked as confidential."

"Then your oath to the King prevents you from acting in the interests of Italy and the Crown; it prevents me from forging a weapon wherewith to fight the enemies of our beloved country."

"The despatch is entirely of a private character, and concerns myself alone," His Excellency protested.

"In other words, you can't trust me—eh?" the Doctor said, with a hard look of dissatisfaction. "I therefore refuse to act further in this affair, and shall leave you to do as you think fit. I must be in possession of all the known facts before I embark upon the perilous course before us; and as you decline absolutely, I am not prepared to take any steps in the dark. The risks are far too great."

The Ambassador was silent for a few moments, his eyes riveted upon those of the secret agent. Then, in a deep, intense voice, he said—

"Malvano, I dare not show you that despatch."

XX

"The Gobbo"

Saturday night in South London is a particularly busy time for the wives of the working classes. The chief thoroughfares in that great district lying between Waterloo Bridge and Camberwell Green are rendered bright by the flare of the naphtha-lamps of hoarse-voiced costermongers, whose strident cries call attention to their rather unwholesome-looking wares, and the crowds of honest housewives with ponderous baskets on their arms are marketing in couples and threes, taking their weekly outing, which is never to be missed. In the Walworth Road on a Saturday evening one can perhaps obtain a better glimpse of London lower-class life than in any other thoroughfare. The great broad road extending from that junction of thoroughfares, the Elephant and Castle, straight away to the site of old Camberwell Gate, and thence to the once rural but now sadly deteriorated Camberwell Green, is ablaze with gas and petroleum, and agog with movement. The honest, hard-working costermongers, with their barrows drawn into the gutters, vie with the shops in prices and quality; hawkers of all sorts importune passers-by on the congested pavements; the hatless and oleaginous butchers implore the crowd to "Buy, buy, buy," and the whole thoroughfare presents a scene of animation unequalled in the whole metropolis—a striking panorama of poverty, pinched faces, shabby clothes, and enforced economy. The district between the Elephant and Camberwell Green has fallen upon evil days. Those who knew the Walworth Road twenty years ago, and know it now, will have marked its decadence with regret; how the lower life of East Street, known locally as Eas' Lane, has overflowed; how fine old houses, once tenanted by merchants and people of independent means, are now let out in tenements; how model "flats" have reared their ugly heads; how the jerry-builder has swallowed up Walworth Common, across which Dickens once loved to wander; how all has changed, and Walworth has become the Whitechapel of the south.

Life in Walworth is the lower life of modern Cockneydom. There are streets in the district which, highly respectable thoroughfares twenty years ago, now harbour some of the worst characters in London; streets which, although a stone's throw from the noisy, squalid bustle of the

Walworth Road, a policeman hardly cares to venture down without a companion; sunless streets where poverty and crime are hand in hand, where filth has bred disease, and where stunted, pale-faced children wallow in the gutter mire. The wreckage of London life now no longer drifts towards the east, as it used to do, but crosses the Thames, and, after struggling in Lambeth, is swallowed in the debasing vortex of wretched, wonderful Walworth.

Those who pass up the great broad thoroughfare from Camberwell citywards see little of Walworth life. Only when one turns into one or other of its hundred side-streets, which spread out like arms towards the Kennington or Kent Road, can one observe how the poor exist. Among these many streets, one which has perhaps not deteriorated to such an extent as its neighbours, is the Boyson Road. The long thoroughfare of smoke-begrimed, jerry-built houses of monotonous exactness in architecture, two stories, and deep areas, is indeed a very depressing place of residence; but there is not a shop in the whole of it, and it is therefore quiet and secluded from the eternal turmoil of Camberwell Gate.

Halfway down this street, in one of the drab, mournful-looking houses, lived a man and his wife who held themselves aloof from all their neighbours. The man was an Italian, whose vocation was that of waiter in a restaurant in Moorgate Street, and he had taken up his residence in Boyson Road only a few months before. His name was Lionello Nenci, the man who had earned such unenviable reputation among the hucksters' shops in Hammersmith, and whom Gemma, on her arrival in London, had tried vainly to find.

An air of poverty pervaded the interior of the house. The hall floor was devoid of any covering save for a sack flung down in place of a mat; the sitting-room was furnished in the cheapest manner possible; and, by the hollow sound which rang through the place, it was apparent that few of the other ten or twelve rooms contained any furniture at all.

Before the fire in the rusted grate of the sitting-room, on this cold, damp Saturday night early in December, Nenci himself, a dark-faced, surly-looking man with scrubby black beard, aged about thirty-five, was seated smoking a cheap cigar, while near him was a younger man, ugly, hump-backed, pale-faced, also an Italian. They were speaking in Tuscan.

"Yes," Nenci said. "I had to clear out of Hammersmith suddenly and come down here, because I thought the Embassy knew too much. She only discovered me a fortnight ago."

"And she is actually living here?"

"Certainly. This house is the safest place. She lies quite low, and never goes out. Here she comes."

And at that moment the door opened, and Gemma entered. She was dressed in shabby black; her fair hair was twisted carelessly, and her small white hands bore no rings, yet, even slatternly and unkempt, she looked strikingly beautiful.

"So you are hiding with us?" the hump-backed man exclaimed, after he had greeted her.

"Yes," she laughed.

"Where is your lover, Armytage?"

She shrugged her shoulders. "He may be abroad again, for all I know. I've neither seen nor heard from him since we parted nearly a month ago," she said, drawing a chair close to the fire and seating herself, her feet placed coquettishly on the rusted fender.

"He knows nothing, I suppose?" Nenci growled, still smoking.

"Not a word. I'm not a fool, even though I may be in love."

Both men laughed. They knew well the character of this beautiful woman before them, and placed the most implicit confidence in her.

"You really love him—eh?" Nenci inquired.

"I've already told you so a dozen times," she answered impatiently.

"But you won't desert us?" the younger man—whom they addressed as "The Gobbo," Italian for hunchback—said earnestly.

"I am still with you," she answered. "It is impossible for me to serve two masters. What time is the consultation to-night?"

"At ten," answered Nenci, glancing up at the cheap metal timepiece on the mantel. "Arnoldo should be here in five minutes."

The door again opened, and Nenci's wife, a dark-haired Tuscan woman of about thirty, entered. The nasal twang of her speech stamped her at once as Livornese. She was good-looking, and, although ill-dressed, her drab skirt hung well, and her carriage had all the grace and suppleness of the South. For a moment she stood chatting to her husband, her visitor, and their companion, then turning down the smoking lamp, placed several chairs around the plain deal-topped table.

"Gemma hasn't yet got used to London," she laughed, as she busied herself preparing for the mysterious consultation which had been arranged. "She pines for her lover, and thinks this place a trifle poor after the big hotel at Charing Cross."

"No, no," Gemma protested. "I don't complain. I'm quite safe here. And I can wait."

"For your lover?" the Gobbo laughed, in a dry, supercilious tone. "It is a new sensation for you to love. L'amore é la gioia, il reposo la felicita—eh?"

Her clear eyes flashed upon him for an instant, but she did not reply. His words cut her to the quick. In that instant she thought of the man she adored, the man who was held aloof from her by reason of her secret.

Presently, after some further conversation, the door bell rang, and Nenci's wife, who promptly answered the summons, admitted two well-dressed men, Romanelli and Malvano.

The appearance of the latter was the signal for congratulations, Gemma alone holding aloof from them. She exchanged a glance with the Doctor, but he in an instant noticed its swift maliciousness, and remained silent.

After some conventional chatter, in which the Gobbo cracked many grim jokes, all six took seats around the table. Nenci had previously assured himself that the shutters were closed, and that the doors both back and front were securely barred, when Malvano was the first to speak.

"There are two of us absent," he observed. "I received a telegram from one an hour ago. He is in Berlin, and could not be back in time. He apologises."

"It is accepted," they all exclaimed.

"And the other cannot come for reasons you all know."

Then Nenci, a stern, striking figure, rather wild-looking, with his black, bushy hair slightly curled, bent forward earnestly, and said—

"Since last we held a consultation in Livorno some months ago, much has occurred, and it is necessary for us once again to review the situation. Most of us have had severe trials; more than one has fallen beneath the vengeance of our enemies; and more than one is now in penal servitude on Gorgona, that rocky island which lies within sight of the land we all of us love. Well, our ranks are thinner, indeed. Of our twenty-one brothers and sisters who met for the first time in Livorno three years ago only eight now remain. Yet we may accomplish much, for not one of us knows fear; all have been already tried and found staunch and true."

"Are you sure there is no traitor among us?" Gemma asked, in a clear intense voice, her pointed chin resting upon her white palm as she listened to his speech.

"Whom do you suspect?" Nenci demanded, darting a quick look at her.

"I suspect no one," she answered. "But in this desperate crisis we must, if we would successfully accomplish our object, have perfect faith in one another."

"So we have," Malvano said. "Here in London we are in absolute security. We have sacrificed enough, Heaven knows! Thirteen of us are already either in prison, or dead."

Gemma sighed. She herself had been compelled to sacrifice a man's passionate love, her own happiness and all that made life worth living, because of her connexion with this mysterious band which had its headquarters among the working class in London, and whose ramifications were felt in every part of Italy. She lifted her beautiful face once again. She was pale and desperate.

"Thirteen is an unlucky number," remarked the Gobbo grimly.

"For the dead, yes. But eight of us are still living," Malvano said.

"By the holy Virgin! it's a desperate game we are playing," Nenci's wife exclaimed.

"Shut your mouth," growled her husband roughly. "When your opinion is required, we'll ask for it." She was a slim, fragile woman, with a pale face full of romance, black eyes that flashed like gems, and a profusion of dark, frizzy hair, worn with those three thin spiral curls falling over the brow, in the manner of all the Livornesi. Even though she existed in squalid Walworth, she still preserved in the mode of dressing her hair the fashion she had been used to since a child. In that drab, mournful street, she sighed often for her own home in gay, happy, far-off Livorno, with its great Piazza, where she loved to gossip; its fine old cathedral, where she had so often knelt to the Madonna; its leafy Passeggio where, with her friends, she would stroll and watch the summer sun sinking into the Mediterranean behind the grey distant islands. When her husband spoke thus roughly she exchanged glances across the table with Gemma, and her dark, sad eyes became filled with tears.

"No," protested Malvano quickly, "that's scarcely the language to use towards one who has risked all that your wife has risked. I entirely agree with her that the game's desperate enough. We must allow no discord."

"Exactly," Nenci admitted. "The reason why I have summoned you here is because the time is past for mere words. We must now act swiftly and with precision. There is only one person we have to fear."

"What is his name?" they all cried, almost with one accord.

"The man whom Gemma loves—Charles Armytage," the black-haired man answered, his eyes still fixed maliciously upon the woman before him.

In an instant Gemma sprang up, her tiny hands clenched, an unnatural fire in her eyes.

"You would denounce him?" she cried wildly. "You who have held me bound and silent for so long, now seek to destroy the one single hope to which I cling; to snatch from me for ever all chance of peace and happiness!" The eyes of the five persons at the table were upon her as she, strikingly beautiful, stood erect and statuesque before them. They all saw how deeply in earnest and how desperate she was.

But Nenci laughed. The sound of his harsh voice stung her. She turned upon him fiercely, with a dangerous glint in her clear blue eyes, a look that none of that assembly had ever before witnessed.

"In the past," she said, "I have served you. I have been your catspaw. I have risked love, life, everything, for the one object so near my heart: the desire for a vengeance complete and terrible. Because of my association with you"—and she gazed around at them as she spoke—"I have been debarred marriage with the man I love. In order that he should leave me, that his daily presence should no longer fill me with regret and vain longing for happiness, I was compelled to resort to self-accusation, and to denounce myself as an adventuress."

"Then you actually spoke the truth for once in your life!" Nenci observed superciliously, a fierce expression in his black eyes.

"Enough!" Malvano protested. "We didn't come here to discuss Gemma's love affairs."

"But this man, who for the last three years has sought my ruin, has made a false denunciation against the young Englishman. I know only too well what passes in his mind. He declares to you that the only person we need fear is Charles Armytage, and the natural conclusion occurs that he must be silenced. I know full well that at this moment our position is one of desperation. Well, you know my past full well, each one of you, and have, I think, recognised that I'm not a woman to be trifled with. You may stir up the past and cast its mud into my face. Good! But, however wrongly I've acted, it is because this man has held me within his merciless grip, and I have been compelled to do his bidding blindly, without daring to protest. You may tell me that I am an adventuress," she cried vehemently; "that my reputation is evil and unenviable; that my friends in Italian society have cast me adrift because of the libellous stories you have so ingeniously circulated about me; but I tell you that I love Charles Armytage, and I swear on the tomb of my dead mother he shall never suffer because of his true, honest love for me."

She had used the oath which the Italian always holds most sacred, and then a dead silence followed. Except the dark wild-looking visage of Nenci, every face betrayed surprise at this fierce and unexpected outburst.

But Nenci again laughed, stroking his scrubby beard with his thin sallow hand.

"I suppose you wish to desert us, eh?" he asked meaningly.

"While you keep faith with me I am, against my will, still your tool. Break faith with me, and the bond which has held me to you will at once be severed."

"How?" inquired Malvano seriously; for he saw that at this crisis-time Gemma held their future in her hands. Nenci's wild words had, alas! been ill-timed, and could not now be retracted.

"Simply this," she answered. "I love; for the first time in my life, honestly and passionately. Through my association with you, my life is wrecked, and my lover lost to me. Yet I still have hope; and if you destroy that hope, then all desire for life will leave me. I care absolutely nothing for the future."

"Well?" the Doctor observed mechanically.

"Cannot you understand?" she cried, turning upon him fiercely. "This man Lionello, has suggested that my lover's life should be taken; that he should be silenced merely because he fears that my love may lead me to desert you, or turn traitor. I know well how easily such suggestions can be carried out; but remember, if a hand is lifted against him it is to me, the woman who loves him, that you shall answer; to me you shall beg for mercy, and, by the Virgin, I will give you none!" And her panting breast heaved and fell violently as she clutched the back of her chair for support.

For a few minutes there was again silence, deep and complete. Then Nenci laughed the same harsh supercilious laugh as before.

"Bah?" he cried, with curling lip. "Your foolish infatuation is of no account to us. Your lover holds knowledge which can ruin us. He must therefore be silenced!" Then glancing swiftly around the table with his black eyes, he asked, "Is that agreed?"

With one accord there was a bold, clear response. All gave an answer in the affirmative.

XXI

AT LYDDINGTON

Outside it was a dry, crisp, frosty night, but in Doctor Malvano's drawing-room at Lyddington a great wood fire threw forth a welcome glow, the skins spread upon the floor were soft and warm, and the fine, old-fashioned room, furnished with that taste and elegance which a doctor of independent means could afford, was extremely comfortable and cosy. "Ben," the Doctor's faithful old black dog, lay stretched out lazily before the fire, a pet cat had curled itself in the easiest of easy chairs, and with her white fingers rambling over the keys of the grand piano sat a slim, graceful woman. It was Gemma.

With Mrs. Nenci as companion, she had been visiting at Lyddington for about a fortnight, and, truth to tell, found life in that rural village much more pleasant than in the unwholesome side street off the Walworth Road. They had both left Boyson Road suddenly late one night, after receiving a note from Nenci, who had been absent a couple of days. This note was one of warning, telling them to fly, and giving them directions to go straight to Lyddington. This they had done, receiving a cordial welcome from the Doctor, who had apparently received word by telegraph, and understood the situation perfectly. So they had installed themselves in the Doctor's house, and led a quiet, tranquil life of severe respectability. Gemma dressed well, as befitted the Doctor's visitor, for she had received one of her trunks which, after leaving the Hotel Victoria, she had deposited in the cloak-room at Charing Cross Station, and her costumes were always tasteful and elegant. She had obtained a cycle from Uppingham, and the weather being dry and frosty, she rode daily alone over the hilly Rutlandshire roads, to old-world Gretton, to long, straggling Rockingham, with its castle high up among the leafless trees, to Seaton Station, or even as far afield as the tiny hamlet of Blatherwycke. The honest country folk looked askance at her, be it said, for her natural chic she could not suppress, and her cycling skirt was just a trifle too short, when judged from an English standpoint. Her dress was dark blue serge, confined at the waist by a narrow, white silk ribbon, its smartness having been much admired when she had spun along the level roads of the Cascine. But English and Italian ideas differ very considerably, and she was often surprised when the country people stood and gaped at her. Yet it was only natural. When she dismounted she could only speak half a dozen words of English, and Rutland folk are always suspicious of the foreigner—especially a woman.

As she sat at the piano on this chilly night, she looked eminently beautiful in a loose, rich tea-gown of sage-green plush, with front of pale pink silk, a gown of striking magnificence, with its heavy silver belt glittering beneath the shaded lamplight. It was made in a style which no English dressmaker could accomplish, and fastened at the throat by a quaint brooch consisting of three tiny golden playing-cards, set with diamonds and rubies, and fastened together by a pearl-headed pin, a charming little phantasy. The pink silk, in combination with the sombre green, set off her fair beauty admirably, yet her face was a trifle wan as she mechanically fingered the keys with all the suppleness and rapidity of a good player. But she was Tuscan, and the love of music was in her inborn. In her own far-off country one could hear the finest opera for sixpence, and there was scarcely any household that did not possess its mandoline, and whose members did not chant those old canzonette amorose. Music is part of the Italian's life.

She stopped at last, slowly glancing around the handsome room, and drawing a heavy sigh. At that moment a sense of utter loneliness oppressed her. Her companion, Mrs. Nenci, had retired to bed half an hour before, and the Doctor was still in his study, where he usually spent the greater part of his time. He was often locked in alone for hours together, and was careful never to allow any one to enter on any pretext. She had, indeed, never seen the interior of Malvano's den, and was often seized with curiosity to know how he spent his time there through so many hours. As she sat silent, she pondered, as she ever did, over her lost lover, and wondered if he were still in England, or if, weary and despairing, he had left for the Continent again.

"He has misjudged me," she murmured—"cruelly misjudged me."

Her fathomless blue eyes glistened with tears, as, turning again to the instrument, she commenced to play and sing, in a soft, sweet contralto, the old Tuscan love-song, "Ah! non mi amava"; the song sung by the contadinelle in the vineyards and the maize-fields, where the green lizards dart across the sun-baked stones—where life is without a care, so long as one has a handful of baked chestnuts, or a plate of polenta di castagne—where the air is sweet and balmy and the very atmosphere breathes of love.

"E mi diceva che avria sfidato,
Per ottenermi tutto il creato;
Che nel mio sguardo, nel mio sorriso
Stavan le gioie del Paradiso.
E mentre al core cosi parlava.
Ah! non mi amava! no, non mi amava!

"Tu sei, diceva, l'angelo mio:
Tu sei la stella d'ogni desio:
Il sol mio bene sei che m'avanza;
Tu de' miei giorni se' la speranza.
Fin le sue pene mi raccontava,
Ah! non mi amava! no, non mi amava!"

Slowly, in a voice full of emotion, she sang the old song she had heard so many times when a child, until its sad, serious air trembled through the room.

Behind her were two long windows, which, opening upon the lawn, were now heavily curtained to keep out the icy draughts. Blasts of cold air seemed to penetrate to every corner of that high-up house, exposed as it was to the chill winds sweeping across the hills. As she was singing, one of the maids entered with her candle, and placing it upon the table, wished her good-night.

"Good-night!" she answered in her pretty broken English; and, when the girl had gone, went on playing, but very softly, so as not to disturb the household. Her voice, full of emotion, had repeated the final words of that passionate verse—

"Non aveva core che per amarmi
Con i suoi detti ei m'ingannava,
Ah! non mi amava! no, non mi amava!"

when the curtains before one of the windows behind her suddenly stirred, and an eager face peered through between them. The slight sound attracted her, and she turned quickly with a low exclamation of fear. Next, instant, however, she sprang up from the piano with a glad cry, for the man who had thus secretly entered was none other than Charles Armytage.

"You, Nino!" she gasped, pale and trembling, holding aloof from him in the first moments of her surprise.

WILLIAM LE QUEUX

"Yes," he replied in a low, intense tone, standing before her in hat and overcoat. "I came here to see the Doctor, but hearing your well-remembered voice outside, and finding the window unfastened, came in. You—you do not welcome me," he added with disappointment. "Why are you here?"

"Welcome you!" she echoed. "You, who are in my thoughts every day, every hour, every moment; you who, by leaving me, have crushed all hope, all life from me, Nino! Ah! no; I—I welcome you. But forgive me; I never expected that we should meet in this house, of all places."

"Why?"

She hesitated. Her fingers twitched nervously.

"Because—well, because you ought not to come here," she answered ambiguously. She remembered Nenci's covert threat, and knew well what risks her lover ran. He was in deadly peril, and only she herself could shield him.

"I don't understand you," he exclaimed. "I have for the past month searched everywhere for you. You left the hotel and disappeared; I have made inquiries in Livorno and in Florence, believing you had returned to Italy, and here to-night, as I passed across the lawn, I heard your voice, and have now found you."

"Why?" she inquired, her trembling hand still upon the piano. "Is not all our love now of the past? I am unworthy of you, Nino, and I told you so honestly. I could not deceive you further."

"Heaven knows!" he cried, "you deceived me enough. You have never even told me your real name." She looked at him with an expression of fear in her eyes. "Ah!" she cried. "You know the truth, Nino. I see by your face!"

"I know that you, whom I have known as Gemma Fanetti, are none other than the Contessa Funaro!" Her breast heaved and fell quickly, and she hung her head. "Well?"

He moved towards her, his hands still in the pockets of his heavy tweed overcoat.

"Well," he repeated, "and what excuse have you for so deceiving me?"

"None," she answered in her soft Tuscan, her eyes still downcast. "I loved you, Nino, and I feared—"

She hesitated, without finishing the sentence.

"You feared to tell me the truth, even though you well knew that I was foolishly infatuated; that I was a love-blind idiot? No; I don't believe you," he cried fiercely. "You had some further, some deeper motive." She was silent. Her nervous fingers hitched themselves in the lace of her gown, and she grew pallid and haggard.

"I now know who you are; how grossly you have deceived me, and how ingeniously I have been tricked," he cried bitterly, speaking Italian with difficulty. "You whom I believed honest and loving, I have found to be only an adventuress, a woman whose notoriety has spread from Como to Messina."

"Yes," she cried hoarsely, "yes, Nino, I am an adventuress. Now that my enemies have exposed me, concealment is no longer possible. I deceived you, but with an honest purpose in view. My name, I well know, is synonymous with all that is vicious. I am known as The Funaro— the extravagant woman whose lovers are legion, and of whom stories of reckless waste and ingenious fraud are told by the *jeunesse doree* in every city in Italy. Ask of any of the smart young men who drink at the Gambrinus at Milan, at Genoa, at Rome, or at Florence, and they will relate stories by the hour of my wild, adventurous life, of my loves and my hatreds, of my gaiety and my sorrow. Yes, I, alas I know it all. I have the reputation of being the gayest woman in all gay Italy; and yet—and yet," she added in a soft voice, "I love you, Nino."

"No!" he cried, drawing from her with repugnance, as if in fear that her hands should touch him; "it is not possible that we can exchange words of affection after this vile deceit. All is now plain why the police of Livorno ordered you to leave the city; why Hutchinson, the Consul, urged me to part from you; why, when we drove together in those sun-baked streets, every one turned to look at you. They knew you!" he cried. "They knew you—and they pitied me!"

She shrank at these cruel, bitter words as if he had dealt her a blow. From head to foot she trembled as, with an effort, she took a few uneven steps towards him.

"You denounce me!" she cried in a low tone. "You, the man I love, declare that I am base, vile, and heartless. Well, if you wish, I will admit all the charges you thus level against me. Only one will I refute. You say that I am an adventuress; you imply that I have never loved you."

"Certainly," he cried. "I have been your dupe. You led me to believe in your innocence, while all the time the papers are commenting upon your adventures, and printing scandals anent your past. Because I did not know your language well, and because I seldom read an Italian newspaper, you were bold enough to believe that I should remain in utter ignorance. But I have discovered the extent of your perfidy. I know

now, that in dealing with you, I'm dealing with one whose shrewdness and cunning are notorious throughout the whole of Italy."

"Then you have no further love for me, Nino?" she asked blankly, after a brief space.

"Love! No, I hate you!" he cried. "You led me to believe in your uprightness and honesty, yet I find that you, of all women in Italy, are the least desirable, as an acquaintance—the least possible as a wife!"

"You hate me?" she gasped hoarsely. "You—Nino!—hate me?"

"Yes," he cried, his hands clenched in excitement, "I hate you!"

"Then why have you come here?" she asked. "Even if you had heard my voice, you need not have entered this room to taunt me."

"I have come to call upon the Doctor," he answered. "Eleven o'clock at night is a curious hour at which to call upon a friend," she observed. "Your business with him must be very pressing."

"It is—it is," he answered quickly, striding to and fro. "I must see him to-night."

"Why?"

"Because I leave England to-morrow."

"You leave England?" she said hoarsely. "You intend to leave me here?"

"Surely you are comfortable enough? Malvano is Italian, and, although I was not aware that you were acquainted with him, he is nevertheless a very good fellow, and no doubt you are happy."

"Happy!" she cried. "Happy without you, Nino! Ah! you are too cruel! If you could but know the truth; if you could but know what I have suffered, what I am at this moment suffering for your sake, you would never treat me thus—never."

"Ah! your story is always the same—always," he laughed superciliously. "I know now why you would never invite me to your house in Florence. You could not well take me to your great palazzo without me knowing its name. Again, you lived in that small flat in the Viale at Livorno instead of at your villa at Ardenza, that beautiful house overlooking the sea, coveted by all the Livornesi."

"I have a reason for not living there," she exclaimed quickly. "I have not entered it now for two years. Perhaps I shall never again cross its threshold."

"And it is untenanted?"

"Certainly. I do not wish to let it."

"Why?"

"It is a caprice of mine," she answered. "To a woman of my character caprices are allowed, I suppose?" Then, after a slight hesitation, she raised her fine eyes to his, saying, "Now tell me candidly, Nino, why have you come here to-night?"

"To see the Doctor. I want to consult him."

"Are you ill?" she asked with some alarm, noticing that he was unusually pale.

"No, I want his advice regarding another matter, a matter which concerns myself." As he spoke he kept his eyes fixed upon her, and saw how handsome she was. In that loose gown of silk and plush, with its heavy girdle, she looked, indeed, the notorious Countess Funaro about whom he had heard so much scandalous gossip.

Slowly she advanced towards him, her small white hands outstretched, her arms half bare, her beautiful face upturned to his. Those eyes were so blue and clear, and that face so perfect an incarnation of purity, that it was hard to believe that she was actually the notorious woman who had so scandalised Florentine society. He stood before her again, fascinated as he always had been in her presence in those bygone sunny days in Tuscany, when he had basked daily in her smiles and idled lazily beside the Mediterranean.

"Nino," she said, in a soft crooning voice scarcely above a whisper—a voice which showed him she was deeply in earnest—"Nino, if it pleases you to break my heart then I will not complain. I know I deserve all the terrible punishment I am now enduring, for I've sinned before Heaven and have sinned against you, the man who loved me. You cast me aside as a worthless woman because of my evil reputation; you credit all the base libellous stories circulated by my enemies; you believe that I have toyed with your affection and have no real genuine love for you. Well, Nino," she sighed, "let it be so. I know that now you are aware of my identity you can never believe in my truth and honesty; but I tell you that I still love you, even though you may denounce and desert me."

He turned from her with a gesture of impatience.

"Tell me, Nino," she went on eagerly, following him and grasping his arm convulsively, "tell me the truth. Why are you here to-night?"

He turned quickly upon her, and made a movement to free himself from her grasp.

"Malvano is Italian," he answered. "I have come to consult him upon a matter in which only an Italian can assist me."

"I am Italian," she said quickly. "Will you not let me render you at least one service, even if it be the last?" She looked earnestly into his face, and her soft arms wound themselves around his neck.

"I have no faith in you," he answered. "I was a fool to enter here, but your voice brought back to me so many memories of those days that are dead, and I couldn't resist."

"Then you still think of me sometimes, caro," she said, clinging to him. "Your love is not yet dead?"

"It is dead," he declared, fiercely disengaging himself. "Gemma, whom I knew and loved in Livorno, will ever remain a sad sweet memory throughout my life; but the wealthy, wanton Contessa Funaro, the woman against whom every finger is pointed in Italy, I can never trust, I can never love."

She fell back, crushed, humiliated, ashamed. A deathlike pallor overspread her face, and her eyes grew large, dark, and mournful. There are some griefs that are too deep, even for tears.

"You cannot trust me, Nino," she cried a moment later. "But you can nevertheless heed one word which I speak in deepest earnest."

"Well?"

"Leave this house. Do not seek this man, Malvano."

"Why?" he inquired, surprised. "He's my friend. We have met once or twice since we shot together in Berkshire."

Again she advanced close to him, so close that he felt her breath upon his cheek, and the sweet odour of lilac from her chiffons filled his nostrils.

"If you absolutely refuse to tell me the reason you have come here to-night, then I will tell you," she whispered. "You are in fear."

"In fear? I don't understand."

"You have enemies, and you wish to consult the Doctor with regard to them," she went on boldly. Then, in a voice scarcely audible, she added, whispering into his ear: "You have received warning."

He started suddenly, looking at her dismayed.

"Who told you? How did you know?" he gasped. "I cannot now explain," she answered breathlessly, still holding his arm in convulsive grasp, panting as she spoke. "It is sufficient for you to know the intention of your enemies, so that you may be forewarned against them."

"Then it is actually true that I'm in personal danger!" he cried. "To my knowledge I've never done an evil turn to anybody, and this is all a puzzling enigma. The letter here"—and he drew from his overcoat a note which had been delivered by a boy-messenger at his chambers in Ebury Street—"this letter is evidently written by an Italian, because of the flourish of the capitals: and I came here to-night to ask Malvano the best course to pursue. I'm staying in the neighbourhood, over at Apethorpe."

"Then leave at once," she urged earnestly. "Tomorrow, get away by the first train to London, and thence to the Continent again. Take precautions that you are not followed. Go to France, to Germany, to Spain, anywhere out of reach. Then write to me at the Poste Restante, at Charing Cross, and I will come to you."

"But why? How do you know all this?"

"Look at that letter, Nino," she said in a low, deep tone. "Look once again at the handwriting."

He opened it beneath the silk-shaded lamp and scanned it eagerly.

"It's yours," he gasped, the truth suddenly dawning upon him. "You yourself have given me this warning!" She nodded.

"Tell me why, quickly," he cried, placing his hand upon her shoulder. "Tell me why."

"I warned you, Nino," she answered, in a soft, hoarse voice; "I warned you because I love you."

"But what have I to fear?" he demanded. "If I'm threatened I can seek protection of the police. To my knowledge I haven't a single enemy."

"We all of us blind ourselves with that consolation," she replied. "But listen. Of all men, avoid Malvano. Leave this house at once, and get out of England at the earliest moment. Your enemies are no ordinary ones; they are desperate, and hold life cheap."

"But you!" he cried, puzzled. "You are here, in the house of this very man against whom you warn me!"

"Ah! do not heed me," she answered. "Your love for me is dead. Yet I am still yours, and in this matter you must, if you value your safety, trust me."

"But Malvano is an excellent fellow," he protested. "I must just wish him good-night. What would he think if he knew I had been here and had this private interview with you?"

"No, Nino," she cried, her countenance pale and earnest. "You must not! You hear me? You must not. If it were known that I had given you warning then my position would be one of greater peril than it now is."

"But surely I need not fear the Doctor? Every one about here knows him. He's the most popular man for miles around."

"And the most dangerous," she whispered. "No, for my sake, fly, Nino. He may enter this room at any moment. I love you, and no harm shall befall you if you will obey me. Leave this place at once, and promise me not to make any attempt to see Malvano." His eyes met hers, and he saw in them a love-light that was unmistakable. By her clear open glance he became almost convinced that she was speaking the truth. Yet he still hesitated.

"Ah!" she cried, suddenly flinging her arms again about his neck. "Go, Nino; you are unsafe here. Leave England to-morrow for my sake—for my sake, caro. But kiss me once," she implored in her sweet, lisping Italian. "Give me one single kiss before you part from me."

His brow darkened. He held his breath.

"No, no," she cried wildly, divining his disinclination, "I am not the Contessa Funaro, now. I am Gemma—the woman who loves you, the woman who is at this moment risking her life for you. Kiss me. Then go. Fly, caro, abroad, and may no harm befall you, Nino, my beloved!" Then she raised her beautiful face to his.

His countenance relaxed, he bent swiftly, and their lips met in one long, tender, passionate caress. Then, urged by her, he wished her a whispered farewell, and disappeared through the heavy curtains before the window as silently as he had come, while she stood panting, breathless, but in an ecstasy of contentment. Once again he had pressed her lips and breathed one single word of love.

XXII

The Unknown

In winter the roads in Rutlandshire are none too good for cycling. When wet they are too heavy; when frosty they are apt to be rutty and dangerous. Once or twice Gemma had been out with the two daughters of the rector of a neighbouring parish, but as she could not understand half a dozen words they said, and discovered them to be of that frigid genus peculiar to the daughters-of-the-cloth, she preferred riding alone. In January the country around Uppingham is bleak, brown, and bare, different indeed from winter in her own sunny land, but it was the exhilarating sensation of cycling that delighted her, and she did not ride for the purpose of seeing the district. The hills around Lyddington were poor indeed after the wild grandeur of the Lucca Mountains, or the Apennines, but on bright mornings she found her ride very delightful, and always returned fresh, rosy, and hungry.

A fortnight had gone by since the night Charles Armytage had visited her, but she had received no word from him, because the address she gave was at the Poste Restante at Charing Cross and she had not been to London. The kiss he had given her before parting reassured her, and now, instead of being pensive, pale-faced, and wan, she had resumed something of her old reckless gaiety, and would go about the house humming to herself the chorus of that gay song, popular to every café-concert in Italy, "M'abbruscia, m'abbruscia, 't capa, signure," or jingle upon the piano for the amusement of the Doctor and Mrs. Nenci, "Pennariale," "La Bicicletta," "Signo', dicite si," and a host of other equally well-known ditties. Both Malvano, who always treated her with studied courtesy, and her female companion were surprised at her sudden change of manner. Neither, however, knew the truth. Armytage had evidently succeeded in leaving the house and gaining the road without having been seen by the servants.

The frosty wind was sweeping keen as a knife across the uplands one morning as she mounted her cycle, and with a laughing farewell to the Doctor, who was just ascending into his high trap to visit a patient some five miles away in an opposite direction, she allowed her machine to run rapidly down the hill for nearly a mile without pedalling. The roads were hard and rutty, but she cared nothing for that, and rode straight as an arrow, taking both hands from the handles in order to readjust the pin which held her neat little toque. Few women rode better than she, and few looked more graceful or pedalled more evenly. In the leafy Cascine at Florence, in the Public Gardens at Milan, in the Bois at Paris, and along the Viale at Livorno, her riding had been many times admired. But here, on these Rutlandshire highways there was no crowd of gossiping idlers, none to remark her beauty, none to whisper strange stories of "the pretty Contessa," and for the first time for months she now felt free from the trammels of her past.

About a mile and a half from Lyddington, she turned off suddenly on to a byroad, rutty and ill-kept, and, still downhill, rode towards Seaton Station. The Doctor expected a small parcel of drugs from London, and, as it could be tied to her handle-bar, she had that morning made it the object of her ride. Malvano, however, had been compelled to scribble a line to the station-master for, as she could not speak English, and the local railway official could not be expected to have any knowledge of Tuscan, the note would obviate any complications.

Shortly before reaching the station, the road crossed the railway by a level-crossing kept by a lame man, one of the company's servants, who had been injured years before, and who now led a life of comparative ease in his snug little cottage beside the line. As she approached, she saw that the great gates were closed, and, riding up to them, she dismounted and called to the cottager for the way to be opened.

The grey-headed old man appeared at the door in his shabby overcoat, shook his head, and cast a glance down the line. Then, almost next instant, the Continental express from Harwich to Birmingham flew past. The gatekeeper drew back one of the levers beside his door, entered the house for a moment, then came forth with something in his hand.

"This letter has been left for you, miss," he said, politely touching his cap and handing a note to her. "It's been here these four days, and I was told not to send it up to the Doctor's, but to give it to you personally next time you passed alone."

"Who gave it to you?" she asked quickly, in Italian, as she took the letter in one hand, holding her cycle with the other.

But the man, unacquainted with strange languages, regarded her rather suspiciously, and answered—

"I don't understand French, miss."

They both laughed, and from her purse she gave the man some coppers. Not until she got to a lonely part of the road, on her return journey, did she dismount to read the secret missive. It consisted of five words only, in Italian, scribbled in pencil upon a piece of that common foreign notepaper ruled in tiny squares. The words were—"Bonciani, Monday, at five. Urgent."

It bore no signature, no date, nothing to give a clue whence the mysterious appointment emanated. She examined its superscription, but utterly failed to recognise the handwriting.

For a long time she stood beneath the leafless oaks with the scrap of paper in her hand, meditating deeply. It was plain that whoever had summoned her to London feared to sign the note lest it should fall into other hands; furthermore, the writer evidently knew that it was unsafe to send a message through the post direct to the Doctor's house. Being unable to speak English, she could not ask the railway watchman to describe the person who had placed it in his hands. She could only act as the unknown writer demanded, or, on the other hand, take no notice of the strange communication.

It was not from Charles, for she well knew his bold, sprawly hand. This was decidedly the writing of one of her compatriots; but as she reflected, she could not think of any one who could desire her urgent attendance at the obscure little restaurant in Regent Street. She had often heard of the Bonciani, even while in Italy, but had never visited it. Then suddenly the sweet, distant sound of church bells, borne to her on the frosty wind, sounded so different to that from the old sun-blanched campanili of the Tuscan churches, and brought to her recollection that the day was Sunday, a festal day in her own land, and that the appointment with the unknown was on the morrow.

Irresolute and puzzled, she tore up both envelope and paper, and cast them to the wind; then, seating herself in her saddle, she rode onward up the long incline which led to Lyddington.

That afternoon there were two or three callers—the wife and daughter of a retired manufacturer living at Laxton, and a couple of young men, sons of old Squire Gregory, of Apethorpe, who had seen Gemma cycling and driving with the Doctor, and who had been struck by her extraordinary chic. One of them, the elder, spoke Italian a little, and they chatted together in the drawing-room, after which tea was served. She did not care for that beverage, and only drank it because it seemed to her the proper thing to do in England. She would have much preferred a glass of menta, or one or other of those brilliantly coloured syrups so dear to the palate of the Italian.

With that ineffable politeness of his race, Malvano entertained his visitors in a manner polished and refined, while Mrs. Nenci, a rather striking figure in black, spoke broken English with them, and did the honours of the house. People often called at the Doctor's in the afternoon, for he was a merry bachelor with the reputation of being the most good-hearted, generous, easy-going man in the county; and on this Sunday the assembly was quite a pleasant one, the more so to Gemma when she found a good-looking young man to whom she could chat.

They were standing together in the deep bay of the old-fashioned window, half hidden by the heavy curtains. The room was filled with the gay chatter of the visitors, and he now saw his opportunity to speak to her.

"Signorina," he said in a low whisper, "a friend of mine is our mutual friend."

"I don't understand you?" she inquired, starting in surprise, and glancing quickly at him.

"Charles Armytage," young Gregory answered. "He was staying with me until about a fortnight ago. Then he left suddenly."

"Well?"

"He doesn't dare to write to you here, but has written to me."

"Where is he?" she inquired eagerly.

"Abroad," the young man replied hurriedly. "In his letter to me yesterday, he asked me to call here at once, see you, and tell you that he is in Brussels; and that if you write, address him at the Poste Restante."

"He is still there?" she asked. "Then a telegram to-day—now—would reach him?"

"Certainly," her young companion replied. "He says he will send me word the moment he changes his address, and asks me to request you to write. He says it is unsafe, however, under the circumstances, for him to respond to your letter."

"Thank you," she answered, breathing more freely. The knowledge that he had escaped to Brussels, and that she could give him further warning, if needed, was to her reassuring. "It is extremely kind of you to bring me this welcome message. I had no idea that you knew Mr. Armytage."

"We were at Eton together," Gregory answered. "I've known him ever since I can remember. But I see my brother is going to drive the

Blatherwycke parson home, so I must say good-bye; and I hope to call again, as soon as I have any further news—if I may."

She answered him with a glance. Then together they returned into the centre of the room, chatting as if no confidences had been exchanged, and a moment later he took leave of her.

Next morning, in a dark stuff walking dress, she mounted her cycle, having announced her intention to ride over to King's Cliffe and lunch with some friends of Malvano's who had invited her. Instead, however, she went to Gretton Station, placed her cycle in the cloakroom, and took a first-class ticket to London, determined to keep the mysterious appointment. It was nearly three o'clock when she arrived, and she at once lunched at the railway buffet, idled there for half an hour, and then took a cab to Regent Street, where she whiled away the time gazing into the windows of the milliners and dressmakers, unaware that a shabby, middle-aged, unimportant-looking man was narrowly watching her movements, or that this man was Inspector Elmes of Vine Street.

At last she glanced at her little watch, with its two hearts set in diamonds on the back—a beautiful souvenir which her absent lover had given her in the early days of their acquaintance—and found it wanted ten minutes to five. She had passed the obscure rendezvous, and glanced at its window with the sickly looking palms and india-rubber plants, the long-necked wine-flasks she knew so well, and the two framed menus; therefore, considering it time to enter the place, she retraced her steps from Piccadilly Circus, and a few minutes later opened the door and walked into the long, narrow salon, with its marble-topped tables and plush lounges.

Two or three men, whom she at once recognised as compatriots, were sipping coffee and smoking. As she passed, they eyed her admiringly; but without a glance at them she walked to the further end, and seating herself at a table on the left, ordered coffee.

Scarcely had it been brought, when the door again opened, and there lounged in leisurely a tall, well-built, handsome man in long dark overcoat and brown soft felt hat. Without hesitation he walked straight to her table, bowed politely, and with a word of greeting seated himself. Her face went white as the marble before her; she held her breath. In that instant she recollected it was the day, the hour, and the place mentioned in that remarkable letter found upon her unfortunate friend Vittorina—that letter which had so puzzled and mystified the Ambassador, the police, the newspaper reporters, and the British public.

She had been entrapped.

XXIII

A Ruler of Europe

W ell?" Gemma exclaimed, quickly recovering herself, and looking keenly into the dark face of the newcomer.

"Well?" he said, imitating with a touch of sarcasm the tone in which she had spoken, at the same time taking a cigarette from his case and lighting it with a vesta from the china stand upon the table.

"What does this mean?" she inquired in Italian, regarding him with a look which clearly showed his presence was unwelcome.

"Finish your coffee and come out with me. I must speak with you. Here it's too risky. We might be overheard. St. James's Park is near, and we can talk there without interruption," he said. Evidently a gentleman, aged about fifty-five, with long iron-grey side-whiskers and hair slightly blanched. His eyes were intelligent and penetrating, his forehead broad and open, his chin heavy and decisive, and he was undoubtedly a man of stern will and wide achievements. He spoke polished Italian, and his manner was perfect.

Gemma kept her eyes fixed upon him, fascinated by fear. Her gloved hand trembled perceptibly as she raised her cup to her lips.

"You had no idea that you would meet me—eh?" he laughed, speaking in an undertone. "Well, drink your coffee, and let us take a cab to the Park." He flung down sixpence to the waiter, and they went out together. She walked mechanically into the street, dumbfounded, stupefied.

By his side she staggered for a few paces, then halting said, in a sudden tone of anger—

"Leave me! I refuse to accompany you."

Her companion smiled. It was already dark, the shop windows were lit, and the hurrying crowd of passers-by did not notice them.

"You'll come with me," the man said sternly. "I want to talk to you seriously, and in privacy. It was useless in that place with half a dozen people around, all with ears open. Besides," he added, "in a café of that sort I may be recognised." Then he hailed a passing cab.

"No, no!" she cried, as it drew up to the kerb. "I won't go—I won't!"

"But you shall!" he declared firmly, taking her arm. "You know me well enough to be aware that I'm not to be trifled with. Come, you'll obey me."

She hesitated for a moment, gazed blankly around her as if seeking some one to protect her, sighed, and then slowly ascended into the vehicle.

"Athenaeum Club," he shouted to the driver, and sprang in beside the trembling woman. It was evident from her manner that she held him in repugnance, while he, cool and triumphant, regarded her with satisfaction.

During the drive they exchanged few words. She was pensive and sullen, while he addressed her in a strangely rough manner for one of such outward refinement. They alighted, and descending the steps into the Mall at the point where a relic of old-time London still remains in the cow-sheds where fresh milk can be obtained, crossed the roadway and entered the Park by one of the deserted paths which ran down to the ornamental water.

"You thought to escape me—eh?" her companion exclaimed when at last they halted at one of the seats near the water. He was well acquainted with that quarter of London, for he had served as attache at the Court of St. James twenty years ago.

"I had no object in so doing," she answered boldly. In their drive she had decided upon a definite plan, and now spoke fearlessly.

"Why, then, have you not answered my letters?"

"I never answer letters that are either reproachful or abusive," she replied, "even though they may be from the Marquis Montelupo, His Majesty's Minister for Foreign Affairs."

"If you had deigned to do so, it would have obviated the necessity of me coming from Rome to see you at all this personal risk."

"It's well that you risk something, as well as myself. I've risked enough, Heaven knows!" she answered.

"And you've found at last a confounded idiot of a lover who will prove our ruin."

"My love is no concern of yours," she cried quickly. "He may be left entirely out of the question. He knows nothing; and further, I've parted from him."

"Because he has ascertained who you really are," the great statesman said.

"For that I have to thank you," she retorted quickly. "If you had been a trifle more considerate and had not allowed the police of Livorno to act as they did, he would still have been in ignorance."

"I acted as I thought fit," her companion said in an authoritative tone, lighting another cigarette from the still burning end of the one he had just consumed.

"You've brought me here to abuse me!" she cried, her eyes flashing fiercely upon him.

"Because you played me false," he answered bitterly. "You thought it possible to conceal your identity, marry this young fool of an Englishman, and get away somewhere where you would not be discovered. For that reason you've played this double game." Then he added meaningly, "It's only what I ought to have expected of a woman with such a reputation as yours."

"Charles Armytage is no fool," she protested. "If he found you here, speaking like this to me, he'd strangle you."

The Marquis, whose dark eyes seemed to flash with a fierce light, laughed sarcastically.

"No doubt by this time he's heard lots of stories concerning you," he said. "A man of his stamp never marries an adventuress."

"Adventuress!" she echoed, starting up with clenched hands. "You call me an adventuress—you, whose past is blacker than my own—you who owe to me your present position as Minister!"

He glanced at her surprised; he had not been prepared for this fierce, defiant retort.

Again he laughed, a laugh low and strangely hollow.

"You forget," he said, "that a word from me would result in your arrest, imprisonment, and disgrace."

She held her breath and her brows contracted. That fact, she knew, was only too true. In an instant she perceived that for the present she must conciliate this man, who was one of the rulers of Europe. The game she was now playing was, indeed, the most desperate in all her career, but the stake was the highest, the most valuable to her in all the world, her own love, peace, and happiness.

"And suppose you took this step," she suggested, finding tongue with difficulty at last. "Don't you think you would imperil yourself? A Foreign Minister, especially in our country, surrounded as he is by a myriad political foes, can scarcely afford to court scandal. I should have thought the examples of Crispi, Rudini, and Brin were sufficient to cause a wary man like yourself to hesitate."

"I never act without due consideration," the Marquis replied. The voice in which he spoke was the dry, business-like tone he used towards Ambassadors of the Powers when discussing the political situation, as he was almost daily compelled to do. In Rome, no man was better dressed than the Marquis Montelupo; no man had greater tact in directing matters of State; and in no man did his Sovereign place greater faith. As he sat beside her in slovenly attire, his grey moustaches uncurled, his chin bearing two or three days' growth of grey beard, it was hard to realise that this was the same man who, glittering with orders, so often ascended the great marble and gold staircase of the Quirinal, to seek audience with King Humbert; whose reputation as a statesman was world-wide, and whose winter receptions at his great old palazzo in the Via Nazionale were among the most brilliant diplomatic gatherings in Europe.

"I have carefully considered the whole matter," he said, after a moment's pause. "I arrived in London yesterday, and from what I have learnt I have decided to take certain steps without delay."

"Then you have been to the Embassy!" she exclaimed breathless. "You've denounced me to Castellani!"

"There was no necessity for that," he answered coldly. "He already knows that you are his enemy."

"I his enemy!" she echoed. "I have never done him an evil turn. He has heard some libellous story, I suppose, and, like all the world, believes me to be without conscience and without remorse."

"That's a pretty good estimate of yourself," the Marquis observed. "If you had any conscience whatever you would have replied to my letters, and not maintained a dogged silence through all these months."

"I had an object in view," she answered in a chilling tone. She, quiet and stubborn, was resolved, insolent, like a creature to whom men had never been able to refuse anything.

"What was it?"

She shrugged her shoulders, and, laughing again, replied—

"You have threatened me with arrest, therefore I will maintain silence until it pleases you to endeavour to ruin me. Then together we will provide a little sensationalism for the *Farfalla*, the *Tribuna*, the *Secolo*, and one or two other journals who will only be too ready to see a change of Ministry."

He hesitated, seeming to digest her words laboriously. She glanced quickly at his dark face, which the distant rays of a lamp illumined, and in that instant knew she had triumphed.

"You would try and ruin me, eh?" he cried in a hoarse menace.

"To upset the whole political situation in Rome is quite easy of accomplishment, I assure you, my dear Marquis," she declared, smiling. "The Opposition will be ready to hound out of office you and all your rabble of bank-thieves, blackmailers, adventurers, and others who are so ingeniously feathering their nests at the expense of Italy. Ah, what a herd!"

Montelupo frowned. He knew quite well that she spoke the truth, yet with diplomatic instinct he still maintained a bold front.

"Bah!" he cried defiantly. "You cannot injure me. When you are in prison you'll have little opportunity for uttering any of your wild denunciations. The people, too, are getting a little tired of the various mare's-nest scandals started almost daily by the irresponsible journals. They've ceased to believe in them."

"Yes, without proofs," she observed.

"You have no proof. You and I are not strangers," Montelupo said.

"First, recollect we are in England, and you cannot order my immediate arrest. Days must elapse before your application reaches London from Rome. In the meantime I am free to act." Then, with a tinge of bitter sarcasm in her voice, she added, "No, Excellency, your plan does not do you credit. I always thought you far more shrewd."

"Whatever so-called proofs you possess, no one will for an instant believe you," he laughed with fine composure. "Recollect I am Minister for Foreign Affairs; then recollect who you are."

"I am your dupe, your victim," she cried in a fierce paroxysm of anger. "My name stinks in the nostrils of every one in Italy—and why? Because you, the man who now denounces me, wove about me a network of pitfalls which it was impossible for me to avoid. You saw that, because I moved in smart society, because I had good looks and hosts of friends, I was the person to become your catspaw—your stepping-stone into office. You—"

"Silence, curse you!" Montelupo cried fiercely, his hands clenched. "I'm too busy with the present to have any time for recollecting the past. It was a fair and business-like arrangement. You've been paid."

"Yes, with coin stolen from the Treasury by your rogues and swindlers who pose before Italy as patriots and politicians."

"It matters not to such a woman as you whence comes the money you require to keep up your fine appearance," he said angrily, for this reference to his political party had raised his blood to fever-heat.

"Even though I have this unenviable reputation which you have been pleased to give me throughout Italy, I am at least honest," she cried.

"Towards your lovers—eh?"

Standing before him, in a violent outburst of anger, she shook both her gloved hands in his face, saying—

"Enough—enough of your insults! For the sake of the land I love, for the sake of Italy's power and prestige, and for your reputation I have suffered. But remember that the bond which fetters me to you will snap if stretched too far; that instead of assisting you, I can ruin you."

"You speak plainly certainly," he said, after a moment's hesitation.

"I do. Through your evil machinations I have no reputation to lose. With artful ingenuity you compromised me, you spread scandals about me in Florence, in Venice, in Rome, scandals that were the vilest libels man ever uttered. In your club you told men that there was something more between us than mere friendship, that I was extravagant, and that I cost you as much in diamonds at Fasoli's in the Corso, on a single afternoon, as the Government paid you in a whole year. Such were the lies you spread in order to ruin me," she cried bitterly. "Never have I had a soldo from your private purse, never a single ornament, and never have your foul lips touched mine. You, who boldly announced yourself my lover, I have ever held in scorn and hatred as I do now. The money I received was from the Treasury—part of that sum yearly filched from the Government funds to keep up your rickety old castle outside Empoli; but bound as I was by my oath of secrecy I could utter no word in self-defence, nor prosecute the journals which spread their highly-spiced libels. You held me beneath your thrall, and I, although an honest woman, have remained crushed and powerless." Then she paused.

"Proceed," he observed with sarcasm. "I am all attention."

"No more need be said," she answered. "I will now leave you, and wish you a pleasant journey back to Rome," and she bowed and turned away.

"Come," he cried, dragging her by force back to the seat. "Don't be an idiot, Gemma, but listen. I brought you here," he commenced, "not to fence with you, as we have been doing, but to make a proposal; one that I think you will seriously consider."

"Some further shady trick, I suppose. Well, explain your latest scheme. It is sure to be interesting!"

"As you rightly suggest, it is a trick, Contessa," he said, in a tone rather more conciliatory, and for the first time speaking without any show of politeness. "Within the past ten days the situation in Rome has undergone an entire change, although the journals know nothing; and in consequence I find Castellani, who has for years been my friend and supporter, is now one of my bitterest opponents. If there is a change of government he would no doubt be appointed Foreign Minister in my place."

"Well, you don't fear him, surely?" she said. "You are Minister, and can recall him at any moment."

"No. Castellani holds a certain document which, if produced, must cause the overthrow of the Government, and perhaps the ruin of our country," he answered in deep earnestness. "Before long, in order to clear himself and place himself in favour, he must produce this paper, and if so the revelations will startle Europe."

"Well, that is nothing to me," she said coldly. "It is entirely your affair."

"Listen!" he exclaimed eagerly. He was now confiding to her one of the deepest secrets of the political undercurrent. "This document is in a sealed blue envelope, across the face of which a large cross has been drawn in blue pencil. Remember that. It is in the top left-hand drawer in the Ambassador's writing-table in his private room. You know the room; the small one looking out into Grosvenor Square. You no doubt recollect it when you were visiting there two years ago."

"Certainly," she contented herself with replying, still puzzled at the strangeness of his manner. The wind moaned mournfully through the bare branches above them.

"You are friendly with Castellani's daughter," he went on earnestly. "Call to-morrow with the object of visiting her, and then you must make some excuse to enter that room alone."

"You mean that I must steal that incriminating paper?" she said.

He nodded.

"Impossible!" she replied decisively. "First, I don't intend to run any risk, and, secondly, I know quite well that nobody is allowed in that room alone. The door is always kept locked."

"There are two keys," he interrupted. "Here is one of them. I secured it yesterday."

"And in return for this service, what am I to receive?" she inquired coldly, sitting erect, without stirring a muscle.

"In return for this service"—he answered gravely, his dark eyes riveted upon hers—"in return for this service you shall name your own price."

XXIV

By Stealth

Before she had parted from the Marquis she had made a demand boldly and fearlessly, to which, not without the most vehement protest, he had been compelled to accede. She knew him well, and was aware that, in order to gain his own ends, he would betray and denounce his nearest relative; that, although a shrewd, clever statesman, he had won universal popularity and esteem in Italy by reason of certain shady transactions by which he had posed as the saviour of his country. The revelations she could make regarding the undercurrent of affairs in Rome would astound Europe. For that reason he had been forced to grant her what she asked in return for the incriminating paper from the archives of the Embassy.

For over an hour they sat together in the darkness engaged in a strange discussion, when at last they rose and together walked on, still deep in conversation. The Marquis had an appointment, and was about to take leave of her when, as they crossed the wide deserted space between the Admiralty and the Horse Guards, a man in a heavy fur-trimmed overcoat and felt hat, in hurrying past, gazed full into the faces of both. At that moment they were beneath one of the lamps flickering in the gusty wind, and he had full view of them.

Gemma's eyes met his, and instantly the recognition was mutual.

It was the man who had attempted to take her life—Frank Tristram. He had evidently arrived from the Continent by the day express from Paris, left his despatches at the Foreign Office, and was walking to his chambers in St. James's Street by the nearest way across the Park. He usually preferred to walk home in order to stretch his legs, cramped as they were by many tedious hours in railway carriages.

When he had passed he turned quickly as if to reassure himself, then, with some muttered words, he strode forward with his hands deep in his pockets and his head bent towards the cold boisterous wind.

"Did you notice that man who has just passed?" Gemma gasped, in a low voice betraying alarm.

"No; who was he?" asked the Marquis, turning back to glance at the retreating figure.

"A man you know; Tristram, the English Foreign Office messenger."

"Tristram!" exclaimed Montelupo quickly. "He's never recognised me?"

"I think so," she replied. "He looked straight into your face."

The Minister exclaimed a fierce Italian oath. "Then the fact that I'm in London will be at once made known," he said.

"That is not of much importance, is it? Castellani already knows, for you've been to the Embassy."

"But he will be silent. I'm here incognito," the Marquis cried quickly, in a changed voice. "I have several matters with regard to Abyssinia and our foreign policy to settle with the British Government, but am procrastinating with an object. If they know yonder at the Foreign Office that I am in London, and have not called upon their Minister, it will be considered an insult, and may strain our relations with England. This we can't afford to do. These English are useful to us. Italy has nothing to fear from the alliance of France and Russia, but nevertheless her only safe policy consists in a firm union with England. The Anglo-Italian naval alliance preserves the peace of Europe by throwing its weight into the scale against any disturber of tranquillity. We shall want English ships to fight and protect us in the Mediterranean when France invades us on the Tuscan shore." Then, after a moment's reflection, he glanced at the illuminated clock-face of Big Ben, and added, "No, I must leave London at once, for in this direction I see a pressing danger. It's now nearly seven. I'll dine and get away by the nightmail for Paris. I must be back in Rome again at the earliest possible moment."

"Am I still to go to the Embassy?" she asked.

"Of course," he answered quickly. "Don't delay an instant. It is imperative that we should obtain that document, and you are the only person who can successfully accomplish the task. When you have done so bring it to me in Rome. Our safety lies in the expeditious way in which you effect this coup."

"In Rome?" she echoed. "That's impossible."

"Why? With us everything is possible."

"You forget that, owing to your absurd and foolish action a few months ago, I shall find myself arrested the moment I cross the frontier," she answered.

"Ah, yes, I quite forgot," he replied. "But that's easily remedied."

They were passing through the square of the Horse Guards at that moment, and halting beneath a lamp where stood a cavalry sentry motionless and statuesque, he took from his bulky wallet a visiting-card and scribbled a few words upon its back. Then, handing it to her, said—"This is your passport. If there is any difficulty in reaching me, present this."

She took it, glanced at the scribbled words, and thrust it into her glove. Then, upon the wide pavement in Parliament Street, a few moments later, he lifted his hat politely, and they parted.

At noon next day Gemma called at the Embassy, and was shown into the waiting-room. She had not remained there five minutes when suddenly the Ambassador's daughter burst into the room with a loud cry of welcome, and kissed her visitor enthusiastically on both cheeks in Italian fashion. Slight, and strange rather than pretty, she had a delicate face, dark eyes, a small quivering nose, a rather large, ever-ruddy mouth, and curling, straggling black locks, which ever waved as in a perpetual breeze.

"I'm so glad, so very glad you've called, dear," Carmenilla said enthusiastically. "Father mentioned the other day that you were in England, and I've wondered so often why you've never been to see us."

"I've been staying with friends in the country," Gemma explained. "I suppose you speak English quite well now."

"A little. But oh! it is so difficult," she laughed. "And it is so different here to Firenze or Rome. The people are so strange."

"Yes," Gemma sighed. "I have also found it so."

In their girlhood days they had been close friends through five years at the grey old convent of San Paolo della Croce in the Via della Chiesa at Firenze, and afterwards at Rome, where Carmenilla had lived with a rather eccentric old aunt, the Marchesa Tassino, while her father had been absent fulfilling the post of Ambassador at Vienna.

"I'm so very glad you've called," Castellani's daughter repeated. "Come to my room; take off your things and stay to luncheon. Father is out, and I'm quite alone."

"The Count is out," repeated her visitor in a feigned tone of regret. Truth to tell, however, it was intelligence most welcome to her. "I'm sorry he's not at home. We haven't met for so long."

"Oh, he's dreadfully worried just now!" his daughter answered. "The work at this Embassy is terrible. He seems writing and interviewing people from morning until night. He works much harder now than any of the staff; while at Brussels it was all so different. He had absolutely nothing to do."

"But this England is such a great and wonderful country, while Belgium is such a tiny one," Gemma observed. "The whole diplomatic world revolves around London."

"Yes, of course," she resumed. "But to sustain Italy's prestige we are compelled to do such lots of entertaining. I'm terribly sick of it all. The situation in Rome began to change almost as soon as father was appointed here, and now it has become extremely grave and critical. The men who were once his friends are now his bitterest foes. He has adjusted several most difficult matters recently, but no single word of commendation has he received from the Marquis Montelupo."

"Perhaps the Marquis is not his friend," Gemma hazarded, for the purpose of ascertaining the extent of her knowledge.

"No. He is his enemy; of that I'm absolutely confident," the girl replied. "I hate him. He's never straightforward. Once, in Rome, he tried to worm from me a secret of my father's, and because I would not speak he has never forgiven me."

"Was it some very deep secret?" Gemma inquired. "Yes. It concerned the prestige of Italy and my father's reputation for probity," she replied. "Why the King trusts him so implicitly, I can never understand."

"If there are serious political complications in Rome, as you seem to think, then the days of his power are numbered," observed her visitor, now master of herself again. "The Ministry will be thrown out."

"Ah! that would be the best thing that could happen to Italy," she declared with a look of wisdom. "Montelupo is my father's enemy; he seeks to fetter him in every action, in order that his reputation as a diplomat may be ruined, so that the King may be forced to send him his letters of recall. Truly the post of Ambassador in London is no sinecure."

Gemma was silent. She hesitated and shuddered, Carmenilla noticed it, and asked her if she were cold.

"No, no," she answered quickly. "It is quite warm and cosy here." The light played on her smooth skin to admiration, and the colour changed in her excited face.

At luncheon, served with that stateliness which characterised the whole of the Ambassador's household, they chatted on, as women will chat, of dress, of books, of plays, and of the latest gossip from Florence and Rome, the two centres of Italian society. They were eating their dessert, when the hall-porter entered bearing a card upon the salver. Carmenilla glanced at it, smiled, and rose to excuse herself.

"A visitor!" Gemma exclaimed. "Who is it?"

Her friend hesitated, blushing ever so faintly.

"An Englishman," she answered. "I won't be more than ten minutes. Try and amuse yourself, won't you, dear? Go back to the boudoir and play. I know you love music." And she left the room hurriedly.

The card was still lying beside her plate, and Gemma, in curiosity reached forward and took it up. In an instant, however, she cast it from her.

The man who had called was Frank Tristram.

In order not to attract the undue attention of the grave-faced man who stood silent and immovable before the great carved oak buffet, she finished her apple leisurely, sipped the tiny cup of coffee, dipped the tips of her fingers in the silver-rimmed bowl of rose-scented water, and rising, passed out along the corridor back to the warm, cosy little room where they had passed such a pleasant hour.

She had detected Carmenilla's flushed cheeks, and had suspicion that this caller was no ordinary friend. This man, whose murderous fingers had not long ago clutched themselves around her own throat, was a friend of this smart, slim girl who was so admired in London society. She stood silent in the centre of the little room, her heart beating wildly, wondering whether she might, without arousing suspicion, retrace her steps along that long, thickly carpeted corridor and secure the document which Montelupo required. The voices of servants sounded outside, and she knew that at present to approach and unlock the door unobserved was impossible.

Therefore she advanced to the grate, and spreading out her chilly, nervous hands to the fire, waited, determined to possess herself in patience. Even now she felt inclined to draw back because of the enormous risk she ran. Castellani was not her friend. If he knew, he might give her over to the English police as a common thief. Her face was of death-like pallor at that moment of indecision. Again she shuddered.

With her hand upon her heaving breast, as if to allay an acute pain that centred there, her white lips moved, but no sound escaped them. She listened. The servants had gone.

Carmenilla was downstairs chatting with Tristram; the house at last seemed silent and deserted, therefore Gemma, losing no time in further indecision, and holding her silken skirts tight around her so that they should not rustle, crept out on tiptoe, holding in her hand the key which Montelupo had given her. At first she proceeded slowly and noiselessly, but, fearing detection, hurried forward as she approached the door of the Ambassador's room.

At last she gained it, breathless. With scarce a sound she placed the key in the lock, and a moment later was inside, closing the door after her.

Unhesitatingly she went straight to the table, and placed her hand upon the drawer containing the document. It was locked. Next instant her heart beat wildly as her quick eye espied the key still remaining in another drawer, and, taking it, she opened the locked drawer and stood examining the great blue official envelope in her hand.

Yes, the blue pencil mark was upon it in the form of a cross, as the Marquis had described. She had gained what she sought. Triumph was hers.

Quickly she turned to make her exit, but next second fell back with a loud wild cry of alarm.

Count Castellani had entered noiselessly, and was standing erect and motionless between her and the door.

XXV

A Woman's Diplomacy

G emma stood immovable; a deathly pallor overspread her cheeks, her eyes fixed themselves in terror upon this tall, well-dressed man, who was her bitterest enemy. With one trembling hand she had clutched the revolving book-stand for support; the other held the envelope containing the secret document. She dared not to breathe; amazement and alarm held her dumb.

"And by what right, pray, do you enter my room?" the Ambassador inquired, after a few seconds of silence, complete and painful. His face was blanched in anger; in his dark eye was a keen glance of suspicion and hatred.

She laughed—that strange hollow laugh which her lover knew so well.

"I came to call on you," she answered. The door was closed, and they were alone together.

"And you entered my room to pry into my private papers?" he said, his blood rising. "What's that you have in your hand?"

She set her lips firmly. She was no longer the sweet, almost childlike girl, but a hard-faced, desperate woman.

"A paper I want," she boldly answered, at the same moment doubling the envelope in half, and crushing it in her palm.

"Then you have at last become so bold that you actually have the audacity to enter one's house and steal whatever you think proper?" he cried, in a towering passion. "Fortunately, I've returned in time to frustrate your latest bit of infernal ingenuity."

"My action is but fair, now that we are enemies," she answered with feigned indignation. "If you could, you'd ruin me; therefore I'm entirely at liberty to return the same compliment."

"I thought you were already ruined," the Count exclaimed. "Your reputation, at any rate, cannot be rendered blacker than it is."

"That's the truth, no doubt." She laughed with an air of gaiety. "But one who makes secret diplomacy a profession, must care nothing for the good will of the world outside the diplomatic circle."

"Those who make love their profession, should be constant, if they would achieve success," he retorted bitterly.

At that moment a recollection flashed across her mind. It had slipped her memory until that instant. This man had on one occasion, in Rome, two years ago, spoken tenderly to her, and she had scorned his attentions. With a woman's quick perception, she now saw that the fact that she had rejected him still rankled within his mind. Yet she was still young enough to be his daughter, and had always held him in dislike. He was a cold, scheming diplomatist, who would stake his very soul in order to get the better of his adversaries.

"Once you spoke of love to me," she said, drawing herself up proudly. "Now you ruthlessly cast my past into my face. Even if I have acted as a diplomatic agent, you know well enough that all these scandalous stories about me are foul libels set about by Montelupo and yourself for political purposes."

"Enough!" he cried, incensed at her words. "We need not discuss that now. I demand to know why I find you prying here, in my room?"

She smiled. "I came to see Carmenilla," she answered.

"And she invited you to lunch?—you whom I have forbidden her to know!" he exclaimed, exasperated. "A woman of your stamp is no companion for my daughter."

"Yet you once told me that you loved me, and I might, if I had felt so inclined, have now been the Countess Castellani, and done the honours of this Embassy. Ah, my dear Conte," she went on, "you are a noted diplomatist, and no doubt as wary and cunning as most of your confreres. But you forget that every woman is by birth a diplomatist, and that in politics I have had a wide and, perhaps, unique experience."

"You possess the ingenuity and daring of the very devil himself," he blurted forth. "Show me that paper."

"No," she answered firmly. "It is in my possession—and I keep it."

"You've stolen it!" he cried, advancing towards her determinedly. "Give it to me this instant."

"I shall not."

From where he stood his eyes wandered to the table, and he noticed that one of the drawers stood open. Within her hand, he saw the envelope was a blue one, secured by seals. In an instant he dashed towards the drawer, rummaged its contents, and finding the document missing, cried—

"Your infernal impertinence is really astounding. You enter my house, commit a theft, and when charged with it refuse to give up the stolen property. If you don't return it to me at once, I'll call in the police, and have you arrested."

"Really?" she exclaimed with a sarcastic laugh which caused his cheeks to become flushed by anger. "I think after so many years of diplomacy, you ought to be aware that such a course is impossible. If you were a young attaché just fresh from Rome, my dear Count, you might be pardoned for not knowing that here, in this Embassy, I am on Italian soil, and, being an Italian subject, the London police are unable to arrest me."

"But they could outside—in the Square."

"Certainly. But if I choose to remain here—what then?"

"Remain here! You speak like an imbecile. Come, give me back that envelope."

"Never!" she replied, still holding it firmly in her small hand, and regarding him in defiance.

Castellani knew well the contents of that envelope, and was aware that Gemma must have been employed by those implicated by the proofs it contained. For months he had held this in his possession as a weapon to use as a last resource, and the manner in which she had entered his room and filched it from the drawer made it plain to him that those to whom he was now opposed were prepared to go any length to gain their own ends. But he likewise knew Gemma well, and was aware that as a secret agent of the Ministry she was without equal— fearless, resourceful, and versed in every art of deception. He had met her often in society in Rome and Florence two years ago, been struck by her marvellous beauty as others had been, and had offered her marriage. In a word, he had made a fool of himself.

The revelations contained in that envelope she held were sufficient to cause the present Government to be hounded from its office and fat emoluments, and possibly force a criminal prosecution against certain ministers for misappropriating the public funds, therefore he was determined to regain it at all hazards and use it for his own advancement. He had, only a month ago, been promised by his party the Ministry of Foreign Affairs in the next Government, and this single document would place him in high office in Rome.

"If you defy me," he said after a pause, his menacing gaze fixed upon that of the pretty, fragile woman, "I must be ungallant enough to wrench it from you."

"I scarcely think you'll do that," she answered. "If you did, we could never come to terms."

"Come to terms?" he echoed resentfully. "I don't understand. I've no intention of coming to any arrangement with you."

He was standing before her in the centre of the room, but she watched his every movement narrowly. She saw that he was desperate, and intended to regain possession of the envelope.

"Once again I ask you to give me that paper you have stolen," he said in a voice that quivered with rage.

"I have already replied, Count Castellani," she responded, "and I wish you good-afternoon." Then with her skirts rustling, she bowed and swept past him towards the door.

"No!" he cried, springing forward and arresting her progress in a moment of fury. "You shall not escape like that. Give me the paper, or—or by Heaven, I'll—"

"Well?" she cried, turning upon him with flashing eyes. "What will you do?"

He drew back abashed.

"I apologise, Contessa," he said quickly. "But give me back that paper. Remember that you've committed a barefaced, unpardonable theft."

"And you, as Ambassador of Italy, utter barefaced lies every day," she retorted.

"Diplomacy is the art of lying artistically," he answered. "It is impossible to achieve success in diplomacy without resorting to realistic perversions of the truth. Every diplomatist must be a born liar—but he need not be a thief."

"Some are," she retorted. "You are one."

His face went purple in anger.

"I—a thief?" he blurted forth. "Have you taken leave of your senses, woman?"

"Not entirely. I believe I have some remaining," she replied. "I again repeat that you, the Count Castellani, His Majesty's Ambassador, are a mean, despicable thief, whom the Tribunal at Rome would sentence to seven years' imprisonment if they became acquainted with the facts."

"Enough! Not another word, woman!" he cried in a towering passion. Then, grasping her arms, he, after a short desperate struggle, succeeded in wrenching from her the envelope for which she had risked so much. "Now you may go," he said, as she stood flushed, panting, and breathless before him, her hair a trifle disarranged, the lace upon one of her cuffs torn and hanging. "If you don't leave at once, I'll ring and have you turned out."

"I shall go when you give me back that paper," she answered, facing him.

"You'll never have it."

"Then, listen," she went on calmly, taking a few hasty steps towards where he was standing astride before the fire. "The worth of that document is to you considerable, I know, but there are others to whom its value is even greater. Just now I charged you with theft, and you feigned to have forgotten. Well, I will recall a fact or two to your memory. A year ago, at Como, there was an inquiry into certain scandals connected with the Bank of Naples." Then she paused. The Ambassador's face had instantly blanched. "Ah!" she went on, "I see that event has not quite slipped your memory. Well, as the result of that inquiry, in which certain statesmen were implicated, two well-known public men received sentences of ten years' imprisonment, and others ranging from two to five years. But, at that inquiry, it was shown that a certain cheque was missing, and it was further proved that this cheque had been drawn for half a million francs. To whom that sum passed remained a mystery."

"Well?" His Excellency gasped, still pale, glaring at her as if she were some object supernatural. All his self-possession had left him.

"The fact is a mystery no longer."

"Why?"

"Because the identical cheque has been recovered and bears your endorsement," she answered, in a slow, distinct voice.

"Who has recovered it?" he demanded quickly. "Who has it?"

She smiled triumphantly. This elegant man who but a moment ago had talked boldly, as became the Ambassador of Italy, was now cringing before her seeking information. His cool demeanour had altogether forsaken him.

"I have that cheque," she said, her clear, unwavering eyes fixed upon his.

In an instant Castellani perceived that he was in the power of this pretty woman he had denounced and condemned. He knew well, too, that she was not the gay, abandoned woman that La Funaro was popularly supposed to be.

"Reflect for a single moment," she continued ruthlessly. "What would be the result of the production of that missing draft about which so much has been written in the newspapers?"

The Ambassador bit his lip. Never in the whole course of his long and varied diplomatic career had he been so ingeniously checkmated by a woman. The estimate he had formed of her long ago was entirely correct. She possessed really remarkable talents.

"The result would certainly be rather annoying," he observed, making a sorry attempt to smile.

"It would throw a very fierce light upon the ways and means of the party of thieves and adventurers who are endeavouring to grab Italy and grow fat upon its Treasury," she exclaimed. "The situation at Rome has, I understand, changed considerably within the past week or so. The public mind is feeling the influence of unfavourable winds. Well, it is possible before long that this missing cheque will have to be produced."

"Which will mean my ruin!" he blurted forth. "You know that well. If that cheque ever gets into the hands of the present Government, I shall be recalled and tried in a criminal court as a common thief."

"That's exactly what I said not long ago. You then declared that you had never touched a soldo of other persons' money," she observed, standing with her hand resting upon the writing-table, a slim, graceful figure in her dark stuff dress.

"No, Gemma, no!" he exclaimed earnestly. "You can't mean to expose this. I—I don't believe you have the cheque, after all. How did you learn my secret?"

"It is my duty to become acquainted with the secrets of those in opposition to the Government," she answered simply. "Remember what you have said of me since we have been together in this room. Of a woman of my evil reputation, what can you expect but exposure?"

"You have resolved upon a vendetta?" he cried in a tone of genuine alarm.

"I have resolved to treat you fairly," she replied, so calm that not a muscle of her face moved. "In return for that envelope and its contents which you've snatched from me, I will give you back your cheque."

"When?" he cried eagerly.

"Now—at this moment."

"You have it here?"

"Yes," she replied. "Give me that envelope at once, and let us end this conversation. It is painful tome to speak like this to one who once offered to make me his wife."

His Excellency frowned, meditating deeply. He saw that La Funaro had entrapped him so cleverly that there was no loophole for escape. She was remorseless and unrelenting as far as political affairs went, and he knew that if he had decided to hand the draft to the authorities, the result must prove utterly disastrous. Not only would he be ruined, but his party who sought office would be held up to public opprobrium and hopelessly wrecked.

"That paper is a purely private one," he said. "I cannot allow you to take it, Gemma."

"You prefer exposure, then?" she inquired, slightly inclining her head. "The Ministry of Justice are exceedingly anxious to recover that cheque, I assure you. Probably they will compel you to disgorge the substantial sum you received from the national funds when you endorsed the draft."

He paused again, his eyes fixed upon the carpet.

"I'm not anxious for any revelations," he answered in a sudden tone of confidence. "But your price is too high. The document which you so nearly secured is to me worth double that which you offer."

"Very well," she said, shrugging her shoulders impatiently. "If that's your decision, I am content." He was silent. His head was bent upon his breast, h's arms were folded.

"Let me see this cheque of yours," he exclaimed at last in a dry, dubious tone.

She unbuttoned the breast of her dress, tore away the switches of the lining, and took out a small envelope, from which she drew a large, green-coloured draft. Then, turning it over, she exhibited his own angular signature upon its back. Afterwards, she replaced it in its envelope, and then said—

"Shall we make the exchange? Or are you still prepared to face exposure? It will not be pleasant for poor Carmenilla if her father is sent to prison for embezzlement."

"Yes, for Carmenilla?" the Ambassador gasped next instant. "For Carmenilla's sake I will deal with you, and make the exchange. You are a truly wonderful woman, Gemma; the most shrewd, the most cunning, and"—he paused—"and the most beautiful in all the world."

"Your compliments are best unuttered, my dear Count," she replied, the muscles of her face unrelaxed. "Remember, like yourself, I'm a diplomatist, and it is scarcely necessary for us to bestow praises upon each other—is it? Give me the envelope."

Slowly he walked over to the table and took the document from the drawer wherein he had placed it. For a moment he hesitated with it still in his hand. By giving it to her he was throwing down his arms; he was relinquishing the only weapon he held against his enemies in Rome.

But in her white hand he saw the piece of green incriminating paper which was such incontestable proof of his roguery and dishonesty in the past. The sight of it caused him serious misgivings. Once that were destroyed he need not fear any other proof that could be brought against him. He had a reputation for probity, and at all hazards must retain it. This last reflection decided him.

He crossed to where Gemma stood, and handing her the sealed envelope with the blue cross upon it, received the cancelled cheque in exchange.

His brow was heavy, and he sighed as, at the window, he examined it to reassure himself there was no mistake. Then, returning to the fire, he lit it at one corner, and in silence held it between his fingers until the flames had consumed it, leaving only a small piece of curling crackling tinder.

XXVI

THE PALAZZA FUNARO

Days had lengthened into weeks, and it was already the end of February. In Florence, as in London, February is not the most enjoyable time of the year, and those who travel south to the Winter City expecting the sunshine and warmth of the Riviera are usually sadly disappointed. At the end of March Florence becomes pleasant, and remains so till the end of May; while in autumn, when the mosquitoes cease to trouble, the sun has lost its power, and the Lungarno is cool, it is also a delightful place of residence. But February afternoons beside the Arno are very often as dark, as dreary, and as yellow as beside the Thames; and as Gemma sat after luncheon in her cosy room, the smallest in the great old palazzo in the Borgo d'Albizzi which bore her name, she shuddered and drew a silken shawl about her shoulders. It was one of the show-places of Florence; one of those ponderous, prison-like buildings built of huge blocks of brown stone, time-worn, having weathered the storms of five centuries, and notable as containing a magnificent collection of works of art. Its mediaeval exterior, a relic of ancient Florence, was gloomy and forbidding enough, with its barred windows, over-hanging roof, strange lanterns of wonderfully worked iron, and great iron rings to which men tied their horses in days bygone. Once beyond the great courtyard, however, it was indeed a gorgeous palace. The Funaros had always been wealthy and powerful in the Lily City, and had through ages collected within their palace quantities of antiquities and costly objects. Every room was beautifully decorated, some with wonderful frescoes by Andrea del Sarto, whose work in the outer court of the Annunziata is ever admired by sight-seers of every nationality, while the paintings were by Ciro Ferri, Giovanni da Bologna, Filippo Lippi, Botticelli, and Fra Bartolommeo, together with some frescoes in grisaille with rich ornamentation by Del Sarto's pupil Franciabigio, and hosts of other priceless works.

It was a magnificent residence. There were half a dozen other palaces in the same thoroughfare, including the Altoviti, the Albizzi, and the Pazzi, but this was the finest of them all. When Gemma had inherited it she had at once furnished half a dozen rooms in modern style. The place was so enormous that she always felt lost in it, and seldom strayed beyond these rooms which overlooked the great paved courtyard with its ancient wall and curious sculptures chipped and weather-worn. The great gloomy silent rooms, with their bare oaken floors, mouldering tapestries, and time-blackened pictures, were to her grim and ghostly, as, indeed, they were to any but an art enthusiast or a lover of the antique. But the Contessa Funaro lived essentially in the present, and always declared herself more in love with cleanliness than antiquarian dirt. She had no taste for the relics of the past, and affected none. If English or American tourists found anything in the collections to admire, they were at liberty to do so on presenting their card to the liveried hall-porter. At the door the man had a box, and the money placed therein was sent regularly each quarter to the Maternity Hospital.

She spent little time in her grim, silent home; for truth to tell, its magnificence irritated her, and its extent always filled her with a sense of loneliness. The housekeeper, an elderly gentlewoman who had been a friend of her dead mother's, was very deaf, and never amusing; therefore, after a fortnight or so, she was generally ready to exchange the Funaro Palace for the *Hotel Cavour* at Milan, the *Minerva* at Rome, or the hospitality of some country villa. Hotels, or even small houses, were not so grim and prison-like as her own great palazzo, the very walls of which seemed to breathe mutely of the past—of those troublous times when the clank of armour echoed in the long stone corridors, and the clink of spurs sounded in the courtyard below where now the only invaders were the pigeons.

The furniture of the small elegant room in which she sat was entirely modern, upholstered in pale blue silk, with her monogram in gold thread; the carpets were thick, the great high Florentine stove threw forth a welcome warmth, and the grey light which filtered through the curtains was just sufficient to allow her to read. She was lying back in her long chair in a lazy, negligent attitude, her fair hair a trifle disordered by contact with the cushion behind her head; and one of her little slippers having fallen off, her small foot in its neat black silk stocking peeped out beneath her skirt. On the table at her elbow were two or three unopened letters, while in a vase stood a fine bouquet of flowers, a tribute from her deaf housekeeper.

Since the day she had parted from Count Castellani in the hall of the Embassy in Grosvenor Square she had travelled a good deal. She had been down to Rome, had had an interview with the Marquis

Montelupo, and a week ago had unexpectedly arrived at the palazzo. As she had anticipated, when she broke her journey at Turin, on her way from London to Rome, and signed her name in the visitors' book at the hotel, a police official called early on the following morning to inform her that she must consider herself under arrest. But the words scribbled by Montelupo upon his visiting-card had acted like magic, and, having taken the card to the Questura, the detective returned all bows and apologies, and she was allowed to proceed on her journey.

Nearly nine months had elapsed since she last set foot within her great old palazzo, and as she sat that afternoon she allowed her book to fall upon her lap and her eyes to slowly wander around the pretty room. She glanced at the window where the rain was being driven upon the tiny panes by the boisterous wind, and again she shuddered.

With an air of weariness she raised her hand and pushed the mass of fair hair off her brow, as if its weight oppressed her, sighing heavily. The events of the past month had been many and strange. In Rome she had found herself beset by a hundred pitfalls, but she had kept faith with the Marquis, and the terms she had made with him were such as to give her complete satisfaction. A crisis, however, was, she knew, imminent; a crisis in which she would be compelled to play a leading part. But to do so would require all her ingenuity, all her woman's wit, all her courage, all her skill at deception.

Suddenly, as she was thus reflecting, Margherita, her faithful but ugly woman, who had been with her at Livorno, opened the door, and, drawing aside the heavy *portiere*, said—

"The signore!"

"At last I at last!" she cried, excitedly jumping up instantly. "Show him up at once." Then, facing the great mirror, she placed both hands to her hair, rearranging it deftly, recovered her lost slipper, cast aside the wrap, and stood ready to receive her visitor.

Again the door opened. The man who entered was Charles Armytage.

For a few moments he held her in fond embrace, kissing her lips tenderly again and again; while she, in that soft, crooning voice that had rung in his ears through all those months of separation, welcomed him, reiterating her declarations of love.

"I received your telegram in Brussels two days ago, and have come to you direct," he said at last. "I did not go to the Post Office every day, hence the delay."

"Ah! my poor Nino must be tired," she cried, suddenly recollecting. "Here, this couch. Sit here; it will rest you. Povero Nino! What a terrible journey—from Brussels to Florence!"

He sank upon the divan she indicated, pale, weary, and travel-worn, while she, taking a seat beside him, narrated how she had left Lyddington for London, and afterwards travelled to Rome. Feeling that the glance of the woman he worshipped was fixed upon him, he raised his head; and then their eyes met for a moment with an expression of infinite gentleness, the mournful gentleness of their heroic love.

"Why did you go to Rome?" he asked. "You always said you hated it."

"I had business," she answered. "Urgent business; business which has again aroused hope within me."

"Still of a secret nature?" the young Englishman hazarded, with a quick glance of suspicion.

"For the present, yes," she replied in a low, intense voice. "But you still love me, Nino? You can trust me now, can't you?" and she looked earnestly into his face.

"I have already trusted you," he replied. "Since that night I left you at Lyddington my life has indeed been a dull, aimless one. You have been ever in my mind, and I have wondered daily, hourly, what was the nature of the grave mysterious peril which you say threatens both of us."

"That peril still exists," she answered. "It increases daily, nay hourly."

"You are still threatened? You, the wealthy owner of this magnificent palazzo!" he exclaimed, gazing around the pretty room bewildered. "Often when I was in Florence, in those days when we first met, I passed this great building. Little, however, did I dream that my Gemma, who used to cycle with me in the Cascine, was its owner."

She laughed. "I had reasons for not letting you know my real name," she replied. "It is true that I have money; but wealth has brought me no happiness—only sorrow, alas!—until I met you."

"And now you are happy?" he asked earnestly. "Ah! yes, I am happy when you are beside me, Nino," she responded, grasping his hand in hers. "I never thought that I could learn to love you so. I am still nervous, still in dread, it is true. The reason of my fear is a strange one; I fear the future, and I fear myself."

"Yourself?" he echoed. "You told me that once before—long ago. You are not very formidable."

"Ah, no! You don't understand," she cried hastily. "I fear that I may not have the strength and courage to carry through a plan I have formed to secure your safety and my own liberty."

"But I can assist you," he suggested. "Your interests are mine, now, remember," he added, kissing her.

"Yes," she said, looking up into his eyes. "But to render me assistance is not possible. Any action on my part must necessarily imperil both of us. No, I must act alone."

"When?"

"Very soon. In a few days, or a few weeks. When, I know not. Very soon I must return to England."

"To England!" he cried. "I thought you preferred your own Italy!"

"I have an object in going back," she answered ambiguously.

"You'll let me accompany you?"

She reflected for a moment; then, without responding, rose, rang the bell, and told the man-servant, who entered resplendent in the blue Funaro livery, to bring her visitor some wine.

"You must be half famished after your journey," she exclaimed. She was standing before him in a white gown, white from head to foot. "I must really apologise for not being more hospitable, Nino."

"I'm really not hungry," he replied. Then he added, "You didn't answer my question."

"I was reflecting," she responded slowly. "I don't know whether it is wise at this juncture for you to return to England, into the very midst of your enemies."

"You haven't yet explained who my enemies are, beyond urging me to be wary of Malvano. True, that man has lied to me about you. He told me a silly, romantic, and wholly fictitious story regarding your parentage; but, after all, he may have been mistaken, especially as it was in answer to my inquiry whether he knew any one named Fanetti in Florence."

"Malvano was well aware that I had used that name more than once," his well-beloved replied. "He wilfully deceived you for his own purpose. He wished to part us."

"Why? He is surely not in love with you?"

"Certainly not," she answered, laughing at such an idea. "His object was not jealousy."

"Then he is actually my enemy?"

"Yes," she replied. "Avoid him. If you desire to return to England with me, I will allow you to do so with one stipulation. The moment

WILLIAM LE QUEUX

we set foot in London we must part. If it were known that we were together, all my plans would be frustrated."

"And I am to leave you to the mercy of these mysterious enemies of yours?" he observed dubiously.

"It is imperative. You must leave London instantly and go away into the country. Malvano must not know that you are in England. Go to your uncle's in Berkshire, and wait there until I can with safety communicate with you."

"But all this is extraordinary," he said mystified, taking from her hand the glass of wine she had poured out for him. "I must confess myself still puzzled at finding you mistress of his magnificent palace, and yet existing in deadly fear of mysterious enemies." He knew nothing of her connexion with the Italian Ministry of Foreign Affairs, and only regarded her as a wealthy woman whose caprice it had been to masquerade, and who had earned a wide reputation for gaiety and recklessness.

"Some day, before long, you shall know the whole truth, Nino," she assured him in deep earnestness.

"When you do, you will be amazed—astounded, as others will be. I know I act strangely, without any apparent motive. I know you have heard evil of me on every hand, yet you still trust me," and again she looked into his eyes; "yet you still love me."

"Yes, piccina," he answered, calling her once again by that endearing term she had taught him in those summer days beside the sea when he knew so little Italian and experienced such difficulty in speaking to her. "Yes," he said, placing his arm tenderly round her waist, "I trust you, although evil tongues everywhere try to wound you."

Only when beside this man she loved was she her real-self, true, honest, loving, and tender-hearted. To the world outside she was compelled to wear the mask as a cold, sneering, crafty, and coquettish woman, the cunning and remorseless adventuress who had won such unenviable notoriety in the political circle at Rome and in Florentine society.

"La Funaro is known by repute in every town throughout Italy," she said brokenly. "My reputation is that of a vain, coquettish woman without heart, without remorse. But you, Nino, when you know the truth, shall be my judge. Then you will know how I have suffered. The foul lies uttered on every side have cut me to the quick, but under compulsion I have remained silent. Soon, however"—and her brilliant eyes seemed to flash with eagerness at the thought which crossed her mind—"soon I shall release myself, and then you shall know everything—everything."

"On that day perfect happiness will come to me," he said fervently. "I love you, Gemma, more deeply than ever man loved woman."

"And I, too, Nino, love you with all my heart, with all my soul."

Their lips met again in a fierce caress, their hands clasped tightly. He looked into her clear eyes, bright with unshed tears, and saw fear and determination, truth and honesty mirrored therein. Her tiny hand trembled in his, and then for very joy she suddenly burst into a flood of emotion.

"When shall we leave for England?" he asked at last, his strong arm still about her waist.

"In a couple of days. I have only waited here for you to join me," she said, drying her eyes. "Life without you, Nino, is impossible."

"So within a week we shall be in London?"

"Yes," she replied. "Soon, very soon, I hope, I may be free. But I have a task before me—one that is difficult and desperate. In order to secure your safety, and my own freedom from the hateful bonds which have fettered me these last two years, I am compelled to resort to strategy, to deception deep and cunning, the smallest revelation of which would wreck all our hopes."

"How?"

"Exposure of my plans would cost me my life," she answered, her face white and set, a shudder running through her slight frame.

"Your life?" he echoed, still mystified. "One would think you feared assassination!"

She made no answer, but, pale to her lips, she held her breath. The flunkey in blue re-entered the room, bearing a telegram upon a salver. His mistress took it and, tearing open the folded pale drab paper, read its contents.

"No reply," she said; and the man, bowing, withdrew. "Nino," she exclaimed in a voice of deep earnestness when the servant had gone, "you may think it extraordinary, but for your sake, because I love no other man but yourself, I have resolved to risk my life and free myself. This telegram makes it imperative that we should leave again for England to-night. You have shown trust in me; you do not believe all the idle tales gossips have littered. I love you, Nino. If I prove victor, I gain your affection, and happiness always with you. If I lose, then I die, unwillingly, but nevertheless in the confidence that to the end you trusted me."

"No, no!" he cried fiercely. "You shall not die! You shall never be taken from me! I adore you, Gemma! God knows I love you, darling!"

"Then you will never doubt me—never!" she cried, clinging closely to him, and raising her beautiful face to his. "You will not doubt me even if, to gain my end, I feign love for another. To him, my kisses shall be Judas-kisses, my smiles mockery, my lips venom, my embrace the chilling embrace of death. Hear me?" she cried wildly. "I go to England with a purpose—a vendetta complete and terrible which I will accomplish by hatred—or, failing that, by love. Both will be equally fatal."

XXVII

ON THE NIGHT WIND

"Y ou still wear your ring, I see," Malvano exclaimed with a merry twinkle in his eyes one morning a fortnight later, while Gemma was sitting at breakfast at Lyddington with Nenci and his wife. The thin-faced, black-haired man had rejoined his wife suddenly a few days before, and since Gemma had returned they had formed quite a merry quartette. She had satisfactorily explained her sudden disappearance, and had concocted a clever story of complications regarding her estate to account for her journey to Italy. Both men, knowing she was "wanted" by the Italian police, marvelled at her audacity in going back and her adroitness in evading arrest.

"I don't always wear the ring," she answered, raising her hand and contemplating it.

"Let me see," exclaimed Nenci, who was seated beside her.

In response she handed it to him. It was unusually large for a lady, but of antique design. In the centre was a large oval turquoise, around which were set two rows of diamonds, all of beautiful colour and lustre, while the gold which encircled the finger was much thicker than usual, the whole forming a rather massive but extremely handsome ornament.

Nenci held it for a moment, admiring it with the eye of a connoisseur, for by trade he was a jeweller, although he had performed, among other duties, those of waiter in a City restaurant. He declared at once that the diamonds were dirty beneath their settings, and, rising from the table, scrutinised it closely at the window.

"I'll clean it for you to-day, if you like," he said, when he returned to his seat. "It is very dull and dusty." She thanked him, and he placed it beside his plate. "Ah!" exclaimed the Doctor suddenly, with a glance full of meaning.

"That was the marriage ring, wasn't it?"

Nenci glanced across at him quickly and frowned—a gesture of displeasure which Gemma failed to notice.

"Yes," she answered rather harshly; "it was the marriage ring—if you like to so term it. I scarcely ever wear it, because it brings back too many painful memories. The bond has been galling enough—Heaven knows!"

"I thought you had no remorse. You always declared you had none," Nenci remarked. "But since you've known that confounded lover of yours you've been a changed woman."

"Changed for the better, I hope," she retorted. "Do you think it possible that I can wear that ring without remembering a certain night in Livorno—the night when all my evil fortune fell upon me?"

Nenci laughed superciliously.

"Come," he said. "You're growing sentimental. That's the worst of being love-sick. When a woman of genius loves, she always throws common sense to the winds."

Her brows contracted for an instant, but, too discreet to exhibit annoyance, she merely joined his laughter, and, with skilful tact so characteristic of her, answered—"Ah, my dear Lionello, you seem to have forgotten our old Tuscan saying, 'L'amore avvicina gli uomini agli angeli ed al Cielo; poiche il paradiso scende con l'amore in noi.'"

"She's had you there," exclaimed the Doctor merrily. "Gemma isn't the person upon whom to work off witticisms." As he sat at table, Malvano looked the very picture of good health and spirits, ruddy, well-shaven, and spruce in his rough tweed riding-coat and gaiters, for, the roads being heavy and wet, he had resolved to ride his round that morning instead of driving. Only the day previous he had been attending upon the customers at the Bonciani, his ears ever open, and, arriving back at Lyddington by the last train from London, he had been a long time closeted with Nenci, prior to going to bed. The two men had held a long consultation, the nature of which Gemma was unable to determine, but it was evident from her close observation of their demeanour that morning that they had resolved upon some line of immediate action.

La Funaro was now playing a dangerous game.

Calm, silent, watchful, ever ready to listen to their nefarious plans, and even making suggestions of deeper cunning and a vengeance more terrible, she had remained there acting a double part with a skill that few other women could accomplish. But her previous training in the wiles of diplomacy and espionage under the crafty, far-seeing Montelupo now held her in good stead. She could conceal all her woman's pity and forbearance, all her repugnance at the terrible plans which were so calmly discussed, and with them grow enthusiastic at the thought of what was to follow. Hers was a strange personality, a curious blending of the grave with the gay. The mask she wore as a heartless, abandoned woman was absolutely without a flaw.

That day Nenci spent most of his hours in the Doctor's study, the room wherein no one was allowed to enter. Sallow-faced, unshaven, wild-haired, he was so striking a figure that the Doctor had advised him not to go into the village, as his presence would at once be remarked. Therefore, when Malvano was absent, he amused himself in chatting to the assistant at work making up mixtures in the dark little room beyond the surgery, in reading in the room, half-study half-laboratory, which Malvano reserved to himself, or in strolling about the extensive grounds walled in against the vulgar gaze.

Gemma that day idled over magazines and newspapers in the morning-room until luncheon, when the Doctor came in, cold and half famished, with an appetite which did justice to his truly British appearance. Afterwards she passed the afternoon in desultory gossip with Mrs. Nenci, while the two men went to smoke; and in the evening, when coffee was served in the drawing-room, she played and sang to them "Duorme, Carme," "Surriento bello!" the humorous "Don Saverio," and other pieces, while Malvano, in his usually buoyant spirits, fetched his mandolino and accompanied her, until the sweet music and the passionate words brought back to each of them memories of their own fair, far-off land.

About ten, Mrs. Nenci and Gemma retired, and that night the woman, whom, all Italy knew as "La Funaro," knelt in the silence of her chamber long and earnestly before her ivory crucifix, praying for courage and for release. Meanwhile, the two men proceeded to the Doctor's study, turning the key in the door after them. The small place, with its shutters closed and barred, smelt overpoweringly of pungent chemicals, the centre table being laden with bottles, test-tubes, retorts, a crucible beneath which a small spirit-lamp was burning, and a host of sundries, which plainly showed that experiments were in progress. At the wall opposite was a side-table upon which a small vice had been fixed, while beside it lay several files and other tools.

Both men threw off their coats and turned up their shirt-cuffs. Malvano taking his seat in the centre of his chemical appliances, while his companion commenced work at the small side-table.

Nenci was smoking a cigarette when they entered, but at sign of the Doctor at once extinguished it.

"Have you given Gemma back her ring?" Malvano inquired as they sat down to work. The reason the Doctor always locked himself within that room was evident. He was making experiments in secret.

WILLIAM LE QUEUX

"Yes; I gave it her just before dinner," the other answered.

"You cleaned it—eh?" the Doctor said, with a grim smile.

"Yes," the other replied briefly.

"It seems a pity—a great pity!" Malvano exclaimed in a tone of regret. "Is there no other way?"

"None," Nenci answered firmly. "She knows too much. Besides, I have suspicions."

"Of what?"

"That she may play us false," the sallow-faced man replied. "Remember, she still loves that man Armytage—the devil take him!"

"Well," Malvano sighed, "it's the only way, I suppose; but it's hard—very hard on a woman whose life has been wrecked as hers has."

"Misericordia! My dear fellow," cried Nenci impatiently. "Surely you won't turn chicken-hearted after all this time? You've never shown the white feather yet."

The doctor remained silent, and turning in his chair, bent over the small crucible beneath which the blue flame was burning; while his companion, casting a keen half-suspicious glance in his direction, also turned to the small vice fixed to his table and commenced work.

A long time elapsed in almost complete silence, so intent were both on what they were doing. Once—only once—did Malvano refer again to the subject of Gemma's ring.

"Is she actually wearing it now?" he inquired.

"She did at dinner, I noticed," Nenci answered. "But whether she wears her rings at night, I don't know," he laughed.

"Isn't it—well—dangerous?"

"Dangerous! Not at all," his companion replied impatiently. "She suspects nothing, absolutely nothing."

Again they lapsed into unbroken silence.

Fully an hour went by, when Nenci rising, still in his shirt-sleeves, folded his arms, and exclaimed in a tone of satisfaction and confidence—

"At last, my dear fellow! I've worked it out completely. Failure has become absolutely impossible." Malvano, still seated in his chair, leaned back and contemplated with admiration the object which his companion had placed before him—an exquisite little marble bust of King Humbert of Italy. It was only about eighteen inches high, but a faithful and beautifully executed copy of that celebrated head by the renowned Pisan sculptor, Fontacchiotti, which is so prominent a figure in the centre of the great reception hall of the Quirinal at Rome. Plaster replicas of this bust can be bought everywhere throughout Italy for half a franc, and are to be found in most houses of the loyal, while larger ones stand in every court of justice. But this miniature reproduction before the Doctor was really an admirable work of art, one such as connoisseur would admire.

Nenci had not chiselled it, but had apparently been doing something to its small base of polished malachite. The hand that had succeeded in reproducing the features so exactly was without doubt a master-hand. On the table where the sallow-faced man had been working stood two other busts exactly similar in every detail, both in little cases of polished wood, lined with crimson velvet, and each bearing the royal monogram in gilt upon its base, exactly similar to the one in the Quirinal.

"It's excellent. The Gobbo has certainly turned them out marvellously well," the Doctor observed.

"He's a genius," the other said enthusiastically. "The reproduction is so exact that detection is absolutely impossible. Look!" And taking up a photograph of a miniature bust standing upon a carved shelf against a frescoed wall, they both compared it with the one before them. "Do you see that small chip in the base?" Nenci said, pointing to the picture. "The Gobbo has even reproduced that."

"A wonderful piece of work," Malvano acquiesced. "Very neat, and very pretty."

"After it leaves our hands it won't want many servants to keep it dusted," his companion observed grimly. "You see, the base being circular is made to move," he added, taking the little ornament in his hand. "You twist it slightly—so, and the thing is done. You see those two scratches across the stone. The base must be so turned as to join them. And then to the very instant—well—" And he broke off without concluding his sentence.

"It will strike the half-hour, eh?" the Doctor suggested with a laugh.

The other raised his shoulders and outspread his palms. Then, regarding his handiwork with the keenest satisfaction, he thrust his hands deep into his pockets, and, leaning against the mantelshelf, gaily hummed the popular Neapolitan chorus—

> *"Pecche. Ndringhete-ndringhete-ndra*
> *Mmiez' 'o mare nu scoglio nce sta!*
> *Tutte venene a bevere cca,*
> *Pecche. Ndringhete-ndringhete-ndra."*

The Doctor, with fingers stained yellow by the acids he had been mixing, the fumes of which filled the small den almost to suffocation, took up the beautiful little bust and examined its green polished base with critical eye, turning it over and over, and weighing it carefully in his hand.

"Devilish cunningly contrived," he said. "It's a pity it must be sacrificed. But I suppose it must."

"Of course," Nenci said quickly. "We must complete our experiments and ascertain that it actually strikes true. Is it quiet enough yet to try, do you think?" Malvano rose. The trousers he wore were old and burned brown where corrosive liquids had fallen upon them, his hair was ruffled, and his face dirty, as if smoke-blackened.

"I hope the thing won't create too much fuss," he said in an apprehensive tone.

"Leave all that to me," his companion answered confidently; and taking the bust, he carefully unscrewed its malachite base, revealing a cavity wherein rested a small square receptacle, oblong and deep, something of the shape of a large-sized snuff-box. It was secured in its place by two springs, which, when released, allowed the box to fall out. Taking it up and opening it, he said to his companion—

"Here you are. Fill it up, while I arrange the tube."

Then, while the Doctor carefully filled the box with some greyish-white powder from a tiny green glass bottle on the table, Nenci took up a tube of thin glass about an inch long, one of the two or three which Malvano had just filled with acid and hermetically sealed by the aid of his spirit-lamp and blow-pipe. This he carefully inserted in the opening, afterwards replacing the closed box of grey compound, securing it deeply in its place by the two little steel springs.

Again he placed it upon the table, and, retreating a few steps, stood admiring it.

"The reproductions are all absolutely perfect," he observed. "We've only now to prove that our calculations are correct. Come, let's go. If anybody meets us, they'll think you've been called out to some urgent case. Therefore we're safe enough."

"Very well," the Doctor agreed; and both put on their coats and went out, Nenci with the bust covered carefully beneath the long ulster he assumed in the hall.

Noiselessly they let themselves out by the servants' entrance, crossed the large paved yard to the stables, and, finding a spade, the Doctor hid it beneath his overcoat. Then, crossing the lawn, they passed through a gap in the boundary fence, and was soon skirting a high hedge-row, proceeding towards the open country, crossing field after field until about twenty minutes later they paused at a lonely spot. The place where they halted was so dark that they could scarcely see one another, but the mossy, marshy ground was soft beneath their feet; therefore the Doctor, knowing the country well, suggested that this was the spot where the experiment should take place. His companion at once acquiesced, and the Doctor, speaking in a low undertone, drove his spade deep into the earth, and worked away digging a hole, although he could scarce see anything in that pitch darkness.

Presently Nenci, placing the bust upon the ground, boldly struck a match, and by its fickle light ascertained the depth of the hole. Malvano was still working away, fearful lest they should be discovered, the perspiration dropping from his brow in great beads.

"I think that's deep enough," he said after some minutes had elapsed. Then, striking another vesta, he glanced intently at his watch to ascertain the exact time. He handed the Doctor the matches, asking him to strike another, and by its aid held the bust upside down and moved the base very carefully round. When at last he had placed it at the exact point, he knelt and slowly lowered it into the hole which had been dug. Both men, working like moles in the dark, quickly replaced the earth, Nenci stamping it down with his feet. At risk of detection—for a lighted match can be seen a long way on a dark night—they struck two more vestas in order that they might the more completely hide the beautiful little work of art upon which Nenci had been engaged so many hours that day.

When it had been entirely covered, and the ploughed land rearranged, both men retreated rather hurriedly across a couple of fields, and at an old weather-worn stile stood and waited, peering back into the darkness.

The chimes of a distant church sounded over the hills; then the dead silence of the night fell again unbroken, save for the mournful sighing of the wind. For fully five minutes they waited, uttering no word.

"It's failed," Malvano at last exclaimed disappointedly, in an excited half-whisper.

"I tell you it can't fail," the other answered quickly. "I ought to know something of such contrivances." Malvano muttered some words expressive of doubt, but scarce had they left his lips when all of a sudden there was a blood-red flash, a loud report, and tons of earth and stones shot skyward in the darkness, some falling unpleasantly close to them.

"Holy Virgin!" exclaimed the Doctor. "It's terrible! By Heaven it is!"

"Nothing could withstand that," Nenci observed enthusiastically, with an air of complete satisfaction. "I told you it was absolutely deadly."

The report had caused the earth to tremble where they stood, and, borne upon the night wind, had no doubt been heard for miles around. Losing no time, they sped quickly forward towards the spot, and there in the gloom discerned that a great oak in the vicinity had been shattered, its branches hanging torn and broken, while at the spot where the little bust had been buried, was a wide, deep, funnel-shaped hole. Some great hazel bushes in the vicinity had been torn up by the roots and hurled aside, while on every hand was ample evidence of the terrific and irresistible force of the explosion.

"The strength of the compound is far greater than I ever imagined! It's frightful?" exclaimed the Doctor, gazing around half fearfully. "But let's get back, or some one, attracted by the report, may be astir. What will people think when it's discovered in the morning?"

"They'll only believe that lightning has done it," Nenci said airily, as, thrusting their hands into their overcoat pockets they retraced their steps, bending against the icy wind sweeping across the open land.

In passing back across the lawn both were too preoccupied with their own thoughts to detect that behind the privet hedge was a crouching figure, and that the person so concealed had probably watched all their mysterious movements and taken the keenest interest in their extraordinary midnight experiment.

XXVIII

THE TRICK OF A TRICKSTER

One afternoon, a week later, Gemma was idling in her cosy private sitting-room at the Hotel Victoria. She had returned there in an involuntary manner, because it was the only hotel she knew in London. It had been a wet, dismal day, and by three o'clock it had become so dark that she had been compelled to switch on the electric light in order to see to write. During two hours she had not risen, but had continued covering sheet after sheet of foolscap with her fine angular writing. She wrote with the air of one accustomed to write, folding down the left-hand edge of her paper so as to create a margin and writing on one side of the sheet only. Before commencing, she had several times read through a long and apparently deeply interesting letter, making careful notes upon it before commencing. Then, drawing her chair closer to the table, she took up her pen and wrote away at express speed, now and then halting to reflect, but quickly resuming until she had filled a dozen folios. At last she concluded abruptly, and without signature, afterwards leaning back in her little Chippendale armchair, turning over the numbered pages, and reading through what she had written. When she had finished, she paused and looked straight before her blankly. Her lips moved, but no sound escaped them. Presently she took from the dressing-bag open beside her a large linen-lined blue envelope, whereon was printed in Italian "Private.— To His Excellency the Marquis Montelupo, Minister of Foreign Affairs, Rome." Into this she placed what she had written, afterwards sealing it at each corner and in the centre, in the manner the Italian Administration of Posts requires insured letters to be secured.

This done, she paused, resting her head wearily on her hands, as if tired out. Suddenly there was a loud rap at the door, and one of the hotel message-boys entered with a card.

"Show him up at once," Gemma answered in her broken English, after she had glanced at the name; and a few minutes later a sour-faced, middle-aged Italian entered, bowing.

"Good-evening, Califano," she said. "It is quite ready" and she handed him the secret despatch. "You leave for Rome to-night—eh?"

"Si—Signora Contessa," the man answered. "I arrived in London only an hour ago, and I leave again *subito*. The Marquis has sent me expressly for this."

"Then see that he gets it at the earliest possible moment," she said quickly. "It is of the utmost secrecy and importance."

"I quite understand, Signora Contessa," the man courteously replied, carefully placing the envelope in the breast-pocket of his heavy frieze overcoat. "His Excellency has already given me instructions."

"Va bene. Then go. Make all haste, for every hour lost may place Italy in greater jeopardy. Remember that your early arrival is absolutely imperative." She spoke authoritatively, and it was evident that they were not strangers.

"I shall not lose an instant," answered the Minister's private messenger. "The Contessa has no further commands?" he added inquiringly.

"None," she answered briefly. "Arivederci!"

"Arivederci, Signora Contessa," he replied; and a moment later Gemma found herself again alone.

"God forgive me!" she murmured as she paced the room wildly agitated. "It's the only way—the only way! I have transgressed before man and before Heaven in order to free myself from this hateful tie of heinous sin; I have risked all in order to gain happiness with the man I love. And if I fail"—she paused, pale-faced, haggard-eyed, shuddering—"if I fail," she went on in a changed voice, "then I must take my life."

She threw herself into a chair before the fire, and was silent for a long time. The dressing-bell sounded, but she took no heed; she had no appetite. The crowded table d'hote, with its glare and colour and clatter, jarred upon her highly-strung nerves. She had dined in the great gilded saloon the night before, and had resolved not to do so again. She would have a little soup and a cutlet brought to her room.

At that moment she was calmly, deliberately contemplating suicide.

She sat in the low chair, her elbows on her knees, gazing gloomily into the fire. The loose gown of pale lilac silk, with deep lace at the collar and cuffs, suited her fair complexion admirably, although it imparted to her a wan appearance, and made her look older than she really was, while the tendrils of her gold-brown hair, straying across her brow, gave her a wild, wanton look. Even as she sat, her eyes fixed upon the leaping flames, hers was still a countenance frail, childlike in its softness, purity, and innocence of expression—a face perfect in its symmetry, and one in which it was difficult to conceive that any evil could lurk.

The diamonds upon her fingers sparkling in the fitful firelight caught her gaze. She looked long and earnestly at the strange ring of turquoise and diamonds upon her right hand, and the sad memories it recalled caused her to sigh deeply, as they ever did. Again she remained plunged in a deep debauch of melancholy, until suddenly the was aroused from her reverie by a loud knocking at her door and her hotel number being shouted by the lad in buttons.

"Gentleman wishes to see you, ma'am," the youngster said, handing her another card.

She glanced quickly at the name, then rising slowly, answered—
"Show him up."

Her breath seemed to catch in her throat, but to her cheeks there came a slight flush, whether of excitement or of anger it was difficult to determine. Her brows were knit, and, as she glanced at herself in the mirror, she felt dissatisfied with herself, because she knew she looked haggard and ugly.

As she turned away from the glass with a gesture of determination, Frank Tristram entered.

"Well," she inquired, turning quickly upon him the moment they were alone. "Why have you the audacity to seek me?"

"Hear me out, Gemma, before you grow angry!" he exclaimed, advancing towards her. "I have come to crave your forgiveness" and he stood with bent head before her, motionless, penitent.

"My forgiveness? You ask that after your attempt to take my life?" she retorted.

"I was mad, then," he declared quickly. "Forgive me. I ask your forgiveness in order that one you know may be made happy."

"I don't understand you."

"Carmenilla. I'm going to marry her," he explained briefly.

"To marry Carmenilla!" she exclaimed, surprised.

He nodded. "Tell me that you forgive my madness that night," he urged. "Remember that both you and I are hemmed in by enemies on every side; that our interests are exactly identical. In return for your forgiveness, I am ready to assist you in any way possible."

Her clear eyes rested upon him with unwavering gaze.

"And you ask my forgiveness," she said in atone of contempt at length. "You—who murdered Vittorina—a helpless, friendless girl."

"I—murdered her!" he cried uneasily, with a look of abject terror. This denunciation was utterly unexpected. "What made you suspect that?"

"To any one who had knowledge of the facts, it's quite plain," she answered boldly. "Ah! do not try to deceive me. The police were in ignorance, therefore they could have no clue, and could make no arrest. I, however, am aware of the reason poor Vittorina's life was taken; I know that her presence was detrimental to all our plans, and that she was enticed here, to London, in order that she might die. It is useless for you to protest your innocence to me." Her face was hard, her eyes fixed immovably upon his.

He shrank beneath her searching glance, and stood before her with bent head in silence.

"You cannot deny that you had a hand in the crime?" she went on relentlessly. "You, a murderer, ask my forgiveness!"

"Ah! Gemma," he cried hoarsely, "forgive me." Then, without heeding the terrible denunciation she had levelled against him, continued, "We have both suffered much, you and I; you perhaps more than myself because you have earned ill repute, and been compelled to pose as an adventuress. But those who know you are well aware that you have always been an honest woman, that your so-called adventures have only been taken in order to act the ignoble part which you were compelled to act, and in every way that you are worthy the love of an upright man like Armytage. Forgive me," he urged in a low, intense voice, stretching forth his hand. "Forgive me!"

Her troubled breast heaved and fell. In that instant she remembered what the black-robed nuns had told her long ago at San Paolo della Croce—that the first step towards penitence was forgiveness. She looked straight into the face of the man before her for several moments in hesitation, then at last, in a low, faltering tone, said—"The evil you tried to do me I forgive freely; but—but I cannot take the hand of a murderer"; and she turned away suddenly, her silken gown sweeping past him where he stood.

"Then you will allow me to marry Carmenilla? You will not denounce me as one who tried to take your life?" he cried eagerly, following her a few paces.

"Your secret will be mine," she answered coldly. "I have forgotten, and bear you no malice."

She was standing beside the fire, once again idly contemplating her rings. The diamonds of the quaint one, with its turquoise centre, seemed to glitter with extreme brilliance and with an evil glint that night.

Presently Tristram advanced swiftly, almost noiselessly, until he reached her side. Then again he proffered his hand, asking—

"May we not be friends?"

"We are no longer enemies," she answered, disregarding his invitation to exchange the hand-clasp of friendship. "This interview is painful," she added. "I have forgiven you. Surely that is sufficient?"

"I believed you to be my enemy—I thought that you had denounced me to the police on that night when my mad passion got the mastery," he said apologetically. "I assure you that I have deeply regretted ever since."

"It is past," she said in a chilly voice. "To recall it is needless."

After reflecting for some moments, he commenced to protest his innocence of the crime she attributed to him; but with a gesture of impatience she held up both her hands as if to shut out his presence from her gaze, and then slowly he left the room without further word.

Afterwards she stood, a slim, graceful figure, leaning upon the mantelshelf, gazing down into the fire. Now and then sighs escaped her; once a shudder ran over her, for her thoughts were still weird and morbid. She was debating whether death by her own hand was not preferable to the strange life she had been for the past two years compelled to lead, still dubious as to whether at last she could secure happiness beside the young Englishman whom she loved with all her soul, and for whom she had risked her life.

Through ten days she remained alone in the great hotel and found London horrible. She went out but little, as the weather was gloomy and wet, and spent her time in her warm private sitting-room in reading, or doing fancy needlework. She had written to Armytage, and received an immediate response, which set her mind at ease. He had urged that he might be allowed to see her, but she had replied firmly in the negative. If she desired him to come to her, she would telegraph. In a couple of hours he could be at her side. Fettered as she was hand and foot, knowing that her lover's enemies sought his life, yet without power to save him, she existed in those days in constant dread lest they should discover his presence in England, and carry out their design. The life of a man is just as easily taken in England as it is in Italy, and she knew well her associates to be desperate, and that they would now hesitate at nothing in order to guarantee success of their plans.

One night, after she had been at the hotel about a fortnight, she dressed her hair as carefully as she could, possessing no maid, and putting on a pretty evening gown of pale blue, cut low and filled with fine old lace drawn round the throat in the manner of evening dresses in vogue in Italy, she wound around her head a pale-blue silken scarf she had purchased in Livorno, one of those worn by the Livornese girls on festive days, and, assuming a rich cape trimmed with otter, drove in a hansom to Lady Marshfield's in Sussex Square.

The man-servant, without taking her name, showed her at once to the drawing-room. He had no doubt received instructions. Upon the threshold she stood for an instant holding her breath, as if in fear; then, bracing herself for an effort, entered the room, a striking figure, proud, erect, handsome, the diamond crescent sparkling in her hair, her silken skirts sweeping behind her with loud *frou-frou*. At that moment she was La Funaro, the notorious woman whose striking costumes had so often been the envy and admiration of fashionable Italy.

In the great apartment there had assembled, in a group near the fire, the Doctor, the Gobbo, Romanelli, and Nenci. All four were in well-cut evening clothes, and were chatting affably, her ladyship, ugly, yet affecting youth, holding a little court about her. On Gemma's entrance there was an instant's silence. Then with almost one voice they welcomed her, crying, "Viva, La Funaro!"

Smiling, she shook hands with each in turn, and sank on the silken settee beside her hostess.

"We are still waiting for one other," her ladyship said, glancing at the clock. "He is late." Afterwards, turning to Gemma, the eccentric old woman began to pay her all sorts of compliments in very fair Italian, while the men stood together smoking and chatting, sometimes in mysterious undertones.

At last the person for whom they had apparently been waiting entered, hot and flushed. It was Tristram. He shook hands with all, except with Gemma. To her he merely bowed.

Lady Marshfield, a few minutes later, rose and passed into the small inner room—a signal for her guests to follow. Then, when they had entered, the door was locked, Romanelli alone remaining outside in the drawing-room to guard against the possibility of any of the servants acting as eavesdropper. A table had been placed in the centre of the apartment, and around this they at once assembled, while Nenci, opening the lady's dressing bag which he carried, took therefrom a small oblong box of polished oak, which he set upon the table, afterwards displaying the exquisite replica of the bust of the reigning sovereign of Italy.

"Beautiful!" they all cried with one accord. "Nothing could be better!"

"Its action is marvellous," Malvano explained. "We have already tried it. The effect is frightful. When set, it contains explosives enough to reduce every house in this street to ruins."

They looked at one another and shuddered.

"It's really very inoffensive-looking," her ladyship remarked, raising her glasses, deeply interested. "I hope it isn't charged!"

"Oh dear, no," Nenci laughed, taking it in his hand. "I've brought it here to show how the mechanism is contrived" and bending towards her, he opened its malachite base, showing the empty receptacle for the explosive compound, the hole for the tiny tube of acid, and the small clockwork mechanism no larger than a watch imbedded deeply in cotton-wool, so as to be noiseless. Standing at the table, he glanced keenly from one to the other as he explained its working. As he handled the bust tenderly, his keen black eyes seemed to shine with an evil light.

When he had concluded, he replaced the mechanical portions he had removed, and put the bust back into the dressing-bag beside him.

"No, no," Malvano said, smiling grimly, some minutes later. "Don't hide it away, Lionello. It's well worth our admiration, and does you credit. This is the last time we shall have an opportunity of seeing it, so let it remain on the table."

All joined in a chorus of laughter and approbation, and Nenci, fumbling in the bag at his side, reproduced it and placed it upon the table in full view of their gaze. At that moment Gemma, deep in conversation with her ladyship, did not notice that the bust was before them, and not until Nenci and Malvano had left the room together in order to consult with the foppishly dressed young man outside in the drawing-room, did she detect its presence.

Then, with a sudden scream of wild alarm, she dashed forward, her bare arms raised in despair, crying—

"Look! Look! This is not the bust he showed us at first, but another! This one is charged! Fly quickly—all of you! In another instant this house will be in a mass of ruins, and we shall all be blown to atoms! This is Nenci's diabolical vengeance!"

With one accord they sprang from their chairs and rushed towards the door. Tristram was the first to gain it, turned the handle.

"God! It's locked!" he shrieked.

Nenci, the sinister-faced man who, with his two infamous companions, had secured them in that room with the frightful engine of destruction in their midst, had ingeniously escaped. Speechless, with faces blanched, they exchanged quick apprehensive glances of terror. Those moments were full of terrible suspense. All knew they they were doomed, and appalled, rooted to the spot by unspeakable terror, none dared to move a muscle or touch that exquisite bust upon the table. Each second ticked out clearly by the Sevres clock upon the mantelshelf brought them nearer to an untimely and frightful end; nearer to that fatal moment when the tiny glass tube must be shattered by the internal mechanism, and thus cause an explosion which would in an instant launch them into eternity.

XXIX

Entrapped

As all drew back aghast and terrified from the little face of carved stone, Gemma, who had tried the door only to discover the truth of Tristram's appalling assertion, dashed instantly back to the table, and, regardless of the imminent risk she ran, took the small image in her hands.

"No, no!" they cried with one voice, haunted by the fear that at any second it might explode and blow them out of all recognition. "Don't touch it! don't touch it!"

"On the night when the two men completed their hellish invention, I watched through the shutters unseen," she cried. "I saw Nenci explain how this deadly thing was charged, and the mode in which it was set. See!" In an instant all had grouped round her, as, turning the bust upside down, she eagerly examined it beneath the shaded lamp. The scratch running across the malachite base and up the outer edge of the removable portion was, she saw, contiguous to a mark higher up. Nenci had turned the circular base until the ends of the almost imperceptible line had joined.

Another instant and nothing could save them.

With trembling hands Gemma grasped it, as Nenci had done on the night when she had watched, and with a quick wrench tried to turn it back.

It would not move!

Next second, however, she twisted it in the opposite direction. As she did so there was a harsh grating sound, as of steel cutting into stone, a crack, as though some strong spring had snapped; and then all knew that the mechanism of the devilish invention had been disordered, and the frightful catastrophe thereby averted.

She bent down, opening Nenci's bag, and took therefrom a second bust, exclaiming—

"He tricked us cleverly. Fortunately, however, I detected the difference in the markings of that green stone, or ere this we might each one of us have been dead." Then, placing the two busts side by side, she pointed out the difference in the vein of the malachite which had attracted her attention, and thus caused her to make the astounding declaration which had held them petrified.

"You've saved us!" the Gobbo cried, addressing her.

"These men must not escape," Gemma cried determinedly. "They shall not! Our lives have been endangered by their villainous treachery, and they shall not evade punishment."

XXX

"I Bear Witness!"

Next morning Gemma stood at the window of her bedroom, looking down upon Northumberland Avenue. She had breakfasted unusually early, and had chosen a dark-green dress trimmed with narrow astrachan—one of her Paris-made gowns which she knew fitted her perfectly and suited her complexion. She had stood before the long mirror in the wardrobe for some minutes, and, with a pride that may always be forgiven in a woman, regarded herself with satisfaction. They knew how to make a woman look her best in the Rue de la Paix.

The recollection of the previous night was, in the light of morning, horrifying. After leaving Sussex Square, she had stopped her cab at the telegraph office opposite Charing Cross Station, the office being open day and night, and had sent a long and urgent message to Rome explaining the situation. Already a reply reposed in the pocket of her gown, but it was unsatisfactory. The private secretary had wired back that the Marquis was away at his high-up, antique castle of Montelupo, "the Mountain of the Wolf," between Empoli and Signa, in Tuscany. She therefore knew that many hours must elapse ere her cipher message was delivered to him. Even his reply could not reach her for four hours or so after it had been despatched from Empoli. But after sending the message to Rome, she had also sent one to Armytage at Aldworth Court, and was now awaiting his arrival.

Her hands were cold and nervous, her eyes heavy and weary, and her face deathly pale and haggard, for she had slept but little that night. She saw plainly that all her desperate efforts to free herself had been in vain. There had been a hitch somewhere, or that night the whole of that assembly at Lady Marshfield's would have been arrested by detectives from Scotland Yard, at the instigation of Count Castellani, acting under telegraphic orders from Rome. Italy would thus have been able to rid herself of as desperate a gang of malefactors as ever stood in the dock of a criminal court. She had kept faith with the Marquis Montelupo, her master, and, in order to gain her freedom, had furnished the Ministry with full details of the plot. Her freedom of action had been promised her in exchange for this information, but with the stipulation that the conspirators must be arrested. The Marquis, cunning and far-seeing, was well aware that this would ensure greater secrecy, and hold her as his agent until the very end.

No arrest had, however, taken place. All her plans had failed utterly, and, in a paroxysm of despair, she told herself that she was still, even at that moment, as far off gaining her freedom as ever she had been. Her tiny white hands clenched themselves in despair.

"I love him!" she murmured hoarsely. "I love him; but Fate always intervenes—always. Shall I never be released from this terrible thraldom? I pray day and night, and yet—"

She paused. Her eyes fell upon the small ivory crucifix standing upon a pile of books beside her bed. She sank upon her knees, clasped her hands, and her thin white lips moved in fervent prayer.

Suddenly, while her head was still bent upon her breast in penitence, as she craved forgiveness for violating the oath she had taken to these men who sought her death, a master-key was placed in the door and the chambermaid entered.

"Pardon, Madame," the girl exclaimed in French, drawing back as soon as she saw her, "I thought you had gone out. A gentleman has just been shown to your sitting-room, and is waiting."

"A gentleman!" Gemma repeated blankly, rising to her feet. Then she recollected. It was her lover who had come in response to her telegram. What could she tell him?

"Very well," she answered. "I'll see him at once" and as the girl withdrew, she stood looking at herself despairingly in the mirror. Again she dare not tell him anything. She was still beneath a double thraldom of guilt.

With both her hands she pushed back the mass of gold-brown hair from the pale fevered brows, sighing; then, rigid and erect, walked down the corridor to her own sitting-room. Her heart beating wildly, but with a glad smile upon her face, she entered.

Instantly she halted. Her look of pleasure gave place to one of hatred. Her visitor was not Charles Armytage, but the man who, only twelve hours before, had secured her and her companions within that room with the terrible engine of death in their midst. It was Lionello Nenci, who stood with his back to the window, his hands idly in his pockets. His sallow face was that of a man haunted by terror, and driven to desperation. His cheeks were pale beneath their southern bronze, and his black eyes glittered with unnatural fire as he advanced towards her.

"You!" she gasped in withering contempt. "You! The mean despicable cur who sought to kill us!"

"Yes!" he answered unabashed. "Shut the door. I want to speak to you."

In involuntary obedience she closed the door, and the *portiere* fell behind her.

"I should have thought, after your infamous conduct last night, you would not ever dare to face me again," she cried in scorn. "Such treachery is only worthy of gaol-birds and traitors."

"You deserved it," he laughed roughly. "You are one of the latter. It was you," he went on mercilessly—"you, with your innocent-looking face, who gave the whole plot away, who exposed us to the Ministry, and put the English police upon us; you who sought our arrest and punishment. It is but what was to be expected of such a woman as yourself, the spy and mistress of Montelupo."

"Mistress!" she echoed, in an instant frenzy of passion. "I'm not his mistress. I swear I've never been. You know that's a foul lie!"

"Every one in Italy believes it," he said, with a brutal laugh. "When they know that you were implicated in the plot, and gave it away to him, it will confirm their suspicions."

She looked at him, intense hatred in her glance.

"And you have come here to tell me this!" she cried. "Having failed in your dastardly attempt last night, you come here to-day to taunt me with the past!"

"No. The reason I've called is to calmly explain the position. The police are already upon us, but the Doctor and Romanelli have left London. I unfortunately, am unable, for I've no money," he added, in a whining tone. "I've come to throw myself upon your generosity; to ask you for some."

"You wish me, the woman whom you denounce as a spy and traitor—whom you and your infamous companions endeavoured to kill—you ask me to furnish you with funds so that you may escape the punishment you deserve?" she cried in scorn, amazed at his boldness. "I shall not stir a finger to save you," she answered promptly.

"Come," he said. "There's no time to lose if I'm to escape. Remember, I'm the man for whom the police of Europe have been searching in vain these last two years, ever since I escaped from Elba; and if I'm again to evade them, it will be expensive. If you're not prepared to sacrifice yourself, then give me money and let us part. You are rich, and can well afford it," he added. "Come. Take my advice, and let the whole thing end here. Assist me this, the last time, and I swear to you that I'll say nothing implicating you, even if afterwards I'm arrested."

"If I give you money, it is on the understanding that you will not in future levy blackmail," she said, eyeing the cringing man before her with contempt. "Recollect that any communication from you will result in your immediate arrest. You know, one word from me at the Ministry and the police will follow you, wherever you may be."

"I agree," he cried eagerly.

She drew from her purse three English notes, each for five pounds, and handing them to him said—

"This is all the money I have at the moment, without drawing a cheque."

"It's not enough—not half enough," he declared in a tone of dissatisfaction, glancing at the clock. "There's little time to lose. A North German Lloyd boat sails from Southampton for New York this afternoon, and the train leaves Waterloo at noon. This money won't even buy my passage and necessaries."

She reflected for an instant, and glanced down at her fragile hands. An instant later, in sheer desperation, she cried—

"Then take my rings!" And twisting them one by one from her fingers, including the antique one of turquoise and diamonds, she laid them, together with her brooch, on the little writing-table where they were standing. "They're worth at least five thousand francs," she said. "Take them, sell them, do what you like with them, but never let us meet again."

Eagerly he took up one—a beautiful diamond half-hoop ring, and glancing at it in admiration, was about to place it in his vest-pocket, when there came a loud rap at the door, and the message-boy, shouting her hotel number, ushered in two men.

Nenci turned quickly towards the door, and shrank back in terror and dismay.

The men who entered were Tristram and Armytage. The face of the latter was dark with determination. He had not expected to find Gemma with a stranger; moreover, the fact that her rings and brooch lay upon the table between her and her visitor puzzled him.

"Ah, dearest!" she cried, rushing towards him, her nervous hands outstretched. "You have come back to me at last—at last!"

Without taking her proffered hands, he looked straight into the sallow, evil face of the Italian. Nenci boldly met his gaze.

"This is the scoundrel who, as I've just told you, endeavoured last night to destroy Gemma, myself, and several other persons at Lady Marshfield's?" Tristram cried, glaring at the black-haired inventor of the terrible engine of death.

"And this," retorted Nenci, pointing at the Captain—"this man is a murderer! It was he who killed Vittorina Rinaldo!"

"You're a liar?" Tristram answered, his face livid and set. "The evidence against me is circumstantial enough, perhaps, to convict me of the crime, but I am innocent—absolutely innocent. I myself was the victim of a dastardly plot. Little dreaming of what was intended, I escorted her from Leghorn to London, and thus unwittingly myself created circumstances which were so suspicious as to fasten the terrible guilt upon me. But I declare before Heaven that I'm in ignorance of both the motive and the secret means by which the crime was accomplished!"

The outlaw laughed a harsh, dry laugh. His demeanour at the first moment of their entry into the room had been one of fear. Now he was fiercely defiant, and affected amusement at their demeanour.

"If you can prove your innocence, then do so," he said grimly. "According to the papers, you left the cab, entered the bar, spoke to your accomplice, the Major, whoever he was, and then escaped by the back entrance."

"True," replied the King's Messenger. "But my hurried flight had nothing whatever to do with the murder of Vittorina, nor did my conversation with the Major bear upon it in any way whatever. I merely expressed surprise at meeting him there after leaving him at the station; and he, too, was surprised to see me. Then, while in the bar, I suddenly recollected that, in the hurry of alighting from the train, I had left in the carriage a despatch-bag given me by one of the messengers of the Embassy in Paris to convey to London; and knowing that the train would be shunted out, perhaps down to the depot at Nine Elms, I made all speed back to Charing Cross, where I found that a porter had already discovered it, and taken it to the lost-property office. I had no fear of Vittorina's safety, for I had already given the cabman the address in Hammersmith, and every second was of consequence in recovering my lost despatches."

"But the Major's photograph was discovered in Vittorina's bag," Nenci cried in a tone of disbelief. "How do you account for that?"

"I don't know. To me, that fact is a mystery, although I have since entertained a suspicion that the Major, when he met me, must have

WILLIAM LE QUEUX

been aware that the girl's life was to be taken. He called upon me afterwards, and we were both afraid of arrest upon circumstantial evidence. I was aware that he was implicated in some shady transactions in the City, for he confessed to me his intention of leaving England secretly."

"Your story is ingenious enough," Nenci replied, "but it will never convince a jury of your innocence. You can't clear yourself. It's absolutely impossible."

"One moment," interrupted Armytage, who, standing beside his well-beloved, had been intently watching the face of this desperate malefactor during this argument—"one moment," he said coolly. "This visit is a very fortuitous circumstance. A face such as yours, one never forgets—never. We have met before."

"I think not, signore," the other answered, smiling with that ineffable politeness which so often nauseates. "I haven't the pleasure of knowing you, save that I presume you are the affianced husband to the Signora Contessa."

"But I know you, although it isn't much of a pleasure," Armytage answered quickly, in a voice that showed that he was not to be trifled with. "You declare that we've never met before. Well, I'll just refresh your memory," he went on, slowly and deliberately. "One night, the night previous to leaving for Italy, while passing the Criterion on my way from the Junior United Service to the Alhambra, I saw a cab stop and my friend Captain Tristram alight and enter the bar, when almost next moment a man brushed past me. Beneath the electric light I saw his face distinctly. I saw him raise his hat, mount the step of the cab, shake hands cordially with the girl sitting inside the vehicle, and at once dart away. I didn't enter the Criterion, as I had an appointment with a man at the Alhambra, and was late. Next morning, however, when in the train between London and Dover, on my way to Italy, I read in the paper that the girl I had seen had been murdered." He paused for an instant to watch the effect of his words; then declared, in a voice which betrayed no hesitation.

"The man who brushed past me and mounted on the steps of the cab was you! It was you who killed her!"

The colour died from Nenci's face. He tried to speak. His lips moved, but no sound escaped them. This unexpected denunciation fell upon him as a blow; it crushed him and held him speechless, spell-bound.

"Is it really true?" cried the Captain, open-mouthed, as astonished as the murderer himself.

"This man before you was the murderer. To that I bear witness!" Armytage replied.

"She was going to his house at Hammersmith," Tristram said, perplexed. "There must have been some motive in killing her before she arrived there."

"Of course. It's easy to discern that such a crime allayed all suspicions. No one would dream that the man calmly waiting at home expecting her arrival was actually the man who murdered her."

The dark-faced outlaw, watching the two men with covert glance, made a swift movement towards the door. But Tristram was too quick for him, and springing forward, placed his back against it, saying—

"No, when you leave this room you will be accompanied by a constable. It isn't safe to trust you out alone." Then, turning to his old college friend, he added, "What you've just said, Armytage, has renewed life within me, old fellow. I knew I was the victim of some foul plot or other, but I never suspected this man of being the actual assassin. His character's desperate enough, as witness his mean, dastardly attempt upon us last night; but I never dreamed it possible for a man to commit murder so neatly as he did."

"You are determined to keep me here?" Nenci cried, his eyes glaring savagely like an animal brought to bay.

"I am determined to give you up to the police," Tristram answered. "Remember, I am suspected, and I now intend to clear myself."

"And risk arrest for the conspiracy."

"There's no proof that I was ever associated with you," the Captain answered. "The word of a murderer isn't worth much."

"You are prepared for the revelations that I can make?"

"I'm prepared for anything so long as you meet with your deserts," the Captain responded.

For an instant the wretched man, his sallow face haunted by a look of unutterable dread, glanced from one to the other. Then, convinced that all were determined, and realising that escape was now utterly impossible, he stepped forward, and, snatching up from the table the antique ring set with the turquoise and diamonds, with a quick movement slipped it upon the little finger of his left hand. They watched him in wonder.

"You think to have a magnificent revenge," he cried, glaring wildly at them. "But I will cheat you yet. Watch!" And with the thumb and finger of his right hand he pressed the large turquoise.

From beneath the ring there escaped a dark red bead of blood.

"Go!" he shrieked hoarsely, his face haggard, deathlike. "Go, call the police! Denounce me, do your worst, but you will only take my lifeless body. May it be of service to you. This you intended should be a fine *coup* of vengeance. But I'll cheat you yet! I'll cheat you—I—"

"Ring, and call in the police," Armytage suggested.

"Useless! useless!" the wretched man gasped, his face drawn and distorted as, clutching the back of the chair, he stood swaying forward slightly. "Can't you see that all your carefully planned revenge is unavailing?"

They regarded him in blank astonishment. Even as they looked his face changed, and he was seized by convulsions which shook him from head to foot.

"Can't you see?" he cried wildly. "I've cheated you, and I'm dying. On my finger is the death-ring—the pretty finger ornament which, when pressed, punctures the skin beneath and injects a poison which is swift, and to which there is no known antidote."

"Heavens!" cried the Captain, glancing at the ring the assassin had assumed. "Now that I remember, Vittorina wore a ring exactly similar to that! Upon her hand after death was a strange discoloration which puzzled the doctors. Then she was murdered by a simple pressure of the hand, which inflicted a puncture beneath the ring, and the latter, being irremovable on account of the post-mortem swelling, the cause of death remained concealed. Truly the means by which she was killed were as cunning and swift as the manner in which the crime was accomplished."

The haggard, white-faced culprit stood swaying forward, holding the chair, his black eyes starting from his head, his parched tongue protruding, his lips drawn, his whole appearance horrible. In those moments of intense agony a jumble of half-incoherent words, like the gibbering of an idiot, escaped him; yet from them it seemed as though he were living his whole evil life again, and that scenes long since past flashed before him, only to be succeeded by this final one—more tragic, more terrible, more agonising than them all.

"I told you that the police should never take me!" he gasped with extreme difficulty. "Montelupo's bloodhounds have already scented me to-day, but I've tricked them as I've tricked you. I'm not afraid of death. I'm no coward. See!"

And again he grasped the ring, and, grinding his teeth, pressed the tiny steel point therein concealed deep into the flesh.

Then he gave vent to a loud, harsh laugh, meant to be derisive, but sounding horrible in combination with the death-rattle in his throat. His life was fast ebbing. Great beads of perspiration rolled off his white brow. Again he tried to speak, but the single word "Vittorina," hoarse and low, was the only one that passed his twitching lips. His bright, glassy eyes, still flashing a murderous hatred in the agony of death, were fixed immovably upon his accuser, when suddenly, almost without warning, he was seized with frightful convulsions, his jaws set, the light died from his face, his legs seemed to give way beneath him, and, reeling, he fell headlong to the floor, carrying the chair with him.

Both men in an instant knelt eagerly beside him.

Tristram quickly loosened his vest, and placed his hand upon his heart. It had already ceased its action.

The subtle Eastern poison—for such it afterwards proved to be—had done its work swiftly, completely. Lionello Nenci—conspirator, murderer, and outlaw, one of the most desperate and dangerous characters that Italy has produced during the past decade, and the miscreant whose arrest had been stipulated by the Marquis Montelupo in his compact with Gemma—was dead.

Le Funaro was free. The terrible thraldom which had compelled her to act as secret agent of the State was for ever ended.

XXXI

Fiori D'Arancio

Nearly a year had gone by.

The strange suicide of an Italian at the Hotel Victoria had been regarded merely as a tragic incident by readers of newspapers, for no word of the motive which led Nenci to take his life had been allowed to leak out.

To the public, the death of Vittorina still remains one of London's many mysteries.

In the few brief months that had elapsed, peace, calm and complete, had come to Gemma and to Charles Armytage; for one morning, in the dimly lit old Church of Santa Maria Novella, in Florence, and afterwards at the Office of the British Consul-General in the Via Tornabuoni, they had been made man and wife. Then, for nearly six months, they had travelled in Austria, Switzerland, and Germany, subsequently spending the winter in a furnished villa high up on the olive-clad hill behind Cimiez, where they were visited by Captain Tristram and Carmenilla, who, too, had married, and were spending their honeymoon on the Riviera. At last, when Carnival had come and gone, the season waned, and Nice and Cannes were emptying, they, too, left and returned to the great old Palazza Funaro in Florence.

They had dined *tete-a-tete* one evening, had strolled arm in arm through these great silent chambers which seemed to speak mutely of the gorgeous pageantry in the days when the Medici had ruled Florence, and entered the room furnished in modern style—the same in which he had a year ago pledged his belief in her.

After the man resplendent in the Funaro livery had brought their coffee, Gemma seated herself upon the settee beside her husband, and, taking up her mandolino, commenced to sing that sweet old Tuscan song he loved so well, which has for its chorus—

> *"O bello mio adorabile*
> *Svenire in se mi par*
> *Vorrei fuggirti rapida,*
> *Non so come mi far!"*

When she had finished, she was silent, as if in hesitation; then, with her clear eyes fixed upon his, exclaimed, in very good English—

"You have trusted me blindly, completely, Nino. You married me in face of all the vile libels which spread from mouth to mouth; yet only to-night am I free to tell you the truth. My story is a strange—a very strange one. Would you like to hear it?"

"Of course, dearest," he cried eagerly. "You know for months I have longed to know the truth."

"Then you shall know. I will tell you everything," she answered. "When I returned here fresh from the convent-school, with unformed girlish ideas, I fancied that the King had slighted my family, one of the oldest in Tuscany, and, finding myself possessor of this place and my father's fortune, became imbued with a deep, implacable hatred of the monarchy. I lived here with a maiden aunt, took sides with the Republicans, and was induced to secretly join a league of desperate malefactors who had in view the establishment of the long-dreamed-of republic in Italy. In my youthful ignorance, I knew nothing of the means by which they intended to accomplish their object, for their action seemed confined in daubing in black paint upon the walls and pavements of the principal cities such as 'Down with the royal robbers! Long live the Republic!' In every town where elections took place the ominous writing on the wall appeared, but the authorities were never able to detect its mysterious authors. With old Lady Marshfield, whose eccentric support of all sorts of wild schemes is well known, and who lived in Florence at that time, I joined this secret league at a meeting held in a house on the Passeggio in Livorno, only a few doors from where I lived when we spent so many sunny hours together. A month later, however, at a reception one night at the British Embassy at Rome, I found myself chatting with the Marquis Montelupo, His Majesty's Minister for Foreign Affairs. Having obtained my sanction, he next day called upon me; but his attitude had changed, for he accused me of being one of the ringleaders of this mysterious gang, and declared that he would order my arrest if I did not consent to become a spy in the service of the Ministry. He saw, I suppose, that I was young, attractive, and could possibly obtain knowledge of certain secrets which would be of use to him. In vain I pleaded, even upon my knees, but he was obdurate. He intended, he said, to stamp anarchism out of Italy, and told me that to avoid imprisonment and disgrace I must furnish complete reports of the intentions and doings of my associates. At last—well, at last I was forced to consent."

"You became a spy?"

"Yes," she answered hoarsely. "I became a mean, despicable traitor, a wretched, soul-tortured woman, whose denunciations caused the arrest and imprisonment of the more dangerous members of the gang, while at the same time, moving in the diplomatic circle in Rome, I furnished constant reports to Montelupo of the feeling existing towards Italy. Friendless and helpless, I became that man's catspaw. He held me for life or death. He spread reports about me, vile scandals which caused respectable people to shun me, but increased my popularity among the faster set in Rome and Florence, to whom I became known as the Contessa Funaro although I was unmarried. When I protested, he merely laughed in my face, saying that he had done so for political reasons, because it had got abroad that I was in the pay of the Ministry, and if I showed myself to be a gay, heartless woman, instead of a patrician diplomatist, this rumour might be refuted.

"So, compelled to suffer this indignity in silence, and maintain the ignominious part he had allotted to me, I went to Livorno under the assumed name of Fanetti, and attended the constant meetings of the league which were taking place there. Was it any wonder that I should, under such circumstances, actually become an Anarchist? Among the members of this band of secret assassins—an offshoot of the dreaded Mafia—was a girl named Vittorina Rinaldo, who, having ascertained by some means that Nenci and Malvano, then in England, had misappropriated the greater part of the funds of the league, resolved to travel to London and denounce them. This she did, being accompanied thither by Captain Tristram, who had been induced to join us by Lady Marshfield, and, I suppose, with some vague hope that the knowledge thus acquired might be of service to the British Foreign Office. Vittorina and myself had taken the oath at the same meeting of the league, and had on that night received from Nenci, the leader, rings of exactly similar pattern—'marriage rings,' he laughingly termed them. Well, you are aware of that scoundrel's devilish ingenuity. It was he who had made those rings so that by a mere pressure of his hand upon the ring the poison was injected, and the girl's life taken. You know how cleverly circumstantial evidence was fastened upon her friend. From recent inquiries, I have discovered that Vittorina's relations on her mother's side were English, and had a villa up at Como, and that Major Maitland, having a couple of years before appropriated a large sum of money belonging to her, was no doubt an accessory to her death, for he has never been heard of since the night of the crime. Remember that his photograph was found among her possessions, and that he was no doubt with Nenci awaiting her arrival that night at Charing Cross."

"There seems to be little doubt, from the fact that Nenci gave you a similar ring, that he intended you should share the same fate as Vittorina," her husband observed, marvelling at her story.

"Certainly he did," she answered. "Time after time I strove to free myself, from the fetters ever galling me and driving me to desperation, but Montelupo was always inexorable. He loved Vittorina, I afterwards discovered, for it was he who had written that mysterious letter signed 'Egisto,' and he was determined to avenge her murderer. Like ourselves he was utterly unaware of the identity of the assassin. Now, however, that you have supplied the information wanting, and the culprit has paid the penalty; now that Malvano, the man who so cleverly acted as secret agent of the Embassy in London, while the same moment he was plotting against the State, and his cunning companion, Romanelli, have been arrested, tried at Rome, and will spend the remainder of their lives in imprisonment on Elba, my master has given me my freedom. I am free to love you, Nino."

"But the little marble image?" he said. "Why was that deadly thing so ingeniously contrived?"

"In order to strike a blow which was intended should paralyse the monarchy and cause a revolution in Italy," she answered quickly. "In the blue boudoir in the Quirinal, on a sideboard behind the Queen's private writing-table, there stands a tiny but exactly similar bust. In collusion with one of the royal servants, it was proposed to exchange this image for one invented by Nenci and Malvano, so that when His Majesty joined the Queen one night after dinner, both would be blown into eternity."

"Then, by your efforts, and by the imminent risks you ran among that desperate gang, you averted the terrible catastrophe—you, indeed, saved Italy."

"I suppose I did," she said. "At that time political feeling ran high, and such a blow at the monarchy would have undoubtedly given the Republicans and Anarchists the upper hand. But I do not now regret," she added, a look of supreme happiness lighting up her beautiful countenance—"I do not regret, Nino, because I have secured your true honest love."

"I believe in your honesty, darling, for I know how terribly you have suffered," he exclaimed, drawing her closer to him, until her head fell upon his shoulder. "Those who now seek to besmirch your good name shall answer to me."

Their hands clasped, their eyes exchanged a love-look long, deep, and intense. Then her eager lips met his in one fierce passionate kiss.

"The years of my bondage are like some half-remembered hideous nightmare, Nino," she murmured, still gazing full into his eyes. "But it is all finished, for you, my husband, true, patient, and forbearing placed in my hand a weapon against my enemies; you brought back to me a renewed desire for life and its pleasures; and you gave me deliverance from the evil that encompassed me. Truly a perfect peace is ours, for the dark Day of Temptation has waned, and has given place to a bright and blissful dawn."

The End

A Note About the Author

William Le Queux (1864–1927) was an Anglo-French journalist, novelist, and radio broadcaster. Born in London to a French father and English mother, Le Queux studied art in Paris and embarked on a walking tour of Europe before finding work as a reporter for various French newspapers. Towards the end of the 1880s, he returned to London where he edited *Gossip* and *Piccadilly* before being hired as a reporter for *The Globe* in 1891. After several unhappy years, he left journalism to pursue his creative interests. Le Queux made a name for himself as a leading writer of popular fiction with such espionage thrillers as *The Great War in England in 1897* (1894) and *The Invasion of 1910* (1906). In addition to his writing, Le Queux was a notable pioneer of early aviation and radio communication, interests he maintained while publishing around 150 novels over his decades long career.

A Note from the Publisher

Spanning many genres, from non-fiction essays to literature classics to children's books and lyric poetry, Mint Edition books showcase the master works of our time in a modern new package. The text is freshly typeset, is clean and easy to read, and features a new note about the author in each volume. Many books also include exclusive new introductory material. Every book boasts a striking new cover, which makes it as appropriate for collecting as it is for gift giving. Mint Edition books are only printed when a reader orders them, so natural resources are not wasted. We're proud that our books are never manufactured in excess and exist only in the exact quantity they need to be read and enjoyed.

bookfinity™

Discover more of your favorite classics with Bookfinity™.

- Track your reading with custom book lists.
- Get great book recommendations for your personalized Reader Type.
- Add reviews for your favorite books.
- AND MUCH MORE!

Visit **bookfinity.com** and take the fun Reader Type quiz to get started.

Enjoy our classic and modern companion pairings!